Before HADLEY

J. NATHAN

CHAPTER ONE

Hadley

He didn't see me watching from the corner of the leather sectional in Katie McGraw's living room. But I'd been watching since he walked through the front door almost an hour before. No, I wasn't some creepy stalker. I'd just lived in the same Georgia town since birth, so I knew everyone. Everyone but him.

He was new, which made me curious. I could sense he wasn't like the guys around town by his relaxed swagger. By the confidence he exuded when he walked into a room full of strangers. By the ease in which he lifted his red cup to his full lips, guzzling his beer like it was a sport. By his tolerance of all the eyes on him and the people approaching, feeling the need to introduce themselves, especially the girls.

He didn't notice me tucked into the corner with my cup filled with warm beer. But why would he? I tended to blend into the scenery. I'd been graced with wavy blond hair and a skinny body I didn't have to work to maintain. But besides that, I was painfully average. I'd had my fair share of boyfriends over the years. But after going to school with most of the guys since kindergarten, a relationship with any of them lacked that spark I'd read about in books and seen in movies. Hence, my curiosity with the new guy.

The fact that he could've been the world's biggest douchebag didn't stop my body from shamelessly reacting the moment he'd walked through the front door, my heart tripping over itself with interest.

That was definitely new for me.

But I wasn't like Katie, party-thrower extraordinaire. She slept with anyone who looked her way. And, as I sat in the corner milking my beer, her skanky hands roamed all over the new guy's chest. And while he may not have been shirtless, he might as well have been. His navy shirt displayed the width of his chest and the sculpted indentations underneath, while his short-sleeves made it impossible to miss the defined lines and hollows in his biceps. He wasn't too tanned or a faux-surfer like the locals. Just the opposite. His dark hair was short on the sides and shaggy on the top like he just rolled out of bed unconcerned with how it looked.

Then, like clockwork, Katie grabbed his hand and whispered something in his ear that garnered one of the biggest grins I'd ever seen. Had she not been giving him the eyes, the ones that said, "You're so getting laid," I would've melted into a pile of goo right there because it was breathtaking. Truly breathtaking.

But I should've known. Guys were physically incapable of saying no to a willing female. And Katie was always willing. She tugged on his hand and led him all too readily upstairs. I'd been to enough parties at her house to know the only rooms upstairs were bathrooms and bedrooms.

What a freaking disappointment.

My hormones clearly weren't in tune with reality. Because in reality, he was the type of guy my father warned me about. The type who drew too much attention. The type who caused girls to become irrational. The type who became bored easily. And while I might've been eighteen, I still listened to my father. Who'd argue with a police detective who'd been profiling people since the start of his career? He assured me more than once, when the truth stared you right in the face, believe it.

I pushed myself up from the sofa and maneuvered around the bodies milling about the kitchen. I dumped my beer in the sink and headed onto the deck to refill my cup with cold beer from the keg. I pulled in a deep breath, the cool March breeze a welcome change from the stagnant air inside.

"Hey, Hadley."

I glanced over my shoulder at Zack Banes, captain of every team at school and one of my biggest mistakes. Sadly, I let him get to second base at a party last year. Not one of my finest moments. But since then, he made it a point to get my attention whenever we ended up in the same place. Which, unfortunately, happened often given the small size of Jacobsville.

"Wanna do a keg stand?" he asked from the corner of the deck.

I shook my head with a smile, as if I actually appreciated his offer, then turned with my filled cup and headed for the back door.

"Did he really think you'd agree to that?" a familiar voice asked.

My head jerked to my right. Michelle, my next-door neighbor, stood by the deck railing wearing a grin. I laughed. "Agree to what? Lifting me so my crotch aligned to his face?"

"So original."

"Guys." I rolled my eyes. "Have you seen Cass?"

She shook her head.

"I'll see you inside." I moved to the living room, dropping down on the sofa to wait for Cass who'd disappeared with her boyfriend Eric. If they didn't turn up soon, I wasn't sticking around.

Unlike the other partygoers, I was over the whole high school scene. I was ready for college. Like yesterday. I'd already been accepted to Georgia State, and with my grades, I thoroughly intended to breeze through my final two months of school.

I finished my beer then headed for the long line at the bathroom. With the groups of girls ahead of me planning to go in two at a time, and knowing there were three other bathrooms on the second floor, I took off for the stairs.

The second floor was dark and eerily still. No sounds trailed into the hallway from any of the rooms as I hurried down it. I avoided the bathroom in the master suite and the one attached to Katie's room—not wanting to interrupt the mistake happening in there. That left the one at the far end of the hallway. The door was wide open, beckoning me toward it. Before I could get there, someone rounded the corner, slamming chest first into me. "*Oomph.*" My body jostled back.

I would've fallen on my butt had two vise-like grips not grabbed hold of my upper arms and steadied me on my feet.

I shook my head, clearing away the surprise as the hands disappeared from my arms. It was then I discovered the new guy staring down at me with the darkest—blackest—eyes I'd ever seen, not to mention the long thick lashes surrounding them.

"Whoa. Are you okay?" he asked with a full-blown British accent.

Forget the midnight eyes and accent, the guy stood there freaking shirtless with his shirt clutched tightly in his left hand.

Mothereffer.

"Um..."

"Um's better than 'Watch it asshole.'" He laughed as he reached down and buttoned his cargo shorts.

My eyes followed his fingers. "You just startled me, that's all." *Shit.* My eyes jumped up, scrambling to avoid his crotch. Face. And, *holy hell,* his bare chest.

"Sorry. I can't seem to stay out of my own way most days, let alone someone else's." I looked up in time to catch his grin and a freaking dimple digging into his right cheek.

Seriously?

Wait a flipping minute. I was Hadley Ryan. I would not be distracted by a hot guy when I knew *exactly* what he was doing up there. Shirtless. With his shorts unbuttoned. "I'm Caynan, by the way. I just moved here."

"I sort of figured that with the accent."

"Yeah. Dead giveaway."

I crossed my arms, unfazed by his easy charm. "I'm sure the girls around here will love it."

He lifted a shoulder. "It hasn't hurt me so far."

Gahhh. The confidence. "Yeah, but you should know…" I glanced around the hallway, making a show of ensuring Katie wasn't lurking nearby. "…It doesn't take much to get Katie to open her legs."

He choked on a laugh, clearly caught off guard by my candor. What could I say? It was a gift. "Good to know."

I shrugged, like helping educate the new guy was my obligation.

He buried his hands in his pockets, apparently in no rush to get back to Katie.

Did his muscles really need to have muscles?

Look away, Hadley. Look away.

"So what should I call you?" he asked.

"Honest."

He cocked his head. "Yeah. Sort of figured that."

"Did you now?"

He nodded. "And bloody adorable."

My head recoiled, horrified by his blatant flirting when he'd taken another girl upstairs. "Is this how they get their flirt on across the pond?"

He laughed, a deep raspy laugh.

"No, I'm serious. Does it actually work?" I asked.

His laughter subsided and his lips slipped into a cocky lopsided grin. "I don't know. Is it working?"

I leveled him with unimpressed eyes, a look I'd perfected a long time ago to ward off guys with bad lines and trouble written all over their good-looking faces. I guess I needed to add guys who had girls in bedrooms and still decided to flirt with me to the list.

"Seriously." The twinkle in his eyes told me he liked my sass. "What can I call you?"

"Don't."

His head whipped back. "Don't?"

"Don't call me."

He fought back a smile. "Thanks for the warning."

"You hang around here long enough, you'll figure out I'm not like the rest of them."

He lifted his brows. "I'd be disappointed if you were."

I laughed to myself. And just in case I wasn't clear on my thoughts of him, I turned on my flip flops and walked the rest of the way into the bathroom. I didn't bother to glance back to see if he was looking. I knew he was. Guys like him couldn't help themselves. They always looked.

Caynan

Well, she was refreshing.

I turned around and headed for the bedroom where I'd left what's-her-name. I slipped inside and there she lay, still passed out on the bed. Thankfully. It wasn't that

I didn't want to screw her six ways to Sunday. She was hot. Curvy. Brunette. And empty upstairs.

Totally my type.

At least with the life I lived.

But tonight, I had other things I needed to take care of. Things these other kids couldn't understand. Couldn't know about. That's if I wanted my teeth intact and my dad to back the fuck off me. He was constantly on my ass. Constantly in my ear. Constantly relying on me to do his dirty work. And it *was* dirty. But I'd gotten used to it—and good at it, as messed up as that sounded. I just wasn't sure how much more I could take without losing my fucking mind. It had been thirteen years of the same routine. And the shit had gotten old. At eighteen, I shouldn't have been stressed and perpetually anxious. Something had to give.

I closed the door behind me and walked over to the bed. I checked the lower pockets on my cargo shorts to be sure they were still buttoned, then dropped my shorts to the floor. I lay down beside the chick in my boxers and rolled onto my side, shoving up her dress and admiring her nice ass as I tucked the hem of her dress into the elastic on her thong. Then I crossed my arms behind my head and lay back to wait for her to wake up.

The feisty little blonde in the hallway had thrown me off my game. I hadn't expected anyone to venture upstairs, especially after making a show of taking the brunette upstairs. It was understood we didn't want visitors, or so I thought. But the little blonde had balls. I could see it in her determination to get to that bathroom. *And* get the hell away from me.

Maybe she had intuition. One that told her to run far away. Because she did. The first one in as long as I could remember.

Most girls were drawn to me. I was a lot taller and broader than other guys my age. I had looks that made girls fall over themselves to get with me. If we stayed in one place long enough, I kicked some serious ass on a baseball field. And since girls loved athletes, I had my pick. Not that I had to worry about ever getting serious. I was always half-way across the country by the time they realized I was gone.

My dad begged me to lay low and stay off the radar, nearly putting me through the wall when I blatantly disobeyed him. Repeatedly. But that just wasn't me. I needed friends. I needed girls. I needed sports to keep me sane in my insane world. But I'd agreed to no social media. Nothing to keep me connected after I left. *And* the reason I stayed home on picture day. No record of me remained longer than the time I stayed in one place. It was easier that way. Lonelier, but definitely easier.

My dad's expression was fucking priceless when I mentioned to my newest principal that I played baseball. He immediately introduced me to the baseball coach, who agreed to let me ride the bench. But once I showed up at my first practice and crushed the ball, the coach's tune changed. I tried holding back at first, not wanting to draw too much attention. But sometimes I just needed to feel like a high school kid again. Feel like everyone else who got to be themselves every day. Not someone who played a different role in every Godforsaken place they ended up.

I had no clue how long we'd be in Jacobsville. I liked it so far. The days had been mid-seventies and the coastline was minutes away. The neighborhoods most of the kids lived in weren't anything like the bungalows by the coast or the trailer we rented. They were mansions. Each bigger than the last. Every town we ended up in had their own social elite. And this town was no different. Being spring break, there'd been some parties, so I'd been to a few houses, but I'd only met the guys on the baseball team and some chicks they partied with.

"Babe." The one beside me stirred. She reached over, her hand eagerly seeking my dick.

I intercepted her hand, linking our fingers together. "Hey."

"Ready for round two?" she slurred.

I turned onto my side, leveling my sober eyes with her drunken ones. "I don't know if I can handle you twice in one night." Sometimes my British accent surprised even me.

She smiled, drawing my attention to her luscious lips. The ones that would've felt so good wrapped around me if I didn't need to get out of there. "Of course you could."

I laughed to myself. "How about a raincheck? I gotta head out." I reached down and untucked her dress from her thong, the small gesture making her purr. I shot her a smile before grabbing my shorts from the floor and carefully slipping them on. She sat up and ran her fingernails up and down my back as I pushed to my feet, pulling her up with me. She wasted no time, throwing her arms around my neck, partially for support and partially to yank my mouth down to hers and jam her tongue down my throat. It took some effort to unlatch her lips from mine before I could move her to the door. She plastered her body to my side, clearly staking her claim, which made it difficult to maneuver the hardwood steps without landing on my ass.

Once we entered the crowded living room, I searched for Pete, the second baseman who'd invited me to the party. Since I'd driven myself, I wanted to let him know I was heading out. I spotted him cozied up with some girl on the sofa. I lifted my chin and motioned toward the front door. Once he acknowledged me, I turned, purposely breaking loose from the clingy chick at my side. She had no other option than to let go of me.

I leaned down and quickly pressed my lips to her forehead, not wanting to look like a total dick to everyone in that room. Apparently, the swift peck wasn't enough for her. She grabbed the back of my head and yanked my mouth down to hers again, her overanxious tongue nearly swallowing my tonsils whole. Whistles and catcalls surrounded us. I pulled back from her claw-like grasp, trying not to look too desperate to escape. I shot her one last smile while working like hell to ignore the sounds around us. "Later."

"Later," she purred all drunk and smitten. It never took long with chicks. Show them a little attention and they were seeing a long-term relationship. Too bad I didn't do relationships. What sensible eighteen-year-old guy did? Especially when he switched area codes like he did boxers.

I hauled ass to the front door, practically running outside. I would've been halfway home had someone not been sitting on the steps. "Shit." I grabbed for the wrought-iron railing, trying to stay upright but face-planting on the lawn instead.

"Ohmigod," a girl gasped, hurrying down the steps. "Are you all right?"

I looked up. The feisty blond from upstairs bent over me, her blue eyes assessing my face while the light by the front door cast a glow around her wavy golden hair. I laughed, more embarrassed than amused. "I'm fine. My pride. Not so much."

Feisty stood there grinning down at me lying on my stomach like a complete tool. It gave me a second to take her in. She wasn't all decked out like the rest of the girls in the wealthy town. Instead, she donned a sexy pair of cut-offs and a band T-shirt. "I'd say your pride went out the window the second you let Katie feel you up in a room full of people." She crossed her arms across her ample chest. "No actually, when you escorted her upstairs, it was gone. *Long* gone."

It was about damn time someone other than my dad put me in my place. "That bad, huh?"

"Well..." Her eyes lifted to the starless sky, considering my question—or at least pretending to. "I guess her dry humping your leg while swallowing your spit would've been worse."

I threw back my head and laughed, amusement washing over me like a nice hot shower. It had been some time since I really laughed and meant it. Even longer since it was triggered by a girl.

"No, seriously, if total player was what you were going for, it's definitely what you got."

I pushed myself up so I sat with my arms behind me as I looked up at her. "And say that's not what I was going for?"

"You're stuck with it now." Without a backward glance, she took off down the walkway, her flip flops clapping with her quick stride. "Later, player," she called.

I stayed on the ground watching the subtle sway of her hips as she made her way down to the sidewalk before finally being swallowed up by the darkness. I wondered if I should've offered her a ride. Isn't that what a player would've done? Gotten her alone? Tried to hook up with her?

Something told me, there was no way in hell that feisty girl would've stepped foot in this player's car.

CHAPTER TWO

Hadley

I slid into my back-row seat in English class, loving that spring break had ended so the home stretch before I left for college could get underway.

"Morning," Cass greeted me, sliding into the seat in front of me. Her short blond hair whipped around as she turned to face me. "Thirty-one days left."

"But who's counting?" I laughed as I placed my iced coffee on my desk.

Cass and I had been locker mates and best friends since freshman year when a senior swiped my locker on the first day of school before I could even get a lock on it. Cass stuffed my things in her locker and made it her mission to make the senior's life a living hell. The senior only lasted a month.

"Want to go look for prom dresses after school?" Cass asked.

"It's probably bad luck to get the dress before the date."

She tilted her head, giving me those 'you're being unrealistic' eyes. "Come on. Guys will be lining up to ask you."

I rolled my eyes as I glanced to the door. I expected Ms. Atwood to stroll in fashionably late with her designer bag and overpriced shoes, but my head snapped back. Caynan strolled into the room. His confident eyes scanned the sea of unfamiliar faces unfazed. *Ugh.* Again with that same frustrating confidence. With his initial sweep nearly complete, he spotted me. His eyes locked in as if on a target. A slow sexy smile slid across his face as he strolled up the aisle toward me, stopping directly beside my desk so I had no other option than to look up at his imposing form. "Nice to see you again..." He paused for me to fill in the blank.

I didn't.

He chuckled to himself. "Okay, then." He ticked his head toward the empty desk beside me. "This one taken?"

I shook my head. "It's all yours."

He slid into the seat with a grin and relaxed into it, stretching his long legs into the aisle and crossing them at the ankles like he owned the place.

I focused my attention straight ahead, coming face to face with Cass and her inquisitive eyes.

"You didn't tell me he was British."

"You've been talking about me?" Caynan interjected.

I turned slowly, raising my brows at his self-assured attitude. "Sorry to disappoint. She asked who Katie hooked up with *this* weekend. I must've neglected to add Brit to your status, player."

He snickered, unaffected by my jab. "Just because I don't know your name…" he said. "…It doesn't mean you don't know mine. Feel free to use it."

"I figured we were past formalities. You know, us being BFFs and everything. I figured nicknames were our thing."

He chuckled low in his throat, his eyes darting guiltily away.

My mouth parted. "What is it?" I demanded.

His brows inverted. "What's what?"

"Your nickname for me. You have one, don't you?"

He shrugged, though the slight tip to his lips told me I nailed it.

"Come on." I picked up my iced coffee, leaving a small puddle of condensation on my desk. "Let's hear it." I lifted the straw to my lips, stifling the smile itching to emerge as I sucked down the much-needed caffeine.

I figured he'd prolong our game. Feign innocence. Deny it some more. But his eyes dropped to my mouth, his tongue darting out and running across his bottom lip. *Oops.* I released the straw and cleared my throat, causing his eyes to lift unapologetically to mine. "Feisty," he said.

"Feisty?"

He nodded.

My lips twisted to the side, considering the name and its implications. It had a certain ring to it and held an unspoken truth. I *was* feisty when I wanted to be. When I could see through someone's bullshit a mile away. When I'd been challenged. And Caynan seemed to challenge me at every turn. "I like it."

He scoffed. "You do?"

I nodded as I placed my cup down on my desk. "I'd like to keep it."

"Only until I get your real name." His eyes shot to Cass who lifted her shoulders and twisted toward the front of the room. *That's my girl.*

Ms. Atwood sauntered into the classroom, dropping her bag down onto her desk. "Good morning. I hope you all had a nice vacation."

Murmurs ensued.

Her twenty-something eyes landed on Caynan, realization flashing in them. "Oh, that's right. An introduction is in order. Caynan, will you please stand up."

I stifled a laugh, wondering how Mr. Confident would do under pressure.

Caynan rose to his feet. I couldn't help but stare at his faded jeans hanging low on his hips and his muscular arms under his black T-shirt. Arrogant or not, he was still ridiculously good looking.

"Ladies and gentleman. I'd like you to welcome our newest Badger. Caynan Abbott. All the way from..." She paused, allowing him to answer.

"Across the pond." He glanced to me, making sure I caught the reference, before clarifying. "Good ol' rainy England."

The girls in the class giggled, undoubtedly swooning over his accent.

Caynan slid back down into his seat.

"Well, I think you're going to enjoy it here, Mr. Abbott," Ms. Atwood offered with a warm smile.

His eyes slid to me. "I think so, too."

Caynan

Feisty bolted at the bell, leaving me to fend for myself. If I had to guess, she did it purposely, wanting to see me sweat. She clearly didn't know me.

Once I stepped into the hallway, trying to decide which way to turn, the girl from the party—Katie, I think—snagged my arm. She practically slammed me into some nearby lockers and sealed her lips to mine before I even knew what was happening. She finally broke the kiss and backed away, fixing her cherry lip gloss while leaving the rest smudged all over my damn mouth. She flashed me the same fuck-me eyes she used at the party. "How's your first day going?"

I shrugged, feeling both violated and embarrassed that anyone who hadn't been at her party and witnessed our make-out session had seen her kiss me now. "As good as to be expected."

She pouted. "I waited for you to call."

For the love of God.

My eyes shifted, snagging on Feisty who'd closed her locker and turned my way. She rolled her eyes before taking off with her friend, leaving no question how she felt about me. "Yeah, well. I've been busy with unpacking and baseball. You know how it is."

Katie nodded like she did, but she had no clue what it felt like to live out of a suitcase. No one in this stuck up, too-rich-for-its-own-good town could possibly know.

"What do you say I walk you to your next class?" she offered.

I handed her my schedule since I really had no idea where to go.

"Oh, we've got calculus together. Lucky you. I'm great at math."

For some reason, I doubted that.

The rest of the day flew by like all the other first days I'd endured. A blur and overwhelming. Baseball practice ended up being the highlight of my day. I took out my aggression and frustration of starting all over again on the ball, sending it firing out of the field more times than I could count.

After practice, I grabbed my shit from the locker room and headed to my black Jeep Wrangler sans its top. It was my baby. I'd rebuilt most of it with my own two hands and would've fought my dad tooth and nail if he made me get rid of it.

I drove through town on my way home with flashes of my old friends flooding my mind. I wondered where they were. What they were doing. How my last team was doing in the standings. I shook off the useless thoughts. To live this life, to move as frequently as we did, you couldn't think like that. You needed to live in the here and now. Not the past. Never the past.

I pulled into the trailer park on the outskirts of town where we'd taken up temporary residency, parking on the dirt front lawn. Inside the small space, I grabbed a sport's drink from the fridge and dropped down onto my bed in the far end of the trailer. No sooner had I closed my eyes, the front door creaked opened and slammed shut.

"Son!"

Ugh. That voice.

That fucking voice.

"Back here," I called, too exhausted to use my accent or get up to see him.

Within seconds, my father's tall frame filled my doorway. "How'd it go?"

I shrugged. "Same ol'."

"I met up with that guy I was telling you about. He may have some jobs for us."

I nodded, wishing I'd pretended to be asleep so I didn't have to have this conversation.

On the outside, my dad looked like a pretty decent guy. Someone who had his shit together. But it was all just a façade. He was anything but a decent guy. He was the man behind the curtain pulling the strings.

My strings.

I played my part, showing up where I was needed. It wasn't like I actually had a choice.

"Did you hear anything I just said?" his irritated voice rose.

I shook off my mind's ramblings. "Yeah. I got it."

"You know, son, this is for both of us. Don't act like you're better than me just because you're ready to graduate. Don't act like you're going off to some college after this. Your future's with the business. We're a pair. A duo. A package deal. Where I go, you go."

I could feel the rage bubbling inside me. It happened every time he felt the need to squelch my future plans. It's not like I actually had any. I knew I couldn't escape the hold he had on me. But I didn't need to be reminded of it. Every. Waking. Second.

"Look at me when I'm talking to you," he demanded through gritted teeth.

Begrudgingly, my eyes shifted to his. As expected, they were cold and detached.

I knew when I needed to get away from him. Far away. I threw my legs off the side of my bed and stood. My dad might've been tall, but I was taller, bulking up even more over the last year. He stepped back when I stood, knowing enough to let me go. I brushed by him, storming out of the trailer and hopping into my Jeep. I peeled out of the dirt front yard, sending dust and rocks kicking up behind me, wishing I had the balls to leave it all behind.

Hadley

I walked out of the guidance office the following morning with a mental list of things I needed to do. I thought once I'd been accepted to college, I'd be done with the online forms. But according to my guidance counselor, if they were offering free money, I needed to jump through hoops to keep it. I hurried into the crowded cafeteria, hoping to grab a drink since I'd been unable to get an iced coffee before my early meeting.

"Hey, Hadley."

I glanced to my left. Monica, co-captain of the girls' soccer team, stood from a table and approached me, her long red hair bouncing with each step. We'd been teammates freshman year for all of three seconds. That's how long it took to realize my soccer skills sucked. Don't get me wrong. I loved sports. Watching them. It was safer that way. For everyone. "How's it going?"

"I saw you talking to the new guy at Katie's party."

My head shot back.

"What's he like?" she asked anxiously.

I shrugged. "I really don't know. He tripped over me. It was more him trying not to look like a fool than really talking."

"But you talked to him. Isn't his accent amazing?"

Her sudden dreaminess threw me for a loop. "If you like that sort of thing."

"What's not to like? Have you seen his body?"

I couldn't stop the unwelcome image of him shirtless in Katie's hallway from invading my brain. "Yup. I've seen it."

"Katie's so lucky she got to him first."

My eyes drifted across the cafeteria, ironically, landing on the man of the hour. He was seated with some baseball players and girls on either side of him all up in his space. "Oh, I wouldn't worry about that. It seems like he gets around."

Monica froze when she spotted what I'd seen. Jealousy brimmed in her eyes.

"See you later." I took off toward English class.

Cass already sat in her seat as I took mine. "Hey," she said, not bothering to look up as her thumbs pounded away at her phone.

I hated talking to the back of her head. "Hi."

"Did you hear the news?"

"What news?"

She swiveled to face me. "Katie's house got robbed."

"Robbed?"

She nodded. "Someone broke into her dad's safe. Apparently, they had something like the freaking Hope Diamond in there and now it's gone."

"Wow."

"Yeah, I heard the cops were questioning her stepmom for hours. I'm surprised your dad didn't tell you."

"You know he's not allowed to talk about work at home." My mother had been brought up by my grandfather, the wealthy senator, and my grandmother, the debutante. You could understand their surprise when she married a cop—even if he did eventually make detective. But she stuck with my dad, making sure his work never interfered with our family. "Do they know when it happened?"

Cass shook her head. "Her dad claimed he hadn't been in his safe in months."

"Geez. That sucks." I dug into my backpack on the floor beside my desk, seeking my notebook and a package of licorice.

"For you," a deep British voice said.

I glanced up at Caynan who stood beside me with a grin. He'd placed an iced coffee on my desk. I nodded toward it. "What's this?"

"I was behind you at the drive-thru before you gave up and took off. Thought you might like one."

My entire face scrunched up. "Why?"

He shrugged as he slid into his seat beside me. "I just thought it was a nice gesture."

"Nice gesture?" I scoffed, wondering what nice gesture he'd done for the two girls sandwiching him in the cafeteria.

He nodded, his lips twitching in the corners. "After nearly plowing you over at the party."

"Nearly? You definitely plowed me over. Lucky I'm still alive to talk about it."

He laughed, a deep throaty laugh. "I just couldn't remember if I apologized. So, I got you the coffee."

My eyes narrowed. "How do I know you didn't slip something in it?"

His brows slanted in. "Like what?"

I shrugged. "I've seen movies. The poor unsuspecting co-ed gets drugged in her iced coffee."

That made him laugh even harder. "And what would I get out of drugging you in the middle of English class?"

"So, you're saying you'd drug me, just not at school?"

"What?" His face was incredulous. "I never said that."

I lifted my shoulders. "Who knows. You could be some crazy Brit on the lam from the…what do they call cops over there?"

He paused.

"You two are adorable," Cass interjected, pulling our attention to her—our one-woman audience.

I willed her with my eyes to zip it. "Are not."

She ignored my plea. "Oh, no. You're definitely adorable."

Ms. Atwood walked through the door already talking about the story she assigned yesterday.

I turned my attention to the front of the room, though the urge to drink the coffee was overpowering.

"*Psst.*"

My eyes shifted to Caynan who stared across the aisle at me.

"You know you want to."

I turned back to the front of the room, resisting the urge to grab it at all costs.

I never backed down from a challenge. I was stubborn like that.

CHAPTER THREE

Caynan

For the most part, the rest of my first week in Jacobsville was just like every other. I got lost. I got propositioned by several willing females. I focused my energy on baseball, not school.

Thanks to my two home runs, we won today's game easily. Coach pulled me aside after and asked me about my future plans. I brushed him off saying I'd been considering the military. That always garnered a look of admiration, but an understanding that college ball wasn't in my immediate future. He assured me, if my plans changed, he had contacts at the local colleges who would come see me play. I thanked him, knowing that would never happen.

I pulled to a stop down the road from my teammate Mark's house that night, the closest I could park with all the cars lining the street. Once I switched off the engine, a pounding on my window startled the hell out of me. Even with my soft-top down, I hadn't heard anyone approach. *Damn.* I must've been slipping. A tall redhead with green eyes stared in at me laughing hysterically with her friends.

I pushed open my door and stepped out, donning my confident grin and accent. "What's up, ladies?"

"Sorry." The redhead twisted her hair around her finger. "Didn't mean to scare you."

"I wasn't scared."

She practically sighed. "I'm Monica."

"Good to meet you."

The girls with her giggled. It had to be the fucking accent. Why couldn't my father have chosen somewhere in the US? "You heading to Mark's?"

I nodded. "Which one is it?"

She linked her arm through mine. "Come on. We'll take you there."

Hadley

The floor beneath my feet trembled with the bass from the band outside. Most were out there listening to the lead singer butcher pop-country songs, but Pete, Cass, Eric, and I were in the middle of a high stakes game of High-Low-Jack at Mark's kitchen table.

"And then the ball flew out of the field," Pete explained, his animated arm pointing to an invisible fence across the kitchen.

"He's that good?" Eric asked as he threw down a card.

"Dude. The guy can crush a ball like nothing I've ever seen. Either he's on some serious 'roids or he's not human."

We all laughed at Pete's exaggeration.

"Speak of the devil," Pete beamed as Caynan stepped into the kitchen with Monica latched to his arm.

Wow. They worked fast. Earlier in the week, we'd seen him between two girls in the cafeteria. Monica clearly wasn't deterred by his player ways.

Caynan scanned the kitchen before his eyes latched onto mine. His smile faltered, but he quickly recovered, stepping up to the table and eyeing the cards in our hands. "Hey."

Pete congratulated him on a great game while I focused on my cards.

"Hey, Hadley," Monica said.

I cringed at the sound of my name. My eyes lifted, just in time to catch Caynan's eyes expanding. I'd made it through the entire week without Ms. Atwood calling on me. Instead of giving Caynan the chance to gloat over the revelation, I glanced to Monica. "Hey."

"You guys heading outside?" Caynan asked.

"After this game," Pete answered for us.

"If Cass and I don't win all their money." I threw down my king. "They always want a rematch when we win."

Eric and Pete groaned, mumbling lame excuses for their poor card playing skills.

Monica tugged on Caynan's arm. "Let's go get a drink."

I looked up briefly, catching Caynan's eyes. Instead of showing excitement to get his buzz on with a willing female, he appeared unaffected—distracted even. But he nodded before following her outside into the crowd.

"Jealous, Hadley?" Cass teased.

My eyes shot across the table at her. "What?"

"*Puh-lease.* Every time you two are in the same room, I can feel the sexual tension."

I cocked my head, drilling her with a fierce glare.

Pete looked to me, his freckled face scrunched up. "Sexual tension?"

I shook my head. "She's delusional."

"Am not."

I wanted to wipe the smug grin right off her face. "We sit next to each other in English class. That's all."

"He bought her a coffee," Cass announced like that would win her case.

"To thank me," I explained.

"*Sure.*"

I scratched my nose with my middle finger and threw down my last card.

"Thank you for what?" Eric asked, completely interested in Cass' theory. Of course he was. Most. Whipped. Boyfriend. Ever.

"Katie's party. We kind of collided."

"Was that when his shirt was on or off?" Cass asked, purposely trying to get a rise out of me.

I jumped to my feet with heat pulsing in my cheeks. "Anyone want a drink?" All three of them thrust their empty red cups my way. I grabbed them by the rims and stepped outside, maneuvering around the bodies filling the massive deck. Beyond it, on the back lawn, the band raged on a stage with flashing lights and huge speakers.

I burrowed my way to the keg in the corner of the deck. There was a line. No big surprise. I kept my eyes on the prize as I inched closer, wondering why I bothered coming to these parties in the first place. I mainly kept to myself, sitting with Cass and Eric the majority of the time.

Once it was my turn, I balanced the cups on top of the keg and rotated them until they were all filled. I picked them up by the rims and maneuvered back through the swaying crowd, spilling beer as I did.

Out of nowhere, the cups were pulled from my hands. My head flew to my right. Caynan strode toward the back door with the cups in his hands.

"I had them," I huffed.

"Now I have them." He grinned over his shoulder as he walked through the open door, setting the cups down on the table in front of each of my friends and handing me mine as I sat down.

"Did someone find a friend?" Cass asked, as irritating as ever. "You wanna play?" she asked Caynan, jumping up from her seat as she did. "You can be Hadley's partner."

My wide eyes bore into hers. Could she not take a hint? I wasn't interested.

"I just need to use the bathroom first," Caynan explained.

"Don't you mean the *loo*?" That was my best attempt at being cultured—which really translated to me catching a few episodes of that show about an English family and their servants.

He shot me a wide grin. "Right. Where is it?"

Pete pointed down the hall. "Last door on the left. Or if the line's too long, there're a few upstairs. Mark won't mind if you use one."

Caynan nodded, before taking off down the hall.

My face shot to Cass. "Seriously?"

She pressed her hand innocently over her heart. "What?"

I shook my head. "I'm not interested."

"Yeah. Okay. What girl wouldn't be interested in that?" She nodded toward the hallway where he'd disappeared.

"Someone who knows it's got heartbreak written all over it," I countered.

"No one said you have to date him." Cass sipped her beer. "Just go out with him and have a little fun. You're entitled, you know."

Monica stumbled through the French doors in her three-inch wedges. "Has anyone seen Caynan?"

I lifted my drink into the air. "I rest my case."

Caynan

My eyes shot around, taking in the dark-wooded, paneled walls in the shadowy office. I'd already searched the closet and the spot on the wall behind his father's framed jersey. I circled the mahogany desk. Framed pictures of Mark and his mom sat at the front and a blotter covered the center. My gloved hands tugged on the desk drawers. They were locked. Typical. But no one kept anything of any real value in a desk anyway.

I stood behind the leather swivel chair, looking at the room from a different angle. I leaned back against the wall, hearing a *click* as the wall unhitched behind me. I stepped away, turning to examine it. My hands moved over the wall until I located the raised portion. I dug my fingertips into the horizontal groove and pulled. A portion the size of a mini-fridge swung open.

Bingo.

I pulled a tiny flashlight from my pocket and stuck it between my front teeth, shining the light on the safe's dial. Unlike most young millionaires who went all high tech, demanding the most expensive electronic locks, Mark's dad was more like the old-money millionaires, sticking with the old-school combination dials. Truthfully, it didn't matter. I hadn't met a safe I couldn't open.

Try putting that on a college application.

Footsteps in the hallway tore my attention away from the safe and to the closed door. I switched off the flashlight, closed the wall panel, and ducked into the closet.

"Caynan? Are you up here," Monica called from the hallway.

I waited, knowing even if she opened the office door, except for the intermittent glow of lights from the stage outside, the room was cloaked in darkness. Her heavy footsteps eventually moved away from the room and clomped noisily back down the stairs.

I didn't have much time.

I slipped out of the closet and hurried back to the safe. With my ear to the metal door and my fingers gripping the dial, I twisted it back and forth, listening for the magical clicks and the scrape of gears unlatching, indicating success was near. Don't get me wrong. Cracking a safe took time. But I had patience. And somehow, a calmness always came over me when the pressure was on.

Having some difficulty hearing with all the noise outside, I slipped my phone from my pocket and pushed my earbuds in. I tapped the mobile stethoscope app and held the phone to the door of the safe, twisting the dial with my free hand. The screen showed each click, while the earbuds carried the sound. I waited for a double click indicating the notch inside had slipped under the lever arm giving me the first number.

I leveled my breathing, drowning out every other sound, until all I heard were the first set of double clicks. Fifty-six. Talk about music to my ears. I took a quick breath, then started again. *Click, click, click-click.* Twenty-four. Another of couple minutes passed before I heard the final *click, click, click-click.* Eighteen.

Knowing I'd been in the office far longer than I should've been, especially with a party raging downstairs, I entered the combination and turned the handle.

The once-locked door swung open.

The flashlight's strobe cast light on piles of envelopes, different sized documents, and stacks of cash. I opened the envelopes quickly, sliding the contents into my hands. I flipped through them: mostly personal documents, contracts, deeds, birth certificates. Nothing of any use to me. I shoved them back in and returned the envelopes to their initial spots, beside the towering stacks of cash.

Not wasting any more time, I grabbed the wrapped hundreds, stuffing them half-way down the front waistband of my boxer-briefs. Reaching around, I tucked more stacks down the back to keep everything even. I left some cash in the safe so it wasn't obvious at first glance that anything had been touched. Digging into the back of the safe, I checked for anything else worth grabbing. My hand grasped a small ring box. I pulled it out and snapped it open. A diamond ring sat tucked inside. Even under the dim flashlight, the massive diamond sparkled like crazy. It had to be at least five carats. I wondered why they kept it hidden away in a safe. I shook off the thought, learning a long time ago not to think about the people I stole from. It made it easier.

I jammed the ring back into the box and returned it to its spot in the back of the safe. My dad would've killed me for leaving it behind. But what he didn't know wouldn't hurt him. I closed the safe quietly and snuck out of the room. I made my way downstairs, my eyes on the front door.

Laughter from the kitchen stopped me in my tracks. Feisty's laugh. Throaty and deep and all woman. *Yup. I just said that.* I glanced down at my jeans. My shirt concealed the cash, but could I really stay with eighty grand tucked into my drawers? I'd done some ballsy shit. But that was pushing it for even me.

Hadley

I threw down my final card, winning the hand for Cass and me. "Pay up, boys. Cash, please."

Pete and Eric groaned, demanding a rematch.

"Look who's back," Cass exclaimed like some celebrity just entered the kitchen.

I looked up as Caynan stepped into the room. I couldn't stop myself. "Monica came down a few minutes ago fixing her lipstick and readjusting her knickers," I explained with my newly discovered British mojo. "I take it she found you?"

Caynan's lips slid into a smile. A freaking smile. Did he have no shame? He glanced to Cass. "Mind if I be Feisty's partner?"

A smile sprang to Cass' face as she bounded up from her seat and onto Eric's lap.

Caynan slipped into her empty seat, directly across from me, as Pete shuffled the cards.

"You know how to play?" Pete asked him.

He nodded, his eyes locked on mine.

I averted my gaze, picking away at my chipped plum nail polish. What had been wrong with me? I sounded like such a jealous bitch. It was like I couldn't stop myself from poking the proverbial bear.

"Don't do that."

I pulled up my gaze.

"Don't avoid me now that you've got me in front of you," Caynan said. "What happened to the Feisty I know and love?" The second the L-word left his mouth, his lips tipped up in one corner, conspiratorially.

I lifted my brows. "Good to know where you stand." I picked up my cards, eyeing the assortment of red and black in my hand.

"Oh, I don't think you have any idea where I stand." The gruff tone in his voice and the flirty glint in his eyes zapped all the way down between my legs.

Screw that.

"Nice try. But I know your game. Haven't you heard that song about players playing?" I picked up my cup with my free hand and dangled it out in front of Cass. "Be a dear and go fetch me some ale."

She lifted a brow. "Sounds like you've been hanging around with the exchange student too long."

"Bugger off, wench."

Caynan laughed, probably at the fact that she just called him the exchange student.

Cass took off outside with my empty cup as Eric threw a card into the center of the table, starting the game. "She just wants you to be happy."

My head flew back as if I'd been yanked by my hair. "What?"

Caynan threw down a card, his attention now on Eric.

"She hates that you're alone. Hates that you're by yourself in that big house most weekends. Hates that you feel like a third wheel whenever you're with us."

I knew she worried about me, but she actually discussed it with her boyfriend? I waited for Pete to throw down his card, then followed suit. "For the record, I don't feel like a third wheel. I love sitting next to you two in the movies while you make out. It's a fun time. Maybe next time I'll try sitting between you."

Caynan and Pete laughed, but Eric didn't. "You know what I mean."

I shrugged, pretending what he said didn't bother me. Like none of what he said was the truth. But it was. I *was* currently alone. I *did* spend a lot of time in that big house by myself while my mother flew off to different functions to support my grandfather and my dad worked long shifts. And I *did* feel like a third wheel with Cass and Eric. How could I not? "Thanks. But I'm fine."

"Keep telling yourself that."

That pushed me over the edge. "Seriously, Eric? Why is tonight the night for everyone to dump on me? I'm just sitting here minding my own business. And I've got Cass trying to hook me up with the town player." My hand shot out at Caynan who sat quietly for a change. "Now I've got you reminding me that I'm alone. Do you think I need reminding?" I jumped to my feet, my eyes jumping between Caynan and Pete. "Sorry, guys. I gotta head home."

"Hadley, wait." Eric pushed his seat back, ready to jump to his feet.

I held up my hand. "Don't. Don't take it back because you think poor Hadley's upset. I told you. I've gotta go."

I took off down the hall, walking right out the front door. The light evening breeze grasped hold of my hair and whipped it around my face as I walked down Mark's driveway.

"Feisty."

Great. I stopped as I hit the road, glancing over my shoulder so I didn't look like a total bitch.

Caynan walked toward me. "Let me drive you."

I shook my head. "I'm fine. I don't live far."

He scratched the back of his head like hot guys always did when they didn't know what to say. "Then let me walk with you."

I crossed my arms. "You can't seriously want to leave a party to walk me home."

He nodded. "Hot girl? Moonlit night? Hell, yeah I wanna."

I laughed, strangely eased by his enthusiasm. I started down the road in the direction of my house.

Caynan's long strides kept an easy pace at my side. "Sorry that guy upset you."

I shrugged. "He's entitled to his opinion."

We walked in silence for a little while, the moonlight and scattered street lights guiding our path.

"Was he right?" Caynan asked.

I shrugged.

He nodded like he already knew the answer. "Well, I felt like he blindsided you, and that wasn't okay."

"He's actually a really good friend. If it came from someone I didn't like, it would've been a different story."

Caynan's dark eyes flickered under the street lights. "Oh, yeah?"

"There would've been definite bloodshed."

He grinned. "I figured."

We shared a quiet laugh in the silent night. Caynan's attention quickly shifted to the neighborhood playground tucked behind some trees. "You've got your own playground?" He took off toward it like an eager little kid.

I followed him, standing on the edge of the beach sand that filled the area. His eyes jumped from the swing set to the seesaw to the jungle gym liked he'd never played on a playground before.

He walked behind one of the swaying swings and grasped the chains to stop it from moving. "Come over here."

I paused for a minute, torn between getting home and not wanting to be a total bitch. *Ah, what the hell.* I kicked off my flip flops, my feet sinking into the grainy sand as I walked toward him. "I take it you like the playground?"

"It's definitely cool sitting smack dab in the middle of the neighborhood like this."

I dropped down onto the swing and grabbed hold of the chains at my sides. "My dad had it built."

"What's he some kind of contractor?"

I shook my head, glad I wasn't looking at him. People made a habit of steering clear of cops, evading them on roads, slowing down when they spotted them hiding with radars. I knew the normal reaction was more disgust than admiration, even if he was a detective. "Well?" I prompted him, wanting to change the subject.

"Well, what?"

I glanced over my shoulder at him behind me. "You planning on pushing me or what?"

He snickered as his hands pressed against my back.

I tried ignoring the almost-electrical zap that shot through his hands, buzzing straight through my body. I really did. But WTF?

"Tell me something about you I don't already know." His question came out of nowhere.

"*Something?* You don't know *anything* about me."

I could hear the smile in his voice. "Yeah, that's why I'm asking."

I stifled a grin as he propelled me forward, each time gaining more momentum. "Fine. I eat red licorice like it's going out of style."

"How about that. I like licorice, too."

I laughed, knowing his game and upping the ante. "I have five guinea pigs."

He paused. "Guinea pigs?"

"Oh yeah. They're so cute and cuddly. I actually sleep with them in my bed every night."

"Oh." Though I couldn't see him, I assumed his repulsed tone mirrored his expression.

"Oh," I said, really getting into it. "I know something most people don't know about me. I *hate* shaving. Like absolutely loathe it. My legs, my armpits. You name it. It's totally annoying. So I don't do it. Do you think that's weird?"

"No." He sounded completely unsettled. "It's totally…cool?"

I waited until I couldn't take it anymore, then burst out laughing.

"Tell me that means you're lying."

"About the guinea pigs? Yes."

"Not the shaving?"

I shrugged. "Depends on the day."

We both laughed.

"You should know," I warned him. "In a game of wits, I always win. You might as well just admit defeat now."

"Defeat? I'd never admit that. And if this were an actual competition, I'd die before backing down."

"Fine. I wouldn't want you dying on me."

"See?" He sounded pleased with himself. "You do like me."

I closed my eyes, enjoying the breeze on my face as I lifted higher into the air. "So, why'd you move here? Your dad's job?"

"Oh…" He cleared his throat like he'd swallowed a bug. "No…He's kind of between jobs right now."

"So, your mom's?" Silence followed my question. A long, awkward, deafening silence. I'd clearly asked the wrong question. *Idiot.* "I'm sorry. Look at me being all nosy. You don't have to tell me."

"No, it's fine. I just haven't really thought about her in a while." His voice came out low, muffled even.

"She passed away when I was five."

"I'm so sorry." *Way to go, Hadley.*

"Nah. It's okay. I'm good."

He didn't sound good and for some bizarre reason, I had the urge to stop the swing and wrap him in a big hug. Not the kind of hug the girls at school wanted to give him. The kind of hug a guy who grew up without a mom deserved.

"She got cancer. And it spread quickly." He continued, catching me off guard. "My dad said it took no more than a month between the time they found it and the day she died."

I dropped my feet, letting my toes drag in the sand until I slowed the swing. When I finally stopped, I swiveled to face him. "That must've been really hard on you both."

He shrugged, his eyes avoiding mine. "I barely remember."

"Well, I'm a good listener—when I'm not being nosy or a smart ass. So…"

His appreciative eyes met mine. In that moment, I saw a real guy. I saw someone who'd endured heartbreak just like everyone else. And as much as I despised guys who slept with anything that walked, I hurt for him.

Needing a subject change—like yesterday—my eyes flashed to my empty driveway three houses away. "That one's mine." I pointed to the monstrosity my mother had designed, with its white bricks and multiple peaks.

"It's kind of small, don't you think?"

"Tell me about it. I only have two walk-in closets."

He laughed. It felt nice to hear him laugh after revealing something so traumatic. "I like you." His words came out of nowhere.

Goosebumps zipped up my arms. I wanted to believe it was the cool breeze, but I couldn't be sure. "You don't know me."

"I know you like iced coffee, licorice, and guinea pigs."

"I don't really like guinea pigs," I assured him.

His raspy laugh and dark gaze blew every thought out of my head.

Dammit.

He reached out and grasped the chains on my swing, positioning himself directly in front of me.

Oh, God. Don't kiss me. Please don't kiss me.

He stared me down, his eyes blazing with something unrecognizable. Something hypnotic. Something I liked more than I should. His hands slid down the chains, meeting my hands. His were large and warm and covered mine completely.

Without warning, he tightened his grip and gave my body a quick twist, spinning the swing around quickly then stepping back. I lifted my legs off the ground and let the momentum twirl me around. I threw back my head and laughed as the night breeze washed over me. I felt free. Free from the concerns of my friends. Free from my loneliness. Free from the need to keep everyone at arm's length—one of my worst flaws.

When the chain twisted all the way up to the top, the swing stopped spinning. I let it take me around in the opposite direction as it quickly unwound. When it threatened to take me back the other way, I dropped my feet and tiptoed it back to the center until I was untwisted and less dizzy. I looked to Caynan standing there with a small grin on his face. "Your turn."

He shook his head. "Maybe some other time."

"Oh, right." I jumped to my feet, holding the chain for a moment longer to be sure my legs were steady. "You need to get back to your date."

He smiled a knowing smile.

What? What did he know? And what wasn't he saying?

"Go. I'll be fine." I released the chain and started toward my house.

Caynan followed after me. "I'm not used to girls running away from me."

I flicked my head over my shoulder. "I told you. I'm not like other girls."

"Oh, believe me. That was clear the night we met." He laughed sardonically as he matched my pace.

We reached my house, stopping at the bottom of my steep driveway. "Well, thanks for the walk. And the swing."

"Let me walk you to your door." He stepped forward, but I kept my feet planted firmly on the pavement.

"You seriously think I'd fall for that?"

His brows knitted together, and, even in the darkness, I could see the little indentation between them. "Fall for what?"

"The lean in for a kiss move once we get to the door."

He appeared truly perplexed. "Who said I wanted to kiss you?"

Every muscle in my face fell slack. My mouth parted. If darkness hadn't cloaked the night, he would've seen my cheeks glowing.

He burst out laughing. "Just so you know, I totally want to kiss you. But I won't."

"Damn right you won't."

"Is that a challenge?"

My eyes widened. "No. It's a fact."

He cocked his head, his eyes doing some crazy twinkling thing reserved for guys in boy bands. "You'd be missing out."

"On what Katie already had—and what Monica is waiting to have again when you get back? No thanks."

That knowing grin reappeared. Damn that grin. "I can't help it if other girls are more susceptible to my charm."

"Susceptible? They're fools. Anyone can see that you wear a mask."

He started to bury his hands in his pockets, but resisted the urge, clenching and unclenching them at his sides. "A mask?"

"No one's that confident."

He snickered. "We can agree to disagree. At least for tonight."

I nodded, slightly embarrassed by my bitchy remark. "Sounds like a plan. Goodnight, Caynan."

Using his actual name brought a grin to his face. "Goodnight, Feisty."

My eyes narrowed. "You know my name. Why don't you use it?"

His lips lifted into a lopsided grin. "It's more fun this way." He turned back toward the way we came, taking a couple of steps before stopping and looking back at me. "Hey. If your dad's not a contractor, what's he do?"

"He's a detective on the police force."

His features stilled.

I laughed, saving him the trouble of searching for something kind to say. "Could've saved you the trouble of walking me home, huh?"

His eyes tightened. "Why's that?"

"Who'd be foolish enough to hurt a cop's daughter?"

He paused for a long moment, and then his lips curved up. "Just so you know, I still would've walked you home."

His words sent an unexpected shiver skimming down my spine. *Damn him.*

"Goodnight." With that, he turned and sauntered back toward the party in no particular rush.

I watched until he disappeared into the darkness, wondering why he really walked me home. And why he pushed my buttons like no other guy.

Caynan

I could barely breathe by the time I turned the corner. Too many times the cash threatened to fall out of my drawers. Like at any second, it planned to reveal itself. It was strange. The entire time we were hanging out in the playground, I felt like Hadley could see through me. Like she knew what I'd done and was just waiting for me to trip up and expose it. And why the hell had I divulged so much to her? I'd never told anyone the truth about my mom. I'd made up some pretty exciting stories about overseas adventures and Bollywood movie stardom, but never once had I ever come close to broaching the truth. Then I met Hadley, and *bam*, I shared my biggest heartache. With the daughter of a fucking cop.

Karma truly was a bitch.

My dad's car wasn't there when I pulled up outside our trailer. Once inside, I walked straight into his room and closed the door, locking the double bolts. I pushed his bed toward the wall and rolled up the area rug, revealing the compartment built into the floor. Grabbing my key from my pocket, I opened the lock to reveal our safe. I twisted the knob and clicked out the combination. Then yanked the cash from my jeans and stuffed it inside with the other stacks of cash we'd collected.

Each time I opened the safe, I envisioned myself filling my backpack with cash, taking off on my own, starting over somewhere new, and being whoever I wanted to be. But it wasn't as easy as it seemed. I didn't have one authentic piece of identification to my name. I'd be expected to live a bogus existence for the rest of my life. And what about my father? He may not have been the father most kids would've wanted, but could I actually abandon him? Where would he go without cash? What would he do without me to rely on?

I usually made quick work of dumping the cash, but after seeing the ring in Mark's dad's safe, I pulled a small velvet pouch from ours. I untied the small rope tie and opened it, pulling out the tiny wedding ring my father had bought for my mom using his own hard-earned cash.

It'll just be the two of you, my mother's weak words echoed through my head.

I remembered holding her frail hand as she lay in the hospital taking her final breaths, trying desperately to get the words out. *Take care of your father. You're all each other have.*

I shook my head, needing to literally shake the memory from my brain. If I didn't, it would've festered, setting me off balance.

My father didn't do the shit we did when my mother was alive. Or so he claimed. He said he did it to pay the hospital bills after she passed. But since he'd yet to pull us out—and was always looking to expand and create new partnerships—I had my suspicions.

I love you, son, my mother assured me before she closed her eyes for the final time. And it was those words I clenched hold of when I was at my lowest.

I closed my eyes and pulled in a shaky breath. If only she had known what would've become of us. The knot in my gut tightened. The pit in the deep recesses grew. It was stress. Anxiety. Anger. I was in a no-win situation with no possible way out.

CHAPTER FOUR

Caynan

Since robbing my teammate, thinking about my mom, and opening up to Hadley like a damn chick, I'd been off-kilter. It was a big fucking mistake to actually allow myself to feel like a normal eighteen-year-old again. It took the entire weekend to get my head back on straight.

Pulling into the school parking lot Monday morning came as a welcome change from the four walls of the trailer. I needed to be surrounded by people whose biggest concerns were what to wear, what to post on social media, and what to do on the weekend. I could handle that superficial shit.

The second I stepped into the parking lot, a few of my teammates joined me, filling me in on our upcoming opponent. I let out a deep cleansing breath. The first in days. And it felt good. Damn good.

I stopped by my locker to grab a few books. While my head was buried inside, fingernails ran up my back causing the hair on my arms to stand on end. I spun around.

An unfamiliar blonde with thick bangs moved into my space. My eyes instantly dropped to her assets. Both of them. Staring me right in the face thanks to her low-cut white shirt. "I'm Shannon. I've been out of town, but I've heard all about *you*." She leaned into me, her soft body pressing into mine and her mouth lingering near my ear. "I'm hoping I get to learn a lot more." Her breathy tone would've put porn stars to shame. But just as quickly as she appeared, she turned and walked away.

I blinked a few times making sure I hadn't imagined her, but when I glanced in the direction from where she came, I spotted her long legs stemming from her short denim skirt strutting down the hallway.

I was really starting to like Georgia.

I made it to English with seconds to spare. Hadley sat in her seat scribbling something down in her notebook. We didn't have homework and the teacher wasn't even there yet, so I wondered what she was doing.

"Hey, Feisty."

Her blue eyes stayed down, her pencil moving furiously across the paper. "Hey."

She shifted a little which allowed a glimpse of her paper. She hadn't been writing. She'd been drawing. Drawing something I couldn't distinguish from my seat. "How was your weekend?"

I expected something witty about the beginning being terrible because some annoying guy wouldn't leave her alone, but she just shrugged.

Ms. Atwood entered, instructing us to clear our desks for a test. Predictable groans ensued. Fifty minutes later, the bell rang. Hadley jumped up and took off with Cass without bothering to even look my way. Something was clearly up with her. We'd had fun together at the playground, no matter how much she'd deny it.

Or maybe it was me. Maybe I'd misread it. Maybe I really did turn her off.

Smart girl.

I wasn't the kind of guy girls like Hadley brought home to daddy. Especially her daddy. She was wise to steer clear of me.

I strolled into art class last period, my eyes sweeping the room. Shannon sat at the back-corner table, her eyes on mine as if willing me to sit with her. I grinned as I made my way over to her. *She* was the type of girl who went for guys like me. The type who didn't expect roses and grand gestures. The type who didn't see forever when she looked into my eyes when I had her pinned beneath me in the backseat of my Jeep. The type who wouldn't be heartbroken when I bailed.

She smiled the way hot girls always smiled when they knew they were hot. When they knew guys were having difficulty not visualizing them naked. "Well this must be my lucky day," she said.

"Or mine." I had no trouble talking to pretty girls. I thrived on it.

She tossed back her blond hair and laughed. I'd like to say her laugh was as hot as she was, but it wasn't. It was high-pitched and phony, nothing like Hadley's throaty laugh.

"What did I miss last week?" she asked as I slid down beside her.

"Not much. Just worked with watercolors."

Our teacher walked in carrying a large drawing. He tacked it up to the front board and turned toward us. "Today, we're going to be discussing tone. I'd like you to examine a drawing created by a student in my Advanced Visual Arts class." He pointed out the lines, shading, and texturing used in the charcoal drawing of a willow tree. He explained that the method the artist used while creating lines established the drawing's tone.

The more I stared at the drawing from my spot in the rear of the classroom, the more I noticed the areas where the artist chose courser lines, or smudged the edges, or deepened the color. The more their anger and frustration became evident.

"Hadley plans to study art at Georgia State in the fall," our teacher explained.

So, Feisty was a tortured artist. Got to admit. Never would've guessed that one.

"She has a true knack for taking an ordinary image and transforming it into something entirely different." He pointed to a spot on the side of the tree. "Notice the way she brings insignificant objects in the background of the image into the forefront by casting light around them. She has a way of seeing past what everyone else sees."

Yeah. It's probably why she stays away from me.

"Do me a favor," he continued. "If you run into Hadley in the hallway, be sure to let her know what you think of her work. She's never truly happy with it, and I think the more she hears it, the more she'll believe it."

On my way out of class, I found myself lingering near the teacher's desk, trying to lose Shannon who rambled on about her trip to Cabo San Lucas over break.

Our teacher finished talking to another student then turned to me. "Can I help you, Mr. Abbott?"

"I was just wondering if any of these other drawings are Hadley's?" It felt weird actually saying her name out loud. I liked how it rolled off my tongue. More than I should.

His eyes scanned the walls filled with student artwork. He pointed to another charcoal drawing in the far corner of the room. My eyes latched onto the small girl with her hair blowing to the side of her head as if standing in the middle of a hurricane. "That's the one she submitted for acceptance to Georgia State's art program."

I stared at the mesmerizing image, wondering if the little girl was Hadley. If she felt like she existed in the midst of a tornado, the same way I did. "She's really good."

Out of the corner of my eye, I could see his head shake. "Actually, she's one of the best to come through these doors in a very long time."

"Ready, Caynan?"

I looked to Shannon, my mind filled with nothing. Nothing but emptiness. She was just like every other pretty girl I'd encountered in my travels. She had no depth. No hidden talent. Nothing but good looks to carry her through life. And for once, I was completely turned off by the notion.

Hadley

"Go out with me."

My eyes shot up from my phone where I'd been reading on the bleachers. Caynan stood on the grass in front of me with his ball cap pulled down low and sunglasses covering his eyes. I tried, unsuccessfully, to ignore the fact that his red baseball uniform fit him like a glove. "I thought Brits only played futbol?"

He grinned, and there was something about the curve of his lips and the confidence in his smile that reminded me of every underwear model I'd ever seen. So bold and self-assured—even while practically naked. Like they knew the secret of what lay beneath their tight fabric and wondered if everyone else did, too. "Well, aren't you clever?"

I lifted my shoulders. "Some may say brilliant."

He shook his head. "You haven't agreed to go out with me. Your brilliance must be slipping."

"Or spot on."

He didn't laugh like I thought he would. He pulled off his sunglasses and hooked them to the top of his ball cap, revealing those deep dark eyes. "So, what do you say?"

"About what?"

His lips pulled up in both corners, his damn dimple dipping into his right cheek. "You heard me." He dropped his bag and climbed the metal bleachers. "I may have an accent, but I speak English." He sat down beside me, his left leg brushing mine.

I ignored the quick tremor surging through me. "Yes, but in the states, the question takes on many different meanings."

"Then let me make it clear." He inched closer, making sure I could read his lips. Hell, I could almost touch his lips. "It's when two people who seem to like each other spend time together outside the confines of the school. Like we did Friday night. Which, by the way, was the highlight of my weekend."

His nearness and the crisp rugged scent rolling off him threatened to blast much of my sanity to shreds.

"So, what do you say?"

I inched back, pretending to readjust the way I sat, but needing to put some space between us. "I've seen the girls you hang out with."

He arched a brow. "Hang out with?"

I nodded. "They all have a lot in common." I'd seen Shannon digging her claws into him that morning. She had the same curves in all the right places that Monica and Katie had.

Caynan laughed. "So, let me get this straight. You've been watching me?"

"It's not like you try to hide it."

His nose wrinkled. "So, you think I'm sleeping with all the girls you've seen—I mean, you've been watching me with?"

I couldn't decide if I was angry at the way he had me pegged or amused by our banter. "It doesn't matter. I don't go out with players."

"Scared?"

"Of getting herpes from just sitting near you? Yes."

He threw back his head and laughed, low and deep. When he laughed like that, his accent was non-existent. And as much as I wanted to deny it, I liked his laugh. It crept into every little crevice, every little girly part of me. And apparently, there were many.

Bastard.

He looked out at the freshly-cut field, with its emerald grass, newly raked dirt, and crisp white lines. "You here for the game?"

I shook my head, caught off guard by the subject change. "I'm driving Cass home. She had to make up a test, so I came out here for some peace and quiet."

He nodded, his eyes trained on the empty field. "Well, you should stick around."

"Why? So, I can see you mash the ball?"

His eyes cut back to mine. "Mash the ball?"

I shrugged. "I've dated a few baseball players."

"So, I've got competition?"

"To have competition, you've actually gotta have a chance."

He snorted as some of his teammates walked onto the field, snatching his attention. "Well, regardless of my chances, I hope you stay."

I cocked my head. "And why's that?"

His eyes slid back to mine. "So I can see you whenever I want to."

Ripples rolled through my belly like a tidal wave on a shore, fast, forceful, and completely unexpected.

Caynan grinned as he stood and made his way down the bleachers. Once he reached the grass, he turned to face me. "Think about it."

I grabbed my bag from beside my feet and stood. "Good luck." I made my way down the bleachers and took off toward the parking lot, needing a quick escape before I did something stupid. Like agree to go out with him.

Caynan

Why did that damn girl make me act all stupid? I had plenty of girls throwing themselves at me. Plenty willing to sleep with me with no strings attached, or at least that's what they claimed. So why, beyond all reason, was the one who was put off by me, the one I wanted to provoke? Make smile? Be around?

The truth was I hated that she didn't like me. No. She didn't *trust* me. What told her I wasn't one of the good ones? What told her I wasn't worth her time? What told her I wasn't worth the trouble? The girl saw through me, without even knowing my secrets. And that didn't sit well with me. I needed to do something to fix it. I had no idea why I needed to fix it. I just knew this girl was different. Different from other girls. Different from me. And if I didn't fix it, I'd always wonder what she really saw when she looked at me.

I entered my trailer feeling on edge. I'd seen my father's car out front, so I knew I'd have to deal with him and his shit sooner rather than later.

"How'd it go?" his gruff voice asked before I even closed the door behind me.

"We won." I dropped my bag onto the floor, glancing to him sitting at our kitchen table.

He placed his pen down on a messy stack of papers and slipped off his glasses. "You hit any out?"

I nodded, searching for the tiniest bit of excitement in his eyes. There wasn't any. "Three RBIs."

He nodded once, then slipped his glasses back on and picked up his pen, indicating the end of our conversation. It always played out that way. As a father, he wanted to be happy for me, wanted to know his son kicked some serious ass out there. But he knew—as did I—my skills on the field were short-lived. I'd never play college ball. I'd never know if I had what it took to make it to the majors. To see my name on the backs of T-shirts. To fill stadiums. To hit my true potential.

The here and now was the extent of my baseball career. So why bother talking about how well I played. It meant nothing.

Absolutely nothing.

Deep down, I wanted to believe my father was a good guy. Because if I allowed myself to believe otherwise, if I saw him for what he really was, I had no one else in this world I could rely on. Then I would've truly been alone. He wanted me to finish high school, even if it had to be under a bogus identity. He just got us wrapped up in the wrong business. He knew, as well as I, that we couldn't just up and quit. We relied on the income. And at times, we relied on bigger jobs from the kinds of people who didn't just let you quit working for them.

At one time, I believed my dad could do it on his own. But once his eyes starting failing him, and I was faster with a safe, he became expendable and I became essential.

Yup. Life sucked.

And while I could've bitched about how I never signed up for it, how I never asked to be involved with the shit we did, how I'd never been given a choice, what good would it have done me? It was my future. And my father had made it perfectly clear on more than one occasion that if I took off, I was on my own. And even if he wasn't the ideal father, he was all I had. *Take care of your father…You're all each other have.*

Those words would be the fucking death of me.

CHAPTER FIVE

Hadley

"Go out with me."

Cass stopped midsentence and we both looked up at Caynan, staring down at us from the aisle in English class.

"Cass has a man," I explained. "I don't think he'd take too kindly to you asking her out."

Caynan smirked. "You know I wasn't asking out your friend."

"How would I know that? My guess is you've already made it through all the single seniors. Why wouldn't you move on to the taken ones?"

He laughed as he slid into his seat. "Why wouldn't I just try the juniors?"

I rolled my eyes, not wanting to admit he had a point.

He leaned out into the aisle, trying to get closer to me. "I'm serious. I want you to go out with me."

My forehead scrunched. "What's the point?"

"The point is…you're beautiful. And I'm hot."

I scoffed. Was he for real?

That just made his smile grow. "And haven't you noticed how we just can't seem to stay away from each other?"

I crossed my arms. "Oh, I can stay away from you. You just keep showing up everywhere I am."

"It's gotta mean something."

"You're a stalker?"

His mouth opened, then snapped shut. "I think we should give it a go."

I leveled him with my best 'don't mess with me' glare. "When hell freezes over."

His head shot back, though his smile never wavered. "Seriously? Because with global warming screwing everything up, I hear anything's possible."

* * *

All week Caynan continued his quest to get me to go out with him. On Wednesday, he slipped a package of licorice on my desk with a post-it note on it: *We have more than candy in common.* On Thursday, he held up a small sign when I walked into class with a guinea pig on it with the words: *Go Out With Him!* To both, I'd rolled my eyes and proceeded like they'd never happened.

I did have to give him props for remembering what I'd told him on the playground. Most guys wouldn't have.

Don't get me wrong. He was a good looking guy and amusing to be around. But I wasn't someone who wanted to be used. And that's exactly what would've happened if I gave in to him. We'd have fun together. I'd develop feelings for him. And then he'd move on. Why put myself through that? And while it would've appeared as though he'd made it his mission in life to pursue me relentlessly, I'd seen him with plenty of other girls. In the cafeteria. In the halls. Even after school before his games.

On Friday, the only day he hadn't asked me out, I hurried out of school, eager to get home. I had lots to do over the weekend and needed a power nap like no one's business.

"Feisty?"

I cringed at the British accent that beckoned me. I stopped in the middle of the busy parking lot and turned around.

Caynan jogged toward me. "Where you heading?"

My brows furrowed. "Home?"

He stopped once he reached me, burying his hands in the pockets of his jeans. "Was that a question?"

"I don't know. Why are you asking?"

"Are you always so paranoid about people or is it just me?"

"It's just you." I didn't crack a smile, though I wanted to.

Caynan's shoulders shook with laughter. "Good to know."

"Well, have a good weekend." I turned toward my car, attempting a quick escape.

"Wait."

I exhaled a long breath before turning back to him.

"There's somewhere I want to take you."

My face scrunched in confusion. "I thought I made it clear—"

"Yeah, I got it. No date. But this isn't a date. I just want you to go somewhere with me."

My eyes narrowed. "What's the difference?"

He lifted his face to the cloudless sky. I wondered if he was praying for strength to deal with me. Good luck with that. "I don't really know." He met my gaze. "I guess I won't try to hold your hand or kiss you at the end of it."

Slightly amused, I grabbed onto my backpack's straps, needing something to do with my hands. "Where?"

His eyes rounded. "Does that mean you're in?"

"Tell me where first."

He shook his head. "I don't want to ruin the surprise."

"Surprise?" I considered it for a minute. I liked surprises. But could I really trust him? Player or not, he definitely worked the whole charming British thing. And forget his body. It wasn't terrible to look at. "Have you taken other girls to this place?"

Bewilderment lined his features. "Other girls? No."

"Because they turned you down or because they knew your true intentions?"

He looked down at the pavement as he shook his head. "Has anyone ever told you that you're challenging?"

I shrugged as Cass' words bombarded my mind. *No one said you have to date him…Just go out with him and have a little fun. You're entitled you know.*

Damn her. I pulled my phone from my pocket and typed out a quick text.

"What are you doing?"

"Texting Cass."

"In the middle of our conversation?"

I nodded, though my eyes remained on my phone. "I'm letting her know I'm with you in case I go missing."

He howled with laughter. "That's fucking hilarious."

"Well? Do you blame me?" I sent the text and lifted my gaze.

"Does this mean you're in?"

I stared into his hopeful eyes. What harm could come from seeing where he wanted to take me? It wasn't like I'd fall for his ways. I was too smart for that.

Caynan

I liked having Feisty in my Jeep. Even with the top off and the wind whipping her hair all around her head, she still smelled flowery and sweet. Most girls would've pulled their hair back in a ponytail or asked me to put on the top. But not her. She didn't even push her hair away from her face. I liked that about her. She didn't give a damn.

And while I liked having her next to me in such close quarters, I couldn't wait to get to our destination. I wasn't sure if she'd been there before or if she'd even like it. I'd made the appointment, hoping I could get her to go. That deep need for her to like me remained present, eating away at me with each passing day.

Once we crossed the county line, her eyes shot around, taking in the surrounding buildings. "Give me a clue."

"No."

Her head whirled my way. "What if I hate it?"

My eyes jumped between the road and her. "Then you hate it."

"You're not worried?"

"Why would I be worried? Even if you hate it, I get to spend time with you."

I watched as she suppressed a grin.

Oh, I'm definitely wearing on her.

The GPS announced our destination five hundred feet ahead on our right. Hadley's head whipped to the right, her eyes searching the storefronts lining the street. I pulled along the sidewalk, parallel parking a couple of blocks away. No way I'd let her in on the surprise without being able to see her reaction.

"Wow. For someone who's used to driving on the opposite side of the road, nice parking job."

"Thanks," I mumbled as I switched off the engine. Why the hell did her references to England make me so damn uneasy? Oh, that's right. Because I was a fucking liar.

I jumped out of my Jeep and hurried to her side. She'd already pushed open her door, but I offered my hand. She smiled down at it, but ignored it and hopped out on her own. Damn independent girl.

Her eyes moved around, taking in the people strolling by us in different directions. "Glad to see there are witnesses."

I laughed, loving the way her sarcasm came so easily. "You really think I'd commit the crime in broad daylight?" My thumb hitched to the right. "I'd take you down one of these alleys where there'd be no witnesses."

She smiled, and I actually felt her enjoying our banter.

Instead of reaching for her hand—like a player would have, I reached for her door and closed it, heading down the sidewalk with her by my side. I spotted the sign a few shops down, loving that she still had no idea where we were headed.

"So, why is it you think I'll like this place?" she asked.

"Well, I stumbled across some very interesting information about you." I stopped in front of the shop.

Her eyes expanded when she spotted *Claire's Art Studio* written in graffiti in the shop window.

"I've seen your art, Hadley." I couldn't disguise the awe in my voice. "It's amazing."

Her gaze shifted. "If we're at an art studio, I'd think you're telling me I need practice."

I laughed as I walked over to the door and held it open for her. "Come on."

Claire, an older woman in a paint-splattered apron, greeted us as we stepped inside. "You must be Caynan and Hadley." She held out her paint-covered hand. Hadley didn't seem to mind, shaking it right away. "I hear you're quite the artist."

Hadley's cheeks pinked. "I dabble a little."

"She's going to college to major in art."

Hadley's entire body whirled toward me. "How do you know that?"

I looked her dead in the eyes. "When I'm interested in something, I make it my mission to find out everything there is to know about it."

She raised her brows in question. "Those stalker tendencies rearing their ugly heads again?"

"Apparently when it comes to you, they can't control themselves."

She suppressed a smile. I wished she wouldn't. She had such a pretty smile.

Claire interrupted our exchange. "So, I'll admit, Caynan's plan for the two of you didn't seem like something an art major would be interested in." Her eyes moved between us. "But now meeting you…I can tell you'll have some fun with it." She pointed to a door at the back of her studio. "Everything's set up for you. Be sure to grab aprons on your way in so you don't ruin your clothes."

"Ready?" I asked Hadley.

A huge smile spread across her lips. "Oh, I can't even begin to imagine what you've arranged."

Her enthusiasm intensified my excitement. "Come see." I grabbed two aprons and handed one to Hadley. I threw the other over my head and opened the door. Hadley walked inside, tying her apron behind her. She eyed the huge sheets of white paper rolled out across the cement floor. Beside them were vats of red, blue, green, and yellow paints waiting to be used. "We're finger painting?"

"I figured, if you were gonna give me a lesson, I needed to start small."

Her eyes cut to mine. Was she angry? Amused? Excited? "You didn't have to do this."

"I know."

She paused for such a long time I wondered if I'd insulted her. "This is awesome."

My smile spread. "Really?"

She nodded, her eyes carrying gratitude she wasn't likely to reveal—at least without a little sass. I was starting to see that was her M.O. "Thank you."

"You don't have to thank me for wanting to hang out with you."

She shook her head. "No. Thank you for taking an interest in me."

I wasn't sure how to respond. Her words caught me off guard. Didn't she have people in her life who took an interest in her? Hadn't there been guys before me who tried to impress her by using her art? "You ready to get dirty?"

She rolled her eyes. "If you do it right, you won't get dirty. But I have a feeling, that's not your style."

I unleashed a cocky grin. "Got that right."

Hadley

He'd taken me to an art studio. *A freaking art studio.*

This guy who'd known me for two weeks had taken me somewhere he knew I'd love, when guys I dated for months never once even asked me about my art. Caynan clearly understood it was my thing. Understood it was one of the most important things in my life. And now he was taking an interest. And though he didn't really want a lesson, he wanted to spend time with me.

What I couldn't fathom was why. He was the new guy. The one with the accent and swagger. He had girls falling all over him. I was work. I was stubborn. I was not one to fall for the player.

Yet there we were.

Maybe he was into the chase. Into the rush of having someone turn him down, knowing he could have them if he just tried harder. But *would* I give in? Would I fall prey to his witty lines and sinfully good looks? Or was I so put-off by the rotation of girls surrounding him that I'd never be able to see past it?

"What do you think?" he asked, halting my internal debate.

I glanced to his finished product. It looked like something a kindergartener would've done by blending colors that never should've been blended. I glanced to him, squatting behind it. Streaks of color lined his face, liked he'd forgotten his hands were covered in paint and wiped them everywhere. "Well, it's certainly interesting."

"So it sucks?"

"Pretty much." I laughed. "But don't give up. Maybe finger painting just isn't your thing. Maybe you'd be better with charcoal or pencils."

His eyes clouded with something I couldn't quite decipher as he climbed to his feet, eyeing me where I sat cross-legged on the floor. "You're awfully clean over there."

My eyes expanded. *Shit.* I scrambled to my feet, trying not to touch anything. "You wouldn't."

He held up his paint-covered hands and inched toward me. "Oh, but I would."

I backpedaled, which only made him pursue me faster. "Just remember, we took your Jeep. If you get paint on me, I get paint on your Jeep."

He paused for the slightest moment, before moving closer. In my quest to escape him, I inadvertently backed myself against a wall. Caynan's lips quirked up in the corners as he stopped in front of me, a devilish glint in his eyes. "I'm not worried about my Jeep." His eyes dropped to my lips.

Quivers rushed through me. Nervous, excited quivers. *Dammit.*

"I'm more worried about you having a good time." His eyes lifted to mine. "Are you?"

I nodded, watching his every move. If I kept talking, he wouldn't touch me. "This was a great idea. How'd you know I'd say yes?"

"I didn't." His eyes dropped to my picture. I'd tried to replicate van Gogh's famous swirls. "You've got to be kidding me."

"What?" I looked down.

"You even work wonders with finger paint."

I laughed, feeling totally self-conscious.

"Do that again," he implored.

"What?"

"Laugh like that."

My forehead creased. "Why?"

"Because it's one of the prettiest things I've ever heard."

A shiver rolled through me as I swallowed down hard. *I will not fall for this. I will not.*

"And I know this isn't a date…" His face inched closer to mine. "But there's something I really want to do."

My breath hitched. I didn't want him to kiss me. Or maybe I did. *Shit.* "What?" My heart sputtered, though I'd deny it 'til the end.

He reached up with both hands and dragged his fingertips down my cheeks, leaving streaks of sticky wet paint dripping down my face. My eyes widened as he burst out laughing.

His laughter was contagious. One, because both of us covered in paint was funny and two, because I'd completely misread the moment. "You do realize two can play the same game?" I reached up and dragged my fingertips across his forehead and chin, leaving streaks of red and blue.

Something flashed in his dark eyes as I pulled my hands away from his face. A look I wasn't used to. A look that told me I might not be the one in charge anymore.

He lifted his hands, cupping my face. His eyes locked on mine. I didn't even care that his paint-covered hands covered my cheeks. The pull between us grew palpable as if electrical waves encompassed only us, zapping and sparking and drawing us toward each other. His breath came out in spurts. My stomach bubbled with excitement. He inched closer. He was going to kiss me. And I was going to let him.

Dammit.

"How's everything going in—oh my." Claire walked into the room, stopping short when she found us face to face and covered in paint.

Instantly, Caynan's hands dropped from my cheeks and he stepped back from me, both of us laughing awkwardly.

Whoa.

And, as much as it pained me to admit it, in that moment, with paint covering our faces and an almost-kiss lingering between us, it wasn't about what hadn't happened in that room between Caynan and me. It was more about what had.

Caynan

I pulled into the empty school parking lot, parking beside Hadley's red four-door sedan. I turned to look at her, but she'd already turned toward me.

"Thank you."

"You already thanked me."

She shook her head. "No. Thank you for trying to change my mind about you."

"Is that what you think today was?"

Her eyes searched my face. "Wasn't it?"

I shrugged. "I knew you were into art, and I wanted to do something with you. It just made sense."

Her lips twitched. "So, you've never taken another girl to an art studio to finger paint before?"

"Oh, yeah. It's totally what I do to get girls to like me."

She sat quietly, probably trying to decide if it had been the truth. "What are you doing tomorrow night?" Her words tumbled out so quickly, I wasn't sure she'd actually asked.

"Not sure. Why?"

Her eyes dropped to her lap like suddenly being close to me unnerved her. I wouldn't lie. I liked that it did. "Would you like to go somewhere with me?"

"Like a date?"

Her eyes flashed up. "No! Definitely not a date."

"Sorry the idea's so repulsive," I teased, though her aversion did nothing to boost my ego.

Hadley laughed. "No, I just meant it's more like I need your help with something."

I could think of a lot of things I'd like to help her with, but I was pretty damn sure those weren't the things she had in mind. "Okay."

The smile that lit up her face made the afternoon so completely worth it. This girl was the real deal. Sweet yet sassy. Confident yet vulnerable. If I wasn't careful, she had the ability to make me feel things. Things a guy like me had no business feeling.

Then I'd be fucked.

CHAPTER SIX

Hadley

I stood outside the Grandview Country Club under the valet overhang, my eyes squinting in the late afternoon sun. Expensive cars pulled up and members jumped out handing off their keys to the eager valets. Thankfully, my green T-shirt, torn skinny jeans, and flip flops deterred any from offering me their keys—though I wouldn't have blamed them. I'd been standing there for quite some time impatiently waiting for Caynan who hadn't shown up yet.

I had no idea what possessed me to invite him in the first place. It had been rash and stupid. But I couldn't take it back. I didn't even have his phone number. Sure, I'd had fun at the art studio. No one besides my parents had ever done something so thoughtful for me. But I wasn't a fool. I knew it was just his latest attempt to get in my pants. Because what else did he gain from getting me to go out with him?

The beeping of a horn snapped me out of my head. I expected to find a disgruntled member waiting for his car to be parked, but Caynan's Jeep passed by, heading toward the parking lot. I hurried over, meeting him halfway. His faded jeans hanging low on his hips and his blue shirt accentuating every dip and indentation underneath did nothing to keep my mind focused on the reason we were there—and not our almost kiss. The one I'd spent too much time thinking about.

"Hey. Sorry, I'm late." Something changed in his eyes. "My dad had something for me to do before I could leave."

"That's fine. Look, I was thinking. Maybe this wasn't a good idea."

His forehead scrunched.

"You're probably gonna hate it. So if you have something else to do—"

He reached out and covered my mouth with his hand. "You actually thought, after all the hard work I put into getting you to notice me, I'd back out?"

I nodded with his hand still covering my mouth.

"You silly girl." He dropped his hand.

I crossed my arms, unintentionally drawing his attention to my chest. "First of all, I've noticed you. That was never the problem."

His eyes lifted to mine, his voice dropping suggestively. "Is that so?"

I cocked my head. "You're pretty hard to miss surrounded by all your admirers all the time."

His bottom lip jutted out in contemplation. "It seems to me, that for the last two days, I've only been surrounded by you."

Unable to argue his point, I did the only thing I could do. I dropped my arms and led us into the building and through the main lobby.

Caynan's gaze lifted to the massive crystal chandelier hanging over the entryway. "Am I underdressed?"

I shook my head. "We're not attending my mom's fundraiser, just helping to set up."

"What kind of fundraiser?"

I clamped down on my bottom lip, unsure how my answer would go over. "It's to raise money for children with cancer."

I watched the information register behind his eyes.

I hadn't considered his mom when the invite flew out of my mouth. That's where my current trepidation stemmed from. I knew he'd either like the idea or be reminded too much of his mom and back out.

He nodded once. "Sounds good."

I exhaled a silent breath, one I hadn't even realized I'd been holding.

"What do you need me to do?"

I led him into the ballroom where busy waiters and waitresses scurried around, setting place settings at large round tables draped in white tablecloths.

I pointed across the room. "That crazy woman over there is my mom." I watched as she bustled around, dropping papers down on long tables that lined the perimeter.

"What's she doing?"

"Honestly? Trying to get home as fast as she can. She needs to get her hair and makeup done before she comes back in a couple of hours."

He gestured to the tables along the wall. "What's going on those?"

"Oh, you're gonna love this." I walked over to the tables, eyeing the place cards. "This is where the autographed sports memorabilia will go. It's a silent auction."

His eyes rounded. "Will they have any baseball stuff?"

"Yeah." I pointed to the place cards in front of the empty spots on the tables. "Signed jerseys. Photos. Baseballs." I glanced over my shoulder at him. "Do you actually follow American baseball?"

Something flashed in his eyes, recollection, surprise maybe. "You do realize I don't live under a rock, right?"

I laughed. "Sorry. I just don't know what's the same for you and what's different."

"Hadley?" My body whirled around. My mother hurried toward us, her fingers pointing all over the room. "I need the decorations to line those walls. Nothing gaudy near those tables. Something bigger near the entrance."

I nodded. "Mom. This is Caynan."

Realizing for the first time that someone stood beside me, her eyes moved to him. "Oh, hello."

He offered his hand. "Nice to meet you."

Her eyes shot to his hand and then to me. "Nice to see you've brought one with manners." She shook his hand. "Pleasure to meet you. Love the accent."

"Caynan's from England."

She smiled. "So I gathered. Listen, I need to get home. I'll be back in a couple of hours."

"Everything will be all set when you return, *Madame*." I loved pushing her overanxious buttons.

Her unamused frown told me she was too tired and restless to sass me back. "You sure I can't persuade you to stay?"

I shook my head. "The hired help will be out of here before you get back."

She laughed. "Then goodnight. Nice meeting you, Caynan."

"You, too." Caynan watched as she hurried toward the lobby. "She's nice."

I nodded. "She is. But when fundraiser time rolls around, don't get in her way."

"Why does she do it?"

I moved toward the supplies my mother had set up for me in the corner of the room. "She has the time and means to help people in need." I lifted a shoulder. "Why wouldn't she?"

Caynan

The ballroom looked amazing. Hadley wasn't just artistic with charcoal and finger paint, the girl could create elaborate life-sized images with nothing more than tulle, ribbon, and portable LED lights.

"Ready to get out of here?" She grabbed a backpack filled with supplies from under one of the tables.

I took the heavy bag from her and swung it over my shoulder. Her appreciative smile immediately sent my mind searching for ways to see it again. "Stand right there."

"What?"

I held up my palm, stopping her from moving. Then slipped my phone from my pocket and held it up. "I just want to get a picture of you and your work."

She tilted her head, a mix of amusement and embarrassment filling her eyes.

I walked over and switched the view so we could see ourselves on the screen. "And me." I leaned my head into hers and smiled, snapping a few pictures before pulling away. "Now I've got proof you hung out with me."

She nudged me with her elbow. "Don't go ruining my reputation."

I laughed, realizing her sarcasm was a cover. A way for her *not* to like me. But she did. I could see it in her gazes when she thought I wasn't looking. In the smiles she tried to hide when I said something funny. In the way her body jumped any time I brushed by her. Oh, yeah. I was chipping away at her tough exterior, whether she wanted to admit it or not.

"I should probably get your number."

I lifted my brows. "Don't you think we're moving a little fast?"

She leveled me with those pretty eyes. "If something had come up tonight, I had no way of getting in touch with you."

"You mean like when you were trying to uninvite me?" I didn't give her a chance to respond. I handed her my phone and let her call herself so we had each other's numbers. "You sure you don't want to stick around for a little bit?" I asked as she handed me back my phone.

Her head recoiled. "You want to stay?"

My eyes scanned the room. Couples in fancy clothes had begun to arrive, and none of them paid us any attention, regardless of how underdressed we were. "Sure. I've never been to anything like this before."

Hadley paused, her eyes searching my face for an ulterior motive. "And you want to start tonight?"

I grinned. "If it means I get you for a little while longer, absolutely."

Hadley

"Dance with me."

I looked up at Caynan who'd just returned from the men's room. "What?"

He ticked his head toward the dance floor. "They're playing our song."

I paused, listening to the instrumental ballad traveling through the speakers. "How do you know? There aren't any words."

He reached down and grabbed my hand. Tiny goosebumps popped up all over my arms as he laced our fingers and pulled me to my feet.

I glanced down at my T-shirt and jeans then out at all the well-dressed couples gliding gracefully across the dance floor.

"Come on." Caynan tugged me toward the dance floor, weaving us through the dancing couples before stopping in the far corner. He turned to face me. I tried not to look into his eyes, so close and penetrating, but my options were limited as he lifted our joined hands, slipping his other hand around my waist and pulling me flush against the hard plains of his chest. *Good God.* I placed my free hand on his left shoulder and before I even realized it, we were dancing. He was actually good, moving me slowly around in the small area. I lifted my eyes, only to find him staring down at me. "See? I knew you could do it."

"Me?" I laughed, trying like hell to hold his gaze. "I was worried you'd step all over my feet." I could feel the vibration of his low snicker as his chest bounced off mine. "Well, thanks for doing this with me," I said.

His voice dropped suggestively. "There are a lot of things I'd like to do with you."

A giant ripple rolled through my already anxious body. It would've been a miracle if he didn't feel me quiver with aftershocks. "I'm sure there are."

Surprise filled his eyes. "You do realize you've got a dirty mind, don't you?"

"I didn't say anything."

"You didn't have to." He leaned down, lowering his lips to my ear. His breath fluttered over the skin on my neck as his voice lowered again. "I've got a confession to make."

You'd think they turned up the air conditioning the way my body responded with chills and quakes. "What's that?"

"Those girls you've seen me with. I haven't done anything with them."

I couldn't see his face but inhaled his crisp, fresh scent. "Define anything."

"They kissed me. I may have reciprocated, but that's it."

I pulled back so I could see his face. "Why are you telling me this?"

"Maybe I want you to see the real me."

His words blew all thoughts right out of my head. *Fan-freaking-tastic.* "Then why'd you let me—"

"I liked that you were watching me."

"What about Katie's party?" I countered. "Did your shirt just magically disappear once you hit the second floor?"

He lifted a brow. "She spilled her drink on me on the way upstairs."

My eyes narrowed. "Come on. You know you went up there with intentions of sleeping with her."

The darkness of his eyes deepened. "Yeah, well, that was a mistake." The music ended and Caynan released me abruptly. "I should probably get going."

"Oh." Talk about a one-eighty. I followed after him, wondering if he really needed to go or if my accusations had just pissed him off. "Let me just go say goodbye to my mom."

He grabbed my backpack from our table, then stayed at my side as I made my way across the room. My mother's smile grew when she spotted us. She excused herself from the group she stood with and met us halfway.

"We're gonna head out."

My mother looked to Caynan. "Thank you for getting her to stay and for helping. This place looks amazing."

He buried his hands in his pockets. "It was all Hadley."

My breath caught at the sound of my actual name on his lips. And as much as I wanted to deny it, I *really* liked the way it rolled off his British tongue. I leaned in and hugged my mom. "I'll see you later."

Caynan and I stepped outside into the unseasonably cool night, walking through the parking lot in silence. I pressed my key to disarm the alarm. My car beeped, its lights flashing and briefly lighting up the dark lot. I stepped up to my door and turned to face him. "Thanks again."

"Stop thanking me." His tone was cold and clipped as he handed me my backpack.

"Sorry. I just meant—"

He stepped into me, forcing my back against the door. He grabbed my cheeks between his hands and stared down at me. "I want to kiss you so fucking bad right now."

My heart slammed against my chest as my voice came out a mere whisper. "Then do it."

His eyes didn't waver from mine. "This isn't a date. I said I wouldn't kiss you if it wasn't a date."

I dropped my backpack to my feet, the *thud* carrying through the silent lot. "I don't care."

He closed his eyes and dropped his forehead to mine. "Part of me wants to prolong this. Make you crazy for me." His eyes opened and he looked me dead in the eyes. "But the other part wants to taste what I've been thinking about doing since the moment I met you."

I couldn't stop my hands from drifting up the front of his shirt, over the solid muscles in his abs and chest. I'd never felt anything so freaking amazing in my life.

He didn't seem to mind my exploration because he groaned deep in his throat. His breath, a mixture of soda and mint, floated between us. "Go out with me," he said.

"I'm out with you right now."

"A date. Then you better believe I'll kiss you at the end of the night."

"Maybe I don't want to wait until the end of the night," I challenged. What the hell was I saying? It was as if I was in a trance. A Caynan-induced trance. And my words were not my own. My body was not my own. My thoughts were not my own.

His lips twitched. "Is that a yes?"

I paused, trying to maintain every last shred of dignity I possessed. But I knew with every fiber of my being that Caynan Abbott would ruin me for all others. And when he finally kissed me, not only would it be explosive, but it would be something no one else would ever live up to.

I was so screwed.

I pulled into my driveway twenty minutes later still reeling from another almost-kiss. I never meant to be so forward, so accommodating, so desperate. But given the hungry look in his eyes and the way his breath came out so quickly—like being around me turned him on—I just needed him to do it. Needed him to prove he had the balls to do it. Needed him to be the guy I thought he was. Not wuss out and leave me panting like a needy fool.

I threw my car into park and switched off the engine. Except for the small light inside by the front door, the house sat dark and empty. I hoped my dad made it to the fundraiser after his shift. My mother would've been so disappointed if he hadn't. And as much as he loved her, he'd disappointed her on numerous occasions by not showing up to events. The life of a detective came with irregular hours. You didn't just leave a crime scene because your shift ended. You stayed until every bit of evidence had been recovered and documented. At times, I felt sorry for my mother. She knew what she was getting into when she married him, but she never asked to fly solo more often than not.

I reached for my backpack and stepped out of my car.

"Hadley."

My body jolted. Caynan jogged up my driveway as I closed the car door.

He stopped in front of me, the toes of his shoes bumping mine. "I forgot something." He grasped my cheeks between his hands and his lips crashed down on mine, forceful and eager. He stepped into me, urging me back against my car. He sucked lightly on my bottom lip. That's all it took. I opened for him, unable to resist him any longer.

His tongue plunged inside my mouth, sweeping and licking away at my tongue. My cheek. Even the roof of my mouth, tangling and sucking and weakening my knees altogether. *Holy hell.* He could kiss. I dropped my backpack and slipped my arms around his neck, arching into him, his chest a concrete wall against me. I needed him to consume me. I needed him to want me. I needed him to need me the way my body seemed to need his.

My fingers traveled up the back of his head, my fingernails digging into his scalp, urging him closer. *Needing* him closer. He groaned into my mouth, the vibration hitting me deep in my belly and every other part of my body that had suddenly caught fire. I loved the softness of his lips and the urgency of his caresses in the dark driveway with only crickets watching.

Without warning, he pulled away, breathless and focused on my eyes. "I would've never been able to sleep if I didn't do that."

I blinked a few times as my arms dropping from his neck, my lips tingling with numbness I'd never felt before. I tried to think of something clever to say, but for once, words deserted me. I lifted my thumb to my mouth, dragging it across my numb bottom lip, wiping away the remnants of the unexpected kiss. The *amazing* unexpected kiss. "I would've slept fine."

A laugh erupted from him. "Good to know. But just so we're clear…" His lips spread into a slow, sexy smile. "I really want to do that again." He lifted my chin, forcing me to look at him. "Would that be a bad thing?"

"Bad?"

He nodded, his lips twitching.

"What if I said yes?"

He moved closer, his gaze straying to my lips. "Then I'd change your mind." His lips sealed over mine, his tongue pushing inside, prodding in the most delicious way. His arms slipped around my hips, tightening as he pulled me into him.

My hands flew back to his head, my own head tilting to fit with his. I wanted to be closer to him. To his lips. They set my body abuzz, and if we didn't stop soon, I wouldn't be responsible for the insanity that occurred right there in my driveway.

I pulled back from his lips, but he didn't release me. He stared down at me. The anxious look in his eyes was alarming. Intense. A major turn-on. I wasn't sure he'd ever let me go—or if I wanted him to. But I knew what I needed to do. And quickly. "I need to get inside."

A grin twisted his lips. "Totally stole my line."

My eyes narrowed as I considered what I'd said. *Ugh.* "I meant inside my *house.*"

"Yup. Totally what I meant, too." His twitching lips said otherwise.

I tilted my head to the side, searching for the truth in his words. In his expression. In his actions. "What are you doing tomorrow?" I asked.

"Why?"

"Just curious if you're going out with someone else."

"*Ohhhh,*" he teased, finally releasing me and burying his hands in his pockets. "So you're wondering what this is."

I wanted to wipe the cocky smirk right off his face. "I didn't say that."

"You didn't have to. I can read you like a book."

"Oh, yeah? What am I thinking right now?" I stared back at him, unblinking.

"You want me to pick you up, carry you inside, and do unmentionable things to you behind closed doors. But, because you think I'm such a player, you won't let it happen."

"You're right."

His eyes expanded.

I crossed my arms. "I still think you're a player."

He chuckled. "Come on, Feisty." He held out his hand for me. "Let me walk you to the door this time."

CHAPTER SEVEN

Hadley

I pulled into the school parking lot Monday morning, parking in my normal spot in the back under the big tree. As soon as I released my seat belt, my door swung open.

I gaped up into eyes as black as coal. And those eyelashes. They were ridiculously thick and long and fanning out with each blink.

"Morning."

I resisted the urge to smile. "Don't you mean *cheerio?*"

Caynan pulled me from my seat, grabbed my bag, and closed the door behind me. He leaned in so closely, I stepped back, curving against my car door. He smelled so damn good. "I'm thinking you brushing up on your British means you're hoping to spend more time with me."

I laughed. "Bullocks."

He smiled, but the intensity of his stare overwhelmed me. "I had a great time Saturday night."

My belly fluttered. "It was all right."

"I think we should do it again."

"Decorate a ballroom?"

His eyes zeroed in on mine as his head moved slowly from side to side.

"Crash a fundraiser?"

His head continued moving.

"Dance?"

Instead of answering, he leaned down and ran the tip of his tongue along the seam of my lips, seeking access that I all too willing granted him. I was so effing-screwed. I fell into the pace of the kiss, slow and body-numbingly good. But since I wasn't into PDA, I pulled away before the kiss had the chance to turn explosive. And, *God*, did I want it to turn explosive.

"I might be up for doing that again," I said, feigning indifference.

His lips tipped up on one side. "Just not in a parking lot where everyone can see."

I nodded.

"So, you're embarrassed of me?"

I tried to pull my bag from his arm, but he resisted, holding the strap tighter. "I just don't want to put too many expectations on…" My hand motioned back and forth in the space between us.

"I think you're more worried about what other people think than what's really happening."

"And what *is* happening?" I raised my brows in question.

His shoulders shook with silent laughter. "What's happening is I'm gonna walk you to English class, flirt with you during Atwood's lecture, then, if I'm lucky, you'll come to my game tomorrow and let me take you out for dinner after."

"A date?" I asked.

"A date," he assured me.

Caynan

Sitting across the booth from Hadley the following night really gave me the chance to absorb her naturally pretty features. The cool slope of her nose. Her colorful pouty lips that didn't need lip gloss. Her dark blue eyes other girls would've given anything to have. The cute way they flashed away when she got embarrassed. And her feisty sense of humor. The girl had me laughing all night.

"What got you interested in art?"

She chewed her last bite of pasta, placing her fork down on her dish. "My mother traveled a lot with my grandfather when I was younger. Fundraisers and campaign stuff."

"More than she does now?"

She nodded. "I found myself alone a lot. Don't get me wrong. In no way was I neglected. I had my dad. But I was just lonely. I needed an outlet for that loneliness."

I found myself leaning closer, hanging on her words. "And art was it?"

She shrugged. "Turns out, some girls write their feelings in diaries, I draw."

My eyes tightened on hers. "And what would you draw right now?"

Her eyes danced with playfulness. I could tell she was working through multiple options. "Licorice."

I cocked my head, unconvinced. "Why's that?"

She shrugged, but I sensed a vulnerability that she didn't usually expose. "Well, for starters it's yummy…and it makes me happy."

There were so many things I could've said to that. So many cocky comebacks I normally wouldn't have been able to contain with her in my presence. But for once, I kept my mouth shut and my words sincere. "I know I've told you before, but you're really talented."

Her eyes flicked away, searching for something on the hardwood floor that wasn't there.

"Don't do that." Her eyes lifted back to mine. "Learn to take a compliment. Especially when it's the truth." Her eyes itched to abandon my face. But I had to hand it to her. She kept them locked on my eyes. "You. Are. Talented."

She rolled her eyes. "Thank you."

"See?" I teased. "You did it."

She cocked her head, her lips twitching. "How about you? What got you into baseball?"

I shrugged. "I'm good at it."

"Wow. Miss Humble and Mr. Confident."

I laughed. "A perfect match."

She shook her head, her eyes rolling again.

I liked that I could make her smile. Truthfully, I hoped I did a whole hell of a lot more than just that. "There's nothing to be humble about. You're talented and I can mash a ball." I purposely used her word so she knew I listened when she talked.

"I agree you can mash a ball."

My head withdrew. "Was that a compliment?"

She shrugged, noncommittal. "You're all right."

"All right like I could make it to the pros, or all right I look good in my uniform?"

Her eyes lifted to the ceiling like she really needed to consider the question. Or knowing Hadley, a witty response.

Our waitress chose that moment to check on us. "Can I get you any dessert?"

I looked to Hadley whose eyes were now on mine. "You want dessert?"

She shook her head, her eyes hiding something I couldn't quite read.

"I think we're all set." I didn't bother looking at the waitress who turned to retrieve our check. My eyes were on Hadley. "Have something else in mind?"

* * *

Hadley pointed to a dirt road in the middle of the woods where she'd inadvertently taken me off-roading. Eventually, we pulled into a clearing that appeared out of nowhere. Hadley gestured to a spot for me to park, throwing her door open once I did. She glanced to me before hopping out. "Come on."

I didn't move. "I never said I liked surprises."

"This from the guy who surprised me with finger paint?" she laughed, pointing to the edge of the clearing. "The night train passes through. If we don't hurry, we'll miss it."

I squinted into the darkness, spotting the old train tracks lining the woods. "That must be the whistle I hear every night."

Her eyes narrowed. "Where do you live?"

Fuck. "Huh?"

"You can't hear it unless you live on the county line."

"Yeah. I'm near there," I said quickly, hoping she'd drop the subject. It wasn't like my zip code embarrassed me. It was temporary and charged by the month. I just didn't want her getting any ideas about stopping by. My dad would've fucking killed me if that happened. "Come on." I threw open my door. "Show me the best place to watch it."

We met in front of my Jeep. I grabbed Hadley's hand, loving the feel of her fragile fingers in my grip. I let her pull me toward the tracks. She stopped twenty or so feet away, dropping to the grassy knoll. I slipped my hand free from hers and dropped down beside her, wrapping my arm around her small waist and pulling her into my side. She fit perfectly, resting her head against my shoulder and exhaling one hell of a deep breath.

"So, you take a lot of guys out here?"

"Oh, yeah…tons."

I squeezed her closer. "Well, thanks for taking me. What do I have to do to make sure it happens again?"

She lifted her head, her eyes searching my face. "Would you want to?"

"Isn't it obvious?"

The foolish girl shook her head.

"I already told you. There are lots of things I want to do with you."

I watched the muscles in her throat wrap themselves around a giant knot as she swallowed down. I loved that I had that effect on her. "Like what?"

Game on, Hadley.

I twisted toward her, rolling her gently onto her back. Instead of pinning her down and kissing the fuck out of her like I really wanted to, I pulled back. I heard her sharp intake of breath as I rolled onto my back beside her. I reached over and linked our fingers in the space between us while taking in the thousands of stars in the black night. "No matter where I am, these are always the same."

"Do you miss home?" The restraint in her voice showed she didn't know if she should ask.

"Sometimes." There. That wasn't a complete lie. "I miss the people I left behind." Another truth.

"Must be hard."

You don't know the fucking half. "Yeah, but right now, I can't think of anywhere else I'd rather be." Another truth.

Her head fell toward me. Mine did the same. "Me neither." I wanted to roll on top of her and press my growing hard-on into her to let her know exactly what she did to me, but she gasped, bolting upright. "Do you hear it?"

I sat up, concentrating on the silence. Except for some bugs humming deep in the woods, I couldn't hear a thing.

"Listen." Hadley's eyes sparkled with excitement. I'd never seen her so animated before.

Sure enough, a soft whooshing carried through the woods as a slight vibration moved the earth beneath us. "I hear it."

Her smile grew. "Just wait."

I couldn't help but stare at her. This girl who had everything in the world going for her. This girl who couldn't accept the fact that she had talent. This girl who couldn't wait to see a bunch of rusted metal boxcars pass by in the night. She was so different than every other girl I'd met. And I liked that idea way too much.

Her face turned toward mine, her enthusiasm morphing to concern. "What?"

I shook my head, dispelling whatever crazy thought she had running through her mind. "You. You're pretty incredible."

She rolled her eyes. "I know. I hear it all the time."

This girl. "Well, once more can't hurt."

We shared a laugh as the train crept upon us, quickly stealing our attention. The locomotive led the way, passing by slower than expected. A rumbling accompanied the enormity of it. I sat enthralled as each car moved by. Boxcars transporting goods. Cattle cars filled with live cattle. Tanker cars of all sizes and shapes. I tried keeping count, losing track somewhere after one hundred, probably because I couldn't keep my eyes off Hadley.

I loved the way the gust from the train whipped her blond hair all around her head and the fact that she didn't move or try to push it out of her face. Just like in my Jeep. And forget about her completely awed expression as the cars moved by us. It just made me want more moments like that with her. And I knew better than to *ever* think like that. To *ever* think of the future.

I squeezed her hand as the cars continued passing by. She squeezed mine back. A silent agreement that the whole scene was cool as shit. It was her thing. And I wasn't too proud to admit, I'd been wrong. The train was so much more than just some rusty boxcars.

I understood the grandeur. The peacefulness. The subtle way it appeared out of nowhere and disappeared just the same—like it had never been there at all.

Hadley

Caynan didn't speak. I couldn't fathom what he was thinking. Why he wasn't interested. Why his attention had been on *me* instead of the train.

"So?" I asked when the train disappeared into the woods after an amazing four-minute show.

He nodded. "Pretty damn cool."

I laughed. "You barely watched."

His eyes dropped to my lips. "Oh, I watched."

If I were standing, my knees might've buckled. He had the ability to unhinge me with a single look. With a comment that took on several meanings. With his mere presence. The guy was good. "So how many cars did it have?"

"One hundred and sixty."

Bastard. "One hundred and sixty *five.*"

He laughed. "I did need to blink."

I laughed as I fell onto my back, turning onto my side and propping myself up on my elbow. I found it difficult not to admire the way Caynan fit into the whole scene. Fit into my life.

"So?" he asked with a devious twinkle in his eyes.

"What?"

"Am I invited back?"

I shrugged. "Maybe."

"That's not really an answer."

"Well…you haven't really given me a reason to invite you back."

His lips pulled up on one side leaving one hell of a cocky grin in their place. Then he lunged forward, rolling me onto my back and following me down, hovering over me, our lips inches apart. "Let me give you a reason."

I barely blinked before his lips were on mine, powerful and urgent. He had something to prove. Something I'd challenged him to prove. And in that moment, in the middle of the woods with the bugs and bats our only audience, I wanted him to prove he wanted to be there. Wanted to be invited back. Wanted me.

Gahhh. The guy could freaking kiss. His tongue dove inside my mouth, lapping and tangling with mine like it was meant to be there. *God.* I wanted it there. I arched into him, slipping my arms around his back, my hands sliding slowly up the dip above his ass to the curve of his spine. I knew he was built, but I had no idea just how much until my fingers dug into the cords of his muscles.

He broke our kiss, pulling back from me. Our heavy breaths mingling in the space between us. "How am I doing so far?"

I laughed, breathlessly. "Seriously?"

He nodded, humor dancing in his eyes.

"Well, I hate to be the one to break it to you—"

His lips crashed down on mine, stealing my breath away. This time he climbed on top of me, his knees digging into the grass on both sides of my hips. *God.* The feel of his body aligned with mine and the bulge in his jeans pressing right where I ached for it, made me yearn to take it further. To feel every inch of him. To touch his bare skin. For him to touch mine. There was something about Caynan. Something about his hands digging into my hair and his amazing ability with his tongue that made me a complete and utter goner. "I want you out of this shirt," he growled against my lips.

Ummm.

I didn't stop kissing him. I wasn't sure if that was my attempt to stop him from stripping me down in the middle of the woods because A, it was too soon. Or B, I didn't want to be like girls who slept with any guy who showed them attention. I was in no way a prude, but I'd only slept with one guy—a guy I'd known for a year. I'd only known Caynan for less than a month.

He pulled back, sensing my trepidation. "I didn't say I was going to. I just said I wanted to."

I exhaled a mix of relief and disappointment. "I guess player habits die hard."

"Nope. I have eyes. And I'd be a fool not to want to see all of you." His charm was so unnerving at times I couldn't help but wonder if he was too good to be true. "But when the time is right…" He flashed a hotter-than-hot smirk. "I plan to do it. Very slowly. Piece by piece. And you're going to love every second of it."

Gulp.

CHAPTER EIGHT

Hadley

"So, Caynan, tell us about London," Cass implored from across the lunch table the next day.

Caynan's leg, which had been pressed against mine under the table, tensed. "It's just like you'd imagine."

"That's the biggest non-answer I've ever heard."

"Come on, Cass. Leave him alone," I interjected. "He's trying to eat."

"Yeah, but we barely know anything about him except he's from London and a good baseball player—"

"A great baseball player," Eric interrupted from beside Cass.

Caynan held out his knuckles and Eric tapped them. "Thanks, man."

My eyes ventured across the cafeteria. Eyes were on us. Jealous eyes. Accusatory eyes. Gossip-spreading eyes. It made me uncomfortable. It made me wonder how many of them had been up close and personal with Caynan, even if he hadn't slept with them like he claimed. I wasn't used to being the center of attention. I wasn't used to having my every move dissected. But given their jealous stares, that's exactly what they were doing.

"So, is the palace as amazing as it looks on TV?" Cass continued.

Caynan popped some French fries into his mouth. "Looks exactly the same."

Cass was relentless with her interrogation. "How about that Ferris wheel where you can eat dinner?"

"I've never eaten there." He lifted his burger and bit into it.

"Have you ever run into the Royals?"

I wanted to kick her under the table. But at the same time, I hadn't missed his vague answers and the absence of his usual wit.

Caynan shook his head. "We didn't exactly run in the same circles."

I laughed, so did Cass and Eric. I hoped that would be enough to shut her up. He clearly didn't enjoy talking about home. I wondered if it made him homesick or reminded him of his mom. "When's your next game?"

His eyes cut to mine, appreciating the subject change. "Why? You planning to cheer me on again?"

"Unless you think it'll distract you."

"Oh, it'll definitely distract me." He leaned over and dropped a quick kiss on my lips. "But no worries. I'll still mash it for you." He lowered his voice so only I could hear. "Meet me after practice today. I have something I want to do with you."

My stomach dipped, my mind instantly jumping back to the previous night and what he'd said.

I was in so much trouble.

I waited for Caynan to finish practice after school. When he walked out of the gym with his hair all wet from a shower, I stood frozen to my spot, admiring his breathtaking good looks and relishing in the fact that this guy seemed to want me. He walked toward me with a knowing grin. "Like what you see?"

I blinked several times. "What?"

"Oh, come on. You think it's the first time I got that glazed look from a chick?"

I couldn't decide if I was insulted he categorized me with other girls or amused by his overconfidence. "You're delusional. I had something in my eye."

He grinned as he stopped in front of me. "Got something for you." He reached into his baseball bag and dug around, pulling out a package of licorice.

I smiled as I grabbed it, tearing into the wrapper without a second thought. "Thanks." I drew a couple out, handing one to Caynan and sticking the other in my mouth. "So, what are we doing?"

"You'll see." He linked his fingers with mine and tugged me toward the baseball field.

"I already know how good you are."

"I get that a lot."

I bumped him with my hip and he playfully stumbled to the side as if I'd been strong enough to move him. "Your confidence never ceases to amaze me."

He laughed as he dropped his bag onto the metal bleachers and pulled out two gloves and a ball. "For you." He handed me one of the floppy old gloves.

"We're playing?"

He nodded. "Thought you should know the game if you're gonna be cheering me on."

I crossed my arms. "Who said I'll be cheering you on?"

"Must you fight me at every turn, woman?"

I paused, wondering if I really did that.

"You said you would at lunch," he reminded me.

"Fine. I'll probably show up to a couple more games."

He smiled smugly.

That! That right there is why I fight him.

"And what planet do you think I'm from anyway? I know baseball."

"Not my rules, you don't." His raspy tone and the mischievous glint in his eyes flushed my cheeks. "Come on."

I followed him onto the field. "What position do you normally play?"

"I can play anywhere. But Coach just has me DH since I came so late in the season."

I nodded. "You planning to play in college?"

He shrugged, his eyes jetting away as he punched his hand into the palm of his glove.

"Have any scouts seen you play?"

"No", he said quickly.

"Think you've got what it takes to make it to the pros?"

His eyes lifted to mine. "Absolutely."

There was something about his cockiness. Sometimes I hated him for it, and other times it carried all the way down to my bones. This was one of those times. "So, is playing in the pros your plan?"

He shrugged. "Maybe in different lifetime."

I left his final comment alone, seeing how his entire demeanor changed when he said it. "So, tell me about these rules."

His eyebrows bounced. "I was hoping you'd ask." He pointed to second base. "Go stand over there."

"Why don't you?"

"Because I want to check out your ass as you walk over there."

I cocked my head. "Do girls really fall for lines like that?"

He did one of those shrug nods. "If it helps, I'm completely serious."

I ignored the shiver scrambling up my spine and strutted across the infield, totally giving him a show.

His laughter traveled from behind me. "Yup. Totally worth it."

I spun around with a smile on my face. Everything he said made me feel so wanted. So beautiful. So overwhelmed. I wasn't blind. I'd seen him look at other girls. But the way his dark eyes danced with playfulness when he looked at me, I knew he saved that look only for me. "All right." I held up my glove. "Let's get this game started."

He lifted his chin toward me, his lips twitching. "Glove's on the wrong hand, Slugger."

My eyes shifted to the glove on my right hand. "I knew that." I tugged it off and buried my left hand in it.

He grinned as he explained his rules. "You miss, you lose a piece of clothing. I miss, I do the same."

I looked around the surrounding grounds. Some of his teammates' cars remained in the parking lot and the gym was a mere hundred feet away. "You took me to the *school* baseball field because you wanted to get me naked?"

He lifted his eyes to the sky as he pondered the question. "Yeah. Hadn't really thought that one through—wait." His eyes shot to mine. "You would've been in if we were somewhere else?"

I lifted my shoulders, letting him believe he actually had a shot. "You'll never know."

He groaned, cursing his missed opportunity. "Okay, fine. Let me tone it back. You miss, I get to kiss you. I miss, you get to kiss me."

My eyes narrowed, squinting in the afternoon sun. "What's the point of the game? Either way, we end up making out."

He laughed. "Exactly."

I rolled my eyes. "Okay. Throw me the ball."

He lobbed me the ball and I caught it easily.

"Seriously? That's all you've got?"

He laughed. "I wanted to be sure I didn't hurt you."

"Hurt me? My grandmother throws harder than that."

"But I'm not trying to make out with your grandmother."

I laughed as I threw the ball back to him. It veered off to his left, but he reached out and snagged it effortlessly. "Remind me why we're catching the ball?" I said. "I thought the object was to miss it."

"Who said I wanted to kiss you?"

I dug the glove into my side, jutting out my hip. "I have it on pretty good authority that you want to kiss me."

"Oh yeah?"

I nodded as I held my glove up again. This time when he threw me the ball, I pulled my glove away, missing purposely.

He stared me down, his face giving nothing away. It took no more than a couple of seconds, but he broke into a sprint, charging at me at full speed. For no other reason than to make him chase me, I dropped my glove, turned, and ran in the opposite direction laughing hysterically.

"You can run, but you can't hide, Hadley."

Caynan moved fast, but I moved faster. I might not have been super athletic, but I could run. Maybe not as quickly in my cute ankle wrap sandals, but fast enough. I set my sights on the outfield fence and then broke left once I reached it. Unfortunately, Caynan broke left first, blocking my way. I stopped, feigning right. He hopped to my right, but I took off left. He'd clearly played this game before because he caught me easily, wrapping his arm around my waist and lifting me right off my feet. I squealed.

"Nice try." He slipped his arms under my knees and arms and cradled me.

"Just trying to prove a point."

His dimple dug in. "How'd that work for you?"

"I'm still waiting to find out."

He gazed down at me. Never had I wanted to read someone's mind so badly. He lowered me to the ground, his lips descending on mine as his body pressed me into the grassy outfield. His lips were soft with just the right amount of pressure. He took his time, making me want for more. A lot more. His hands dug into my hair, moving my head to fit with his. He eventually pulled back, his eyes remaining on mine. "I like that you challenge me."

"But you just said I fight you on everything."

He smirked. "I didn't say I didn't like it."

"Is that all you like?"

His head moved from side to side, his eyes still locked on mine.

I lifted my brows. "Care to share?"

"Right now, I need to get what's owed to me." This time his lips captured mine and there was nothing soft or gentle about it. Which was fine by me.

* * *

"We had two more break-ins," my father explained.

My eyes shot up from my scrambled eggs. Thursday breakfast on the patio was a family ritual since it was the only time all three of us were home together in the morning. "Where?"

"Joe Richards' house, the VP of Chronotech."

My eyes latched on to the birds soaring high above us. I expected them to be ravens to mirror my father's somber tone, but they were only seagulls.

"And that hockey player, Mike Roberts' house."

"I've been there. It's gorgeous."

He nodded, his eyes assessing my mother to be sure he could talk about work at the table.

"What'd they take?" she asked.

"Cash. Over a hundred grand combined."

My mother sipped her coffee as if the news hadn't been unsettling. "Are you any closer to finding who's behind them?"

He pushed a link of sausage around his dish with his fork. "I wish we were. It's like they already have the combinations. The safes are undamaged. There aren't any fingerprints on them and they're not tripping the alarm systems. We're dealing with professionals."

"Did they take anything other than money?" my mother asked.

He shook his head. "There were other valuables, but they left them. Either they got spooked and needed a fast getaway, or it was just about the money."

"I heard they took jewelry from Katie's dad's safe," I added.

He popped his sausage into his mouth. "Where'd you hear that?"

I shrugged. "People talk."

"Yeah. They took jewelry and money from that one."

"Could it be different people? Like, unrelated crimes?" If art didn't work out, maybe crime-solving could be my thing.

He shook his head. "I just don't know." I'd never seen him so stumped. He always carried himself with such confidence. Never letting anything stand in his way or cause him to falter.

My mother looked to me. "Honey, we're supposed to leave next Friday for your grandfather's fundraisers. But I'm not so sure we should leave you alone now."

"I'll stay home," my dad offered, using any excuse to get out of going to a bunch of fundraisers for a politician—even if the politician was his father-in-law. Even more so when the fundraisers were during one of his few weeks off.

"We have an alarm system," I assured them. "And I know where the guns are kept."

My parents exchanged an uncertain look.

"I'll be fine. Besides...who'd be stupid enough to break into a detective's house?"

"I'll have the guys patrol the neighborhood," my dad offered.

I nodded. "Good idea. When are you coming back?"

"The following Friday. Then we have that two-night event in Bunkerson that you're attending."

"Will you be all right?" my dad asked. Given the hopeful look in his eyes, he wanted me to say no so he had an excuse to stay home.

"I think I can handle it. Just a wild party. Three hundred people or so."

He laughed, while my mother lifted her brows. "Will Caynan be there?"

My dad's eyes jumped between us. "Caynan?"
Shit.

"Hadley didn't tell you she's been dating a new boy? He's from London." Damn her. She knew exactly what she was doing. Let the inquisition begin.

"Why is this the first I'm hearing of it?" He sounded at a loss for words, as if he assumed he knew everything that happened in my life.

I shrugged. "It's nothing serious."

"Looked serious at the fundraiser." The traitor's eyes shifted to my dad's. "He got her out on the dance floor."

"When am I going to meet this boy?" he asked.

Oh shit. "He's really busy with school and baseball right now."

"He any good?" I could tell by his tone he was genuinely interested.

I nodded. "Really good."

"I'll have to tag along to one of his games."

I smiled, though I planned to never let that happen.

"And invite him for dinner." He stuffed another sausage into his mouth. "Tomorrow."

I swallowed down my horror. "It's a little early for family dinners. We've only been on one date."

"I'm working every night until we leave," he explained between bites. "And I need to know who my daughter's hanging out with."

Meeting a girl's father was tough. But when her father was a detective…yeah, it sucked. "No promises."

Caynan

"They're impressed by how fast you work," my dad explained over a breakfast of cold pizza.

"Three houses in a matter of weeks? Or my skill with a safe?" I asked, realizing how fucked up it was to be discussing this with my dad over breakfast.

"Both."

"Do we really need them?"

"Your talents are wasted with these trivial jobs," he said with a mouthful of pizza.

"These trivial jobs are what pay our bills." I couldn't hide my frustration. "Dad. I need a real job."

"You have a real job," he snapped.

"Something I can put on a resume. I need normal experiences. This shit is getting old fast."

"Watch it."

I felt my rage building. "What? Does the truth hurt?"

"What truth?" He scraped his chair back with his feet and stood up, pointing into my face. "This is it for you. How many times do I have to tell you?" I saw in his face something I wasn't used to seeing. Fear. The fact that I wanted out scared the hell out of him. He needed me. His eyes were shit. And without me, he couldn't disarm an alarm. He couldn't crack a safe. He couldn't do anything.

Take care of your father.

"When do we meet with them?" I ground out between gritted teeth.

He shrugged. "Whenever they call." With that, he turned his back on me and walked out of the trailer.

You're all each other have, my mother's voice taunted me.

I growled, turning and punching my fist into the nearest wall.

Hadley

I stepped out of my car, this time with no help from Caynan. I glanced around the crowded parking lot. His Jeep was parked across the way, but there was no sign of him. I made my way inside the school and into English class. Caynan already sat in his seat as I slid into mine.

"Hey." I noticed scratches on the fingers of his right hand and discoloration on his knuckles. "What happened?"

He glanced up, confusion in his eyes.

"Your hand."

His eyes dropped to it. "Oh, it's nothing."

"Looks like something."

His jaw clenched. "I was just fixing something on my Jeep." His eyes flashed away.

Uh, huh.

"You sure you're okay?"

He nodded.

Here goes nothing. "So…my dad wants to see you play."

His eyes nearly burst out of his head as he broke into a coughing fit.

"What's wrong?" I laughed. "Scared he might jinx you?"

He controlled his coughing, but he didn't smile. "You were talking about me?"

"My *mom* was talking about you."

Ms. Atwood entered the room with a guest speaker, silencing the room and ending our conversation before I could even think of broaching the subject of dinner with my parents. If his reaction to my dad checking out his game was any indication, dinner was even more unlikely than I'd initially thought.

At the bell, Caynan made some excuse about having to talk to his coach and bolted out of the room.

"What's up with him," Cass asked as she scooped up her books and walked into the hallway with me.

"I might've mentioned my dad wanted to see him play."

"Yup, that would definitely scare a guy."

"That's not the worst of it. My dad wants him to come over for dinner."

Cass exploded into hysterics. "Well, that relationship was nice while it lasted."

I bumped her with my shoulder. "Thanks a lot."

"Did he find out he was a detective before or after the date?"

"Before."

Cass nodded. "I give him credit for taking you out in the first place. Maybe he's just scared a second date will mean a lie detector test."

The rest of the day passed with no sign of Caynan. I knew when I was being avoided, and he'd been avoiding me like I'd just told him I was pregnant. I guess I couldn't blame him. It was way too fast to be talking about him to my parents—forget bringing my dad to one of his games.

At the final bell, I grabbed my books from my locker. When I stepped back to close it, Caynan stood there.

"So, what did you tell your dad about me?" He sounded unsure, vulnerable even.

My stomach bubbled with hope. "That you're good at baseball."

"Just good?" He stepped toward me, backing me into my locker.

I couldn't even smile, mesmerized by his nearness—especially after assuming I'd scared him away. "Really good."

He lowered his mouth toward mine, but I pushed him back.

"You done avoiding me?"

His head reeled back. "I wasn't avoiding you."

"Sure you were. Look. Fathers are scary. Even more so when they're cops. But it really was innocent. My mom mentioned you in front of him and he just—"

"Wanted to make sure you were hanging out with good people. I get it. You're lucky he cares."

I nodded, realizing that having two involved parents was more of an anomaly these days.

"Can I at least have a heads up when he's gonna be there?" Caynan asked.

"So you can be sure to mash it?"

He leaned forward, and this time I let him press his lips to mine. They were warm and held the reassurance that I hadn't blown everything.

Caynan

After breakfast with my dad and then Hadley mentioning her dad wanted to see me play, it sent me into a slight tailspin. I tried putting some distance between us. But then I felt like crap for avoiding her. She didn't deserve to have to deal with me and all my bullshit. But I didn't have the nerve—or the strength—to let her go. Not yet anyway. Not when she made me feel more like the real me than I'd felt in a long time.

"Pig."

I stared up at the puffy clouds floating above Hadley and me. I didn't see anything even close to resembling a pig. We'd been lying on a wool blanket on the beach for the past two hours. Sadly, we were both fully clothed. I pointed to a darker cloud to the left. "That one kinda looks like a frog."

"A frog?" Hadley's laugh mixed with the crashing of the waves on the shore. "You're pathetic at this game."

I linked my hands behind my head, the fabric of the blanket scratching the backs of my fingers. "Never claimed to be good at everything."

"Oh, I'm pretty sure you have."

I laughed. "Yeah, you're probably right. Once my mouth gets moving, I just can't seem to stop it."

"Oh, yeah?" Hadley rolled onto her side, her head resting in her palm. "Prove it."

I smiled, loving the sassy way she challenged me. "Prove what?"

"How long your mouth can move without stopping. Preferably with mine."

Oh, fuck yeah. My dick twitched as I rolled onto my side, scoping out the surrounding area. Aside from the few seagulls swooping down in search of food and a man a mile down the beachcombing the sand with a metal detector, the beach was deserted.

I took a moment to get my head and…well…the other one in check.

But Hadley wasn't having it.

She moved forward, her lips colliding with mine. The eager swipe of her minty tongue in my mouth sent my body buzzing. If I was going to hell—which chances were I was—I might as well have fun doing it. I immersed myself in the kiss. In the taste of cherry on her lips. In the feel of her soft body pressed against mine. All of her. Every. Sexy. Inch. She controlled the kiss, and it was damn sexy.

I pulled back, knowing I needed to stop whatever my body was screaming at me to continue.

Hadley's eyes flared. "You're such a liar."

Every part of my body tensed as I swallowed around the sudden lump in my throat. "What?"

"You said you couldn't stop." She dragged her thumb along my bottom lip, wiping away the ChapStick she'd left there. The pressure of her soft finger left an indelible numbness in its wake, something I wasn't used to. "And you stopped. Way too soon."

If I didn't want to kiss the hell out of her before, I did now. The girl wanted to push me. Wanted to wrap her tiny hands around my heart and never let go. I was in way over my head.

No. I was *screwed.*

"Come over for dinner tomorrow night."

My head flew back, her words an instant icy shower. "What?"

Nervousness grabbed hold of her features. "I figured if I took you by surprise, you'd say yes." Her eyes flashed away. "My dad invited you."

Oh, fuck. "I thought he wanted to come to my game?"

"He wants you to come for dinner, too."

I swallowed. Hard. "Ummm."

Her words flew out in a single breath. "I don't want to freak you out. I told him we've only been out once, but my parents are heading out of town and, like you said earlier, he just wants to know who I'm hanging out with."

I could tell she needed me to know it wasn't her idea. She clearly didn't have a choice.

I knew that feeling all too well.

"I don't know…" I couldn't even look at her. Lying to her face was a lot harder than I thought it would be. "…I—"

"Oh, come on."

My eyes cut to hers.

She cocked her head, her nervousness replaced by that feisty spunk that made her who she was. "You scared?"

"Scared? I'm not scared of anything." More like freaked the fuck out.

"Then say yes."

My internal battle raged, thoughts whizzing through my head at rapid-fire. How could I meet her dad? He'd profile me the second I walked through the door. How could I get out of it without hurting her feelings? How could I get away from her without agreeing to anything?

Dammit. I knew I'd been playing with fire. I'd let things get too far. "I have to check with my dad."

"Say yes." Her puppy dog eyes begged me.

I closed my eyes, praying for the strength to get out of it unscathed. I needed to put a stop to what was happening—what I was *letting* happen. This shit was supposed to be fun. Pushing Feisty's buttons had started off like a game. I liked watching her squirm. I liked having her put me in my place. But now I needed to figure out how to push her away before we both ended up hurt.

"Say yes."

The hope in her voice nearly crushed me. I wasn't being fair to her. There was no future for us. And Hadley was the type of girl who deserved an amazing future. Hell, she was the type of girl *I'd* see a future with if I actually had one of my own. My eyes popped open and, with the powerful waves crashing nearby and her at my side, I did the only thing I could.

I nodded.

Hadley

I hurried to English class Friday morning, eager to see Caynan. When I passed through the door, my eyes shot to his empty seat. I slipped into my mine, waiting for him to show. I'd become one of those girls. The type whose happiness revolved around the presence of a guy. *Dammit.*

Cass entered the classroom. "Hey, girl."

"Hey."

She lifted her chin toward Caynan's desk. "Where's lover boy?"

I shrugged.

She dropped into her seat, twisting to face me. "So, is tonight the night?"

I inhaled a deep breath. "Yup."

"Is your dad planning to clean one of his antique guns at the table?"

I laughed. "He's not like that. You know that."

"I picture him whipping it out and laying it down all nonchalant before asking lover boy to pass the peas."

I snorted at the ridiculous image in my head.

"I'd give anything to see lover boy's face."

"Stop calling him that."

Her eyes tightened. "Why?"

I titled my head. "It's too early. I barely know him."

"Oh, I'd say you're getting to know him. And he *really* wants to get to know you. *All* of you."

I rolled my eyes.

"I'm serious, Hadley. The way he looks at you…the guy's got it bad."

CHAPTER NINE

Hadley

"Maybe he didn't realize you said tonight," my mother offered as I stared down at my phone.

It was eight-thirty. We'd been outside on our back patio for two hours. The food was cold no matter how many times my mother reheated it.

Caynan hadn't texted. Hadn't called. Hadn't given me the courtesy of an excuse for blowing me off. For making me look like an idiot. I knew he didn't want to meet my dad. But to blow me off completely? Who did that?

"He's probably sick." My dad finally picked up his fork and gnawed into the cold piece of filet. "You said he wasn't in school."

"He could've called," I mumbled, beyond pissed and completely humiliated that the first boy my dad took any interest in stood me up.

"Don't jump to conclusions," my mother warned. "I've met him. Something serious must've happened to keep him from showing up."

I pushed back my chair and stood. "Well, I don't feel like waiting any longer. Sorry I ruined your night." With that, I took off for my room, hearing my parents' pleas for me to wait. But for what? He wasn't showing up. He never intended to.

* * *

The weekend had come and gone and still no word from Caynan. I'd prepared myself on my way into school on Monday, ready to confront him during English class. But he was a no-show there, too.

I looked out across the crowded cafeteria during lunch. People passed by in a blur.

Cass moved her face to block the cafeteria from my view. "Stop sulking."

"This from the person who pushed me to go out with him."

"He's clearly sick."

I cocked my head. "And he couldn't send a text?"

"You think he's missed school just to avoid you?" She mirrored my cocked head.

A few hours later, with Cass' words in mind, I struggled to focus on the homework spread out all over my bed.

Maybe something *had* happened to Caynan. Maybe, while I was moping and hating him for blowing me off, he was in some hospital somewhere. Maybe he was hurt. Or maybe it wasn't him at all. Maybe he was off caring for his sick father. He'd lost his mom; maybe something had happened to his dad.

Sending a quick text to check if he was okay didn't seem like such a terrible idea anymore. I grabbed my phone and sent a message. **Just checking that you're all right…**

I waited.

Hours passed before I finally gave up and went to bed without any response.

* * *

Tuesday morning, I pulled into the school parking lot. My hands tightened on the steering wheel and my stomach churned like I'd eaten something bad. Caynan's Jeep was there. It had been *five* days. Five days since I'd seen him. Since I'd spoken to him. Since I'd wanted to strangle him.

I hopped out of my car and marched into the building, knowing I was moments away from coming face to face with him. My heart rate sped up exponentially as I trudged down the busy hallway. I grabbed the books I needed from my locker and walked into English class. I tried to appear unfazed, but I couldn't help myself. I looked right to Caynan, reading over notes in his notebook. He didn't even bother to glance up when I entered.

I forced a smile at Cass as I made my way up the aisle toward my seat, my pulse pounding in my ears. She gave me wide eyes and nudged her head toward him. Like I couldn't actually see him for myself. *Thanks, buddy.*

I slipped into my seat, turning my head toward Caynan. "Hey." I tried to keep my voice steady, but I couldn't disguise the quiver.

His head shot up like he hadn't seen me walk in. "Hey."

I bit my tongue, trekking through the awkward conversation. "You feeling okay?"

He nodded. "Yeah. I'm fine." His eyes dropped back down to his notes.

I can't believe this is happening.

I can't believe this is freaking happening to me.

I was too smart to be one of those girls. Too smart to fall for empty words. Too smart to fall for disingenuous actions. Too smart to get tossed to the side for the next big thing. "You're an asshole."

Cass' head spun around. Caynan's whipped up, his eyes narrowed.

"You're exactly what I thought you were," I ground out, trying desperately not to cause a scene as I jumped to my feet. "I knew better." I hurried out of the classroom, not bothering to look back.

I needed to breathe. I needed to process the fact that I'd been just like every other girl to him. I'd been played by the God damn player.

"Hadley, wait." I heard the slapping of his sneakers jogging down the nearly empty hallway as I quickened my pace. "Would you just wait?"

Heads of stragglers twisted in our direction. That wasn't enough to stop me. I reached an exit door and threw it open. Two strong hands grasped my shoulders, stopping me from stepping outside. I closed my eyes, shielding them from both the bright morning sun and the owner of the hands. "Let go of me."

"What the hell is wrong with you?" he asked.

I spun around, pulling free from his hands as the door slammed shut behind me. "What's wrong with *me*? You've gotta be freaking joking."

His guilty eyes stayed on mine, though they clearly itched to move away.

I stepped forward, more rage than I'd ever felt rushing through me as I pointed my finger into his chest. He stepped back. "*I'm* not the one who stood somebody up. I'm not the one who didn't return a text checking to be sure you weren't lying in some ditch somewhere. And *I'm* not the one who blew *everything*."

He buried his hands in the pockets of his cargo shorts, his shoulders relaxing and his eyes softening. His suddenly calm demeanor irked every part of my irritated body.

I threw my hands out. "Am I wrong?"

His lips slid into a cocky grin.

Seriously? A flipping grin?

"Glad to see you care."

My eyes flared. "You can't be serious?"

"Oh, but I am." His dimple dug into his cheek. "I've been out of town."

"So?" My voice rose.

"So, I knew when I saw you I'd be able to explain what happened. And we'd be good."

I scoffed, amazed by his brazenness. "Five days later?"

He lifted a shoulder.

My entire face scrunched in repulsion. "I hate you."

He laughed. "No, you don't. I won't let you."

I leveled him with a serious glare, hoping every ounce of disgust I felt for him was relayed in my eyes. "No, really. I hate you."

He stepped closer, causing me to step back. "I got your text." He took another step forward. I took another step back. "Thank you for checking on me." He stepped forward again. I stepped back, this time banging into the set of lockers behind me. "My dad sprung a last-minute trip on me. I planned to call you once we got on the road. But as soon as we hit the town limit, I had no service." His arms shot out, his hands bracing the lockers at the sides of my head, caging me in. "I'm sorry I missed dinner."

Having him that close made my skin crawl, but I matched his gaze, my eyes riveting between his. Did I believe him? Did his story line up? My dad taught me early on that a liar's eyes shifted to their right when they lied. It was a subconscious thing, but a dead giveaway to those attuned to it. Caynan's eyes remained fixed on mine.

"I thought about you the entire time I was away," he continued.

I scoffed.

"I thought about the feel of your skin," he continued. "The taste of your lips. The vibration of your heartbeat when it presses against my chest." His lips sealed over mine without warning. Without permission.

I braced my hands on his chest and shoved as hard as I could. He didn't even shift. His arms stayed locked. His hips held me in place. His mouth devoured mine. I wanted to scream. I wanted to bite his tongue and draw blood. I wanted to tell him this was never going to work. But his tongue relentlessly thrust deeper. Voices materialized in the distance. Were teachers calling us? Were people gawking at us? I finally broke loose, dislodging my lips from his and gasping for air. "Are you nuts?"

He seemed shocked by my anger. "What?"

"I'm not someone you can mess with, Caynan."

He nodded. "I know that."

I assessed the surrounding hallway. Classroom doors were closed, and the last-minute stragglers were hurrying to class, taking no interest in us. "I'm not someone who deals well with being blown off. Or being made to look like a fool. I'm not one of those girls."

His face grew even more serious. "I know that."

"If you don't want to hang out anymore, let's be done right now."

He paused, his eyes holding indecision. "Is that what you want?"

"Oh, no. You might be able to get away with non-answers with Cass, but I can see right through them. The question is 'Is that what *you* want?'"

He dug his fingers through his dark hair, scratching away at his scalp as he stepped back from me, leaving the once warm space around me uncomfortably chilly. "I like hanging out with you."

I remained quiet so he had no choice but to continue.

"I know you're different than other girls."

I cocked my head. That wasn't an answer. "I need someone honest, Caynan. If you can't be, then we're cool. We can go back to bantering in class and then go our separate ways. You're a guy. What eighteen-year-old guy really wants to be exclusive anyway?"

His eyes shifted from mine. "Yeah." It came out so softly I almost missed it.

Part of me wished he hadn't agreed so quickly. But the other part knew it was for the best. The last few days had been torture. The not knowing. The dwelling. The worry. The anger. Who knew what more time spent with him would do to me. It was better to get out before my feelings were any more invested. "It's better this way."

His eyes cut back to mine like he wanted to say something. But his lips slammed shut like he didn't actually have the guts to say it.

I forced an insincere smile. "No worries, player." I stepped around him and started toward English class. My heart thrashed with each step away from the guy I'd begun to let into my life. The guy I believed in. The guy who clearly felt something for me, but was incapable of committing.

"Hadley?"

Caynan's deep voice immobilized me. I jerked a glance over my shoulder.

He stood there staring down the hallway at me for a long time, his arms hanging uselessly at his sides. Indecision had overtaken his features. Had he surprised himself by calling out to me? Because he seemed to be at a loss for words.

I saved him the trouble, turning away and continuing toward class.

"Wait," he called.

I didn't.

The slapping of his sneakers on the floor filled the silence. I didn't stop or turn around. He rounded me, stopping in front of me. "Don't think you're getting rid of me that easily." He grabbed hold of my hand and pulled me into his chest, hugging me in the middle of the empty hallway.

I wanted to resist. To explain we were better as friends. To fight what was happening. But the fact that he wouldn't allow me to walk out of his life, even after I'd urged him to, wouldn't allow me to let it be over either.

* * *

Cass slid her lunch tray onto the table and pegged Caynan with her eyes. "You planning on skipping town again without a word?"

He glanced to me beside him. But I glanced away. He was on his own with that one. "No."

"Hadley's not like other girls. She's not gonna follow you around like a lost puppy if you decide to call it quits."

"I know that." His words were soft.

"If you want to be with her, if you really want to hold onto one of the best people I know, man up and treat her right."

Caynan stared across the table, his eyes a mix of fear and respect. He nodded his response. "Good. Are you taking her to the carnival this weekend?" she asked.

His eyes shot to mine. "You want to go?"

I shrugged, still feeling out of sorts. I hadn't had much time to process the fact that I'd gone from hating him for days to worrying something had happened to him. Not to mention, feeling like a fool for falling for the player to thinking we were over. My head was all over the place.

"Hi, Caynan. Missed you in art." Shannon stopped at the end of our table, her eyes batting like she had something in them.

"Oh," Caynan said politely but not overly friendly. Smart guy.

She nodded. I could've sworn she shifted just to give him a better to look at her boobs.

I opened my mouth to respond, but Cass beat me to it. "If you hadn't noticed, he's dating Hadley. And she's too nice to send your ass back to the corner of the cafeteria where you and your slutty friends belong. But I'm not Hadley. And I'm not too nice to say it."

Shannon's eyes nearly popped out of her head. I wondered if anyone had ever spoken to her that way before.

Cass motioned with her finger in a circle. "Keep it moving."

Shannon actually did what she was told, spinning on her high wedges and strutting across the cafeteria.

I stared across the table at Cass, not knowing what to say. Thank you? You're nuts?

"If you're with Hadley, and I mean really with her," she warned Caynan. "You will keep your eyes and hands off that one and all the rest of the vultures waiting for their chance to move in for the kill."

He grabbed my hand under the table and linked our fingers. "I'm definitely with Hadley," he assured her, squeezing my hand tightly as he did.

CHAPTER TEN

Caynan

I lay on my bed Sunday afternoon considering how I fucked everything up with Hadley. Five days had passed since she nearly sent my ass packing. And even after making amends with her, things had been different. Like she didn't completely trust me. Not once had I seen her outside of school. And during school, she kept me at arm's length—like at any moment she expected me to disappear again.

The irony was not lost on me.

This weekend had been a turning point. She'd agreed to go out with me, but only on Sunday. Who the hell goes to a carnival on a Sunday? But I'd agreed to go. Because time spent with Hadley was better than time spent without her.

And for the record, I had been away like I told her, and it wasn't by choice. My dad forced me to go to that business meeting with him. And as much as I didn't want to go, it gave me an out. The no service thing had been bullshit. I knew I should've called her, but I convinced myself that putting distance between us would make me forget about her. Make her forget about me.

Then her text came.

And it slayed me. I mean...I knew I'd hurt her by not showing up for dinner and not calling. But instead of being angry—like I knew she really was—she asked if I was okay. That's why the harder I tried staying away from her, and the more I tried pushing her from my head, the harder it became. Especially when my fucking head was battling another part of my body.

The front door slammed shut. I checked my phone. It was just after three. Footsteps moved toward my room. My door flew open, slamming against the wall. My father stood there glaring down at me. "You're home?"

I nodded. "Heading out in a few minutes." He didn't need to know anything about my personal life. That was mine.

He raised a brow. "I hope you're being careful. Don't need you leaving your seed behind in every town we end up in."

If I wasn't lying down, my head would've shot back because he was clearly drunk. And while he could be blunt, the slur to his voice and the crass remark wasn't him.

"You know what today is?"

"Huh?"

"The date." His voice grew louder, colder. "You know what today is?"

I shook my head.

"Your mother's birthday."

My stomach rolled over. He hadn't spoken about her in years. With him, it was as though she never existed. I didn't understand it. But I knew enough never to bring her up. It was probably the reason I'd stopped thinking about her. Except, of course, when her uninvited words popped into my head like some fucked-up, otherworldly conscience. I'd never even visited her grave. Not that I knew where it was. We'd never been back to the same place twice. Just like Jacobsville one day. I'd never return.

* * *

"Why you so quiet?" Hadley asked.

I turned toward her in the passenger seat of my Jeep, licking away at her chocolate ice cream cone. "Just enjoying the view." Flirting was easier than telling her about my prick of a father. Spending time with her gave me a reprieve. It made it all disappear. How I thought I could push her away was beyond me.

As opposed to actually going *to* the carnival, Hadley preferred parking on a hill overlooking it. We'd spent the early-evening staring out at the carnival all aglow. The dreamy look in her eyes made it clear how much she enjoyed the colorful flashing lights of the rides and the screams from the people on them. Just one more thing that made her so different from every other girl. She grinned. "Yeah, it does look beautiful."

I reached over, placing a hand on her bare thigh right where her cutoffs stopped. "I was talking about you."

She smiled and when she smiled at me like that—like I was the prince in her own private fairy tale—it made me happier than I'd been in a long time. It also scared the shit out of me. "How's your ice cream?" she asked.

"I bet yours tastes better." I leaned over and kissed her, sucking on her chocolate-coated tongue. She moaned into my mouth, causing me to deepen the kiss, licking away at her mouth like the cone in her hand. She reciprocated, playing a game of push and pull. It was as though my fuck-up never happened. Like this kiss was meant to show me she forgave me for being such a douchebag. It took everything in me not to pull her into my lap so I could kiss the hell out of her all night.

She broke away first, needing to catch a breath, but her eyes stayed on mine as her chest heaved. "I liked yours better."

I laughed, knowing in that moment that things were returning to normal. Thank God.

She tilted her head, her eyes absorbing the details of my face like she'd never really looked that closely before. "Will you tell me something?"

I shrugged. "Depends."

"What's really bothering you?"

"Besides messing things up with you?"

She nodded.

I wanted to say, "I've got plenty of issues. Take your pick." Instead, I shrugged. Being honest with someone was completely foreign to me. I'd never been able to be fully open with anyone before. Never been able to let anyone in. I wondered if Hadley was the one. The one I could actually be myself with. Because I really needed someone to confide in. Someone who could know my demons and still care about me. "It's my mom's birthday."

I heard her sharp intake of breath. "Oh, Caynan, I'm so—"

"Don't. I'm okay. It just gave me something to think about, that's all." My eyes latched onto some lightning bugs deep in the woods beside us. I bet Hadley spent summer nights as a kid bottling them up so she could harness the beauty for just a little while longer. I, on the other hand, was probably already knee-deep in shit I wanted nothing to do with at that point. Sure, at first having everyone excited about what "the kid" could do, made me feel like a king. But soon admiration turned into expectations. And expectations turned into more jobs. Which turned into me losing my childhood way too soon.

"I don't understand." Hadley's voice broke through my thoughts.

"My dad. He hasn't mentioned her in years. Then, out of the blue, he did. It just kind of fucked with my head."

I could see her nod out of the corner of my eye as if she understood. "Can I see a picture of her?"

"I don't have one."

"None?"

I shook my head. "Lost in the move." She didn't need to know which move. It's not like I even remembered.

Hadley finished off her cone then wiped her lips with her napkin. "Let's go."

I thought she'd changed her mind about the carnival since it was only six o'clock, but within minutes, we were at her house. She led me through the elaborate foyer, our footsteps echoing off the high ceilings. If the house looked impressive from the outside, the inside was even more impressive. Everything was sleek and expensive.

From the furniture to the art work, it all sat polished and orderly. We climbed the main staircase to the second floor. We passed the first open door on the right. "That's my room."

"Will I be getting the tour?"

She grinned. "Maybe later."

Yup. That's all it took for my body to respond. Especially with her parents away and knowing we had the entire house to ourselves. I slowed up, readjusting myself in my jeans until we stopped at the next room. That door was open, too, but it was completely dark inside. Hadley switched on the light. I stood in awe as my eyes absorbed the colorful paintings and drawings of people, landscapes, and abstract shapes filling the walls.

An easel sat by the window overlooking the backyard. Carts filled with paints, pencils, chalk, and charcoal sat beside it. Hadley pointed to a sofa pushed against the inside wall. "Sit."

I did as requested and dropped onto the cushy sofa.

Hadley sat down on the small wooden stool in front of her easel. She picked up some colored pencils. "Tell me what she looked like."

My head recoiled so quickly you'd have thought she slapped me across the face. "What?"

"Your mom. What did she look like? Start with the shape of her face. I always draw that first."

My skin tightened. Was she serious? Did she know what she was asking me to do?

"I'm gonna need your help, Caynan." She lifted a nude-colored pencil to the white paper, nudging me on.

I closed my eyes, letting my head drop to the back of the sofa. I could do it. I could explain the hazy image of my mom on Christmas morning. The one of her passing me a gift she couldn't wait for me to open. "Long. Oval. Kind of like mine." My eyes cracked open. Hadley wasn't looking at me. Her pencil flew across the paper. I couldn't see the drawing, but she worked quickly.

"How about her eyes? Were they close to her forehead?" She shook her head before I could answer. "Okay, that sounded weird. Did she have a high forehead?"

I shrugged. "Normal, I guess."

She nodded. "Were her eyes close together or far apart?"

I thought for a moment, trying to picture her pretty brown eyes. Not the way they looked in the hospital when they'd become sunken and dark once the cancer invaded her body. "My dad used to say I looked a lot like her."

Hadley stared across the room at me for a long time. She pulled her hair back into a ponytail and her eyes danced across my face. She was beautiful. Like *really* beautiful. Natural and perfect. At least perfect to me. "Were her eyes the same color as yours?"

I nodded, a vision of my mother laughing materializing in my mind. "And her smile. It was so wide. It showed all her teeth when she laughed."

Hadley nodded then began drawing again. "Hair color?"

"Dark like mine."

Her eyes and hand stayed focused on the paper, long strokes moving quickly to all corners of the paper. "Long or short?"

"Long, but wavy like yours. Not curly."

She nodded her understanding. "I think I can take it from here."

I watched for the next twenty minutes while she worried her bottom lip as different colored pencils moved across the paper. I knew exactly what I wanted to do with that lip, but held off making any moves while she was so focused on doing something so nice for me. Her little body was capable of such genius. I'd seen it in the art room at school, and I could see it there in her art studio. The way she saw things. The way she contorted normal objects, giving them shadows and depth. The way she shined light on her subjects or even the insignificant background objects, spoke of her eye for detail. And the way she saw something no one else did…it's what made her the person she was. The unique person she didn't allow everyone to see.

When her hands finally dropped to her sides, she stared at her work, idle for a long time. I couldn't tell if she was satisfied or if she'd had difficulty working with the limited details I'd given her. After a long pause, her eyes jumped from the drawing to me.

"So?" I asked, leaning forward from my spot on the sofa.

Her eyes grew big and round as she chewed on her bottom lip. "I'm scared."

I stood up. "Why are you scared?"

"I just want it to be perfect for you."

I tilted my head, staring back at this nervous, amazing, talented girl. "You drew it. It'll be perfect." I walked over and stopped beside her, brushing my hip against the side of her arm. I stared at the drawing, mesmerized by the woman with flowing dark hair and deep brown eyes staring back at me. It wasn't quite my mom, or at least what I recalled of her, but it was as if Hadley had taken *my* features and made them softer—more feminine. She even added the light freckles on my nose and the dimple in my cheek. It floored me. Absolutely floored me. She'd barely looked at me while drawing, yet she saw me. She knew me. "I love it."

She turned her head, looking at me over her shoulder. "You do?"

I met her eyes. "No one's ever done something this nice for me before."

She laughed. "I'm sure plenty of girls have done *nice* things for you."

I leaned down and wrapped my arms around her from behind, loving the soft feel of her body against my chest. I rested my head on her shoulder and burrowed my nose in her hair, inhaling her strawberry scent. "You sure you want to go there?" I asked.

She laughed softly. "I can handle you."

I moved my lips up the side of her neck, nibbling a soft path up to her ear. "You *think* you can," I purred into her smooth skin.

Her head rolled to the side, giving me easier access. "I know I can."

I released her body and grabbed her hand. She gasped as I tugged her off the stool and walked us to the sofa. I dropped down first, pulling her onto my lap so she had no choice but to straddle me. God, I loved her body. The way her breasts crushed into me when I pulled her close. The way her entire being just relaxed into me like it was the safest place she'd ever been.

"See?" She tilted her head thoughtfully. "I can handle you."

My head fell back and I laughed, feeling myself getting hard with her seated directly on my growing erection. She wiggled her ass, knowing exactly what she was doing to me. I groaned. "Don't start something you have no intention of finishing."

"Who said I wouldn't want to finish?"

Fuck me.

She gripped the hem of her top and peeled it over her head.

My lips parted as I stared at the lacy pink bra molded perfectly to her ample chest. *Shit.* My eyes jumped to her eyes. I needed to remember this was Hadley. The girl who'd just drawn my mother. She wasn't like the others. She was the one girl who made me feel things I wasn't used to feeling. And I wasn't going to blow it.

She stared down at me, meeting my eyes like she wasn't straddling me without a top on in her big empty house. I don't know why I expected her to be nervous, but there was a confidence in her eyes as she took the opportunity to convince me she'd forgiven me. "I believe this was your request by the train."

A deep guttural groan rumbled in the deep recesses of my gut. "Look. I'm in no way a saint who has any kind of restraint. So please don't make this hard on me."

She lifted a brow. "Hard?"

I laughed. "Yeah. I just want you to see that you're different. I want you to see I'm not here for one thing."

Her nose wrinkled. "Are you serious?"

I swallowed back what I really wanted to say. Especially since we were all alone with no chance of interruptions.

She assessed my features, searching for any indication that I was bluffing. When she found none, she huffed her frustration and reached for her shirt. It was fucking adorable.

I clasped my hand over hers, stopping her from grabbing hold of the shirt. "There is no way in hell you're putting that back on. I want to look at you."

As if a cold front swept in, her cheeks flushed. "Well then look." Even with her cheeks glowing, her voice remained confident. "And if you feel your restraint slipping, just go with it. I promise not to complain."

I laughed as I yanked her toward me, our mouths colliding fiercely. Hadley's hands slipped under my shirt, trailing over my bare chest as our tongues melded together. Her smooth hands explored my body. I imagined them wrapped around another part of me and I grew harder.

How long could I do this with her? *Just* this? How long could I—

Hadley moved her body—make that her hips. Grinding slowly on the bulge in my jeans as she kissed me, her hands braced on my chest.

I deepened the kiss, threading my fingers in her hair and tugging back just enough for her to groan into my mouth. The vibration rocked through me, coursing through my body as she continued to rub up on me. I was hard as a rock and pretty sure if I didn't lose my jeans soon, I was going to do some serious damage to my favorite body part.

I released my hands from her hair and skimmed them over her neck and shoulders, lightly brushing the sides of her bra with my thumbs as I continued down. She hummed against my lips as I moved over the bare skin on her sides before gripping her hips. The ones that were still circling my hard on. Good God she was amazing. I coasted my hands over the tops of her thighs, sliding them slowly between her legs.

She gasped into my mouth. We both knew all I had to do was slip my fingers under her shorts. Shift in just the right angle to feel her wet panties. Insert a couple of fingers to hear her scream my name. The voice in my head told me I couldn't do it. Told me if I went any further, I wouldn't be able to stop. Instead of relieving her need, I reached for my fly and unbuttoned my jeans.

Hadley pulled away from my mouth, her lips swollen and eyes glazed. Her soft panting and flushed cheeks told me she was close. "Change your mind?"

I reached for my zipper. Her anxious eyes followed my fingers as I drew it down. There was no disguising my tented boxers. Hadley slipped her right hand out from under my shirt and placed it on my dick. *Sweet Jesus.* Her hand moved slowly over my boxers, experimenting with the pressure that made me hiss. She tightened her grip, increasing the speed. The pressure of her hand and the friction of my boxers tainted my vision with black spots. My head fell back as I moaned my appreciation. Every part of me wanted to beg her to slip her hand underneath my boxers and put her hand—better yet her mouth—directly on me.

Hold up.

This wasn't about me. For once. I wanted it to be about Hadley.

I grabbed hold of her hand, stopping it from moving. Given the surprise on her face, I wasn't the only one feeling needy.

"Do you trust me?" I asked.

Hadley

Captivated by the wild look in Caynan's eyes, I nodded.

"Lay down," he requested, his voice insanely raspy.

My pulse throbbed in every part of my body, especially the spot between my legs. I couldn't believe I'd been brave enough to shed my shirt and make the first move—especially after being distant for the past week.

But how far was I willing to go? Was I ready for whatever he had in mind?

My sudden apprehension wasn't enough to stop me. I climbed off Caynan's lap. He slid down to the end of the sofa and waited for me to lie down. Once my back hit the sofa, he pushed himself to his knees at my feet. "If I do anything you're not comfortable with, you need to tell me."

I nodded, expecting him to cover me with his body. Maybe strip down so I wasn't the only one missing clothing. But instead, he reached for the button on my shorts and slowly peeled them down my legs, revealing the cute pink panties that matched my bra.

Caynan's tongue shot out, sweeping along his bottom lip as his eyes roamed over my body. My eyes were riveted on his, awaiting his next move. He gripped my knees and spread them gently. My skin prickled with anticipation. He leaned down, his lips pressing against my inner thigh. I gasped as he kissed a path up my skin. He was so close to my core. So close to the incessant throbbing mere inches away. My heart rate accelerated as he switched to the other thigh, kissing a similar path up my skin, but not quite reaching my center.

"I trust you," I whispered, urging him on.

His lips continued their assault, alternating between my thighs as his right hand slid up my leg, stopping when it reached the bottom of my panties. His thumb brushed softly over the strip of fabric between my legs. I closed my eyes, enjoying every glorious sensation. Caynan's thumb didn't stay there long. It swept underneath the damp fabric, gliding over my wet skin. Tremors rippled through me as I chewed on my bottom lip, stopping myself from moaning shamelessly.

"Fuck, you're wet," he whispered, as his thumb continued to move, now in a long delicious path from the back of my folds to the front, circling the nub that pounded at the peak—a heartbeat of its own. The pad of his thumb was rough and focused on the pleasure it was bringing me as he circled the spot over and over again. Then his finger disappeared from my skin.

I whimpered at the loss, but just as quickly it reemerged, sliding all the way down my seam before making its way back to the peak again where he repeated the same glorious torture. Over and over again.

"Pull them down," I said, shocked by my boldness.

Caynan's head lifted from between my thighs, his eyes meeting mine. "You sure?"

I nodded.

"Tell me you know you're not like other girls to me."

I nodded. "I know." And even if I didn't know that for absolute certain, there wasn't a chance in hell he wasn't finishing what he started.

His eyes stayed on mine as he slipped his pinkies into the sides of my panties and peeled them down my legs.

I didn't look away. My cheeks didn't pink. My palms didn't dampen. For some reason, I was at ease. I was completely on board with everything that was happening. It felt right.

Without warning, Caynan lowered his head, burying his face between my legs.

Oh. My. God.

I grabbed the sofa cushions at my sides. I'd never had a guy go down there before. Not like that.

His tongue touched exactly where I ached for it. I nearly screamed out at the pleasure but bit back down on my bottom lip to stifle it. Caynan mirrored the pulsing already happening there with steady pressure as he lapped away at it. Over and over again. *Good Lord.* He was relentless. Flicking. Swirling. Sucking.

My eyes crossed and my body arched off the sofa. He held my hips, stopping them from bucking him off me. I whimpered as he abandoned the nub. But like his thumb moments before, he licked a trail down the wet seam of my body. I couldn't be embarrassed by the intimate action when it felt so good. So. Damn. Good. He licked back up to the top, hitting the throbbing spot.

Flick…Swirl…Suck.

My legs began to quiver. "Oh my God," I breathed.

Flick…Swirl…Suck.

He hummed into my wet skin, causing sensations to bubble up. With one last hard suck, heat shot to the center of my core. My body splintered into pieces as I half whimpered, half moaned at the pleasure rushing through me. But that didn't stop Caynan. He milked my body for all it had until I'd nearly crushed his head with my thighs.

I didn't open my eyes as my chest heaved and I gulped in a lungful of air. I felt the cushions beneath me shift as he moved, but my limp body was incapable of movement. "Where did you learn to do that?" My heavy eyelids split apart. "Wait. I don't want to know."

He laughed as he held my panties at my feet and slipped them back on me. "Was it okay?"

"Okay?" I scoffed at the ridiculousness of his question. "Seriously?"

Before he could respond with some smug comment, his phone vibrated in his pocket. His face sobered, his eyes looking torn whether he should answer it or not.

"Go, ahead," I urged.

He pulled it out and checked the screen. "Fuck," he growled through clenched teeth.

"What's wrong?"

His eyes stayed on the screen. "My dad. He needs me home." His eyes lifted to me. "I'm sorry."

As much as I didn't want him to leave, especially after what just happened between us, I didn't want to be that girl. He'd promised me I wasn't like other girls. I had no reason not to believe that. "No worries. We'll just pick this up another time."

Surprised, he lifted his brows as he leaned down toward my face. "Oh, yeah?"

"Oh, hell yeah." With my taste still on his tongue, he closed the distance between us and made sure I knew how sorry he was for bailing.

Caynan

My father sat at the kitchen table when I walked in. He looked less wasted than he had earlier, but he didn't say a word, just tossed a manila envelope toward me on the table.

"What's this?"

"Apparently, our meeting went well. *Really* well." He nodded toward the envelope. "Open it."

I picked it up and flipped open the flap, pulling out an eight by ten colored picture of a gun. A very elaborate gun. More like a pistol.

"It's a Colt Walker. It went for over a million dollars at an auction."

I studied the picture of the old gun. "So?"

"So, we get it. We get twenty percent of street value."

"Where is it?"

"The address is inside."

I reached inside the envelope, pulling out a torn piece of paper. I stared down at the address scribbled across it. Every part of my body froze.

Fuuuuuuck.

* * *

I flashed one of my many fake IDs at the bouncer at the bar two towns over. I walked inside, sliding down onto one of the few empty barstools around the four-sided bar. The bartender approached, her black biker tank top leaving very little to the imagination.

"What can I get ya?" she asked.

"One of everything."

She laughed. "That bad?"

"Times ten." I tunneled my fingers through my hair.

"How about I surprise you?"

"I'm not a big fan of surprises."

"Then I'm guessing you haven't been properly surprised." She winked, before turning and strutting her ass over to the rows of liquor bottles on the illuminated shelves.

No. I'd been surprised all right. That night. By Hadley—sweet Hadley—who'd allowed me to do things I wasn't sure she'd let me do to her. *And* by my fucking father who'd dropped the bomb of all bombs. Twenty percent of one million dollars was no chump change, so telling him I wouldn't get the pistol wasn't an option.

It seemed like every time he got into my head, it was a reality check urging me to distance myself from Hadley. We were from completely different worlds. My life was one big lie. Hers held so many possibilities. My future would take me to another rich town. Hers would take her off to college then a career in art. It had been my brilliant plan to let her in. Now I'd never be able to look her in the eyes again.

But how could I push her away when I saw how much it hurt her last time? That was easy. I was selfish. And selfishly I wanted her. I wanted to see her smile and laugh and fall apart with my face between her legs like earlier that night. Selfishly, I wanted to know I was the cause of every bit of her pleasure.

The bartender walked over, lining three shots in front of me. Without a word, I opened my mouth, downing one after another. I needed the liquor to work its magic. I needed it to carry me into utter oblivion.

No sooner had I finished off the shots, more lined the shiny oak bar in front of me thanks to the giggling girls across the way. I lifted one of the shots in their direction to show my appreciation.

Whiskey. Vodka. Rum. Anything that stung going down, I guzzled. In no time, the girls relocated, parking their asses around me, laughing at every stupid thing I said. Soon, my words became ridiculously jumbled. Too jumbled for even me to make sense of them. But it felt good not to worry or feel guilty. At least for a little while.

Inevitably, the room began to spin, the bar lights transforming into a distorted kaleidoscope of shapes and colors moving faster with each rotation. I lay my head down on the sticky surface in front of me. I just needed a minute to get my shit together. A minute to make it all go away.

A long strand of buzzing in my ears muffled the loud music, replacing the cacophony of chatter around me and the voices in my head with nothing.

Nothing but glorious silence.

CHAPTER ELEVEN

Caynan

Bright sunlight pierced my closed eyelids. My head pounded like a mother fucker, and my mouth tasted like cotton. My arm shot out to the space beside me in bed. Empty and cold. Thank God. But where the hell was I? The mattress was too comfortable to be my crappy bed. And the pillow underneath my head was more like a cloud than my pancake. I braced myself, ready for the infiltration of light as I opened my eyes. I squinted back the intrusive rays as my eyes shot around the enormous bedroom where I lay in a king-sized sleigh bed.

What the hell?

My eyes stopped on the body curled up in the chair in the corner of the room, a fluffy blue blanket wrapped snuggly around her.

Hadley.

Normally, that was the moment I threw on my clothes and bailed before the girl woke up. But not with Hadley. I just wished I knew how I got there. I could only imagine the shit I put her through to end up in her bed without her beside me. I was either off my game, too wasted to perform, or a total asshole.

I kicked my bare feet out from under the soft as hell down-comforter and dropped them to the hardwood floor. I looked down at the wrinkled boxers and T-shirt I still wore, wondering if Hadley attempted to undress me and I'd put up a fight.

I stared across the room, wishing she'd slept in bed with me. Would she have moved all night or stayed in one spot? Would she have snuggled up beside me or wanted her own space? The mattress creaked slightly as I stood and crept across the room, trying not to make any noise in case her parents had returned earlier than expected.

I reached the oversized chair and stared down at her. So peaceful. So beautiful. So fucking perfect. Her blond hair fell over her shoulders as her breath moved in and out softly. I reached out, gently brushing a strand of hair off her face. She startled, jerking up and dropping the blanket to the floor. "Ohmigod."

"*Shhh.*" I knelt in front of her, my hands on her bare legs to steady her. *Good God.* She slept in barely-there shorts and a tight tank top that showed all her curves. "It's just me."

Her sleepy eyes settled on mine, realization hitting them. "Morning."

"Are your parents back yet?"

Her eyes searched the room as she considered my question. "They're probably downstairs."

My eyes widened.

"My dad'll want to meet the guy who slept in my bed."

I clenched my teeth, the tick in my jaw pulsing.

Without warning, she burst out laughing. "Oh, my God. You should see your face."

"So, they're not here?"

She shook her head. "Not until Friday. Then they pick me up for that fundraiser, remember?"

A shaky breath slipped out of me, wishing she hadn't reminded me of that. "Hadley, what am I doing here?"

She rubbed her palms into her sleepy eyes. "You don't remember?"

I shook my head, my mind searching for any sliver of recollection. "I know I got wasted at the bar, but after that, it's all pretty much a blur."

She dropped her hands on a sigh. "Mine was the last number you dialed. The bartender called and said you needed a ride home."

My eyes took in her orderly bedroom. Her makeup and hair products organized by size on her vanity. Her neatened desk. Her matching chair and sofa. "But I'm not home. I'm here."

She nodded. "You asked me to take you here."

"And you listened?"

"I don't know where you live." She shrugged, her eyes flicking away like she was hiding something.

Fuck. My heart thrashed around, rattling my insides at the thought of what I might've done, said, or revealed during my drunken stupor. "Did anything happen?"

Her eyes slid to her bed. "No. But not for your lack of trying."

Though it wasn't what I meant, I laughed. "I didn't say anything that upset you, did I?"

"No." Her answer lacked conviction.

Fuck, fuck.

"But you've got a great American accent when you're drunk." She grinned, though it went no further than her lips.

Fuck, fuck, fuck. I evened our eyes, needing to see the truth in hers. "You'd tell me, wouldn't you?"

She crossed her arms as if she'd just realized how exposed she was in that tight top. "Tell you what?"

"If something happened. If I said or did something that…hurt you."

She nodded. "Yeah, of course." As much as I wanted to believe her, the distant look in her eyes made me doubt her words.

I coasted my hands lightly over her bare thighs, thoughts of us on the sofa in her art studio rushing me all at once. Her sounds. Her smell. "Thanks for getting me."

"Someone had to."

I stood up, pulling her up with me and wrapping my arms around her small body. I buried my nose in her hair, loving the strawberry scent that always rolled off her. "I'm glad it was you."

"It would've been pretty embarrassing if you were expecting someone else."

I laughed, pulling back just enough to see her face. "Care to explain why you slept in that chair?"

She shrugged, looking just as pretty—if not prettier—without makeup and her hair fixed. "You were really out of it. Especially by the time I managed to get you upstairs. I just figured you needed space."

"Let me make something *perfectly* clear. The only space I'm concerned with when it comes to you is my space. And you being in it."

She cocked her head, skepticism etched in her features. "Is that why you went out drinking alone? Because you didn't need space?"

There's the truth. "Oh, I needed space all right. But not from you."

"Then who?"

"My dad. My past. My future. Take your pick."

The sympathy in her eyes sucker-punched me. She was showing *me* sympathy. *Fuck me.*

I ticked my head toward her bed. "Since no one's here, what do you say we go lay down so I can hold you?"

"Just hold me?"

I laughed, pulling her against my chest and tightening my arms around her. I wished the thought of what I needed to do could've somehow been wiped from my brain. "You've gotta take me to get my car. *And* I've got a game tonight. No school means no game." While I knew it was smarter to get us out of the house quickly so I wouldn't be tempted to slip out of her room to find the pistol, I wanted to be with her. At least for a little while longer. "For now, I just plan on holding you. But be warned. Next time I get you alone, I've got different plans." I ran my finger under the spaghetti strap on her top. "Especially when you're wearing things like this to bed."

She laughed, a sleepy raspy laugh.

I walked us toward her bed, turning unexpectedly so I landed on my back and pulled her down on top of me. She yelped, causing us both to laugh. Our lips were so close. I could've easily worked my magic and picked up where we left off the previous night. But things had changed. She may not have realized it, but they had. And I had no idea what I was gonna do about it.

I rolled us onto our sides. Hadley instantly tucked herself into my chest, resting her head under my chin. I almost wished she hadn't. It just made everything harder.

"Are you gonna tell me what happened last night?"

I swallowed down a guilty knot and tried to distract her. "I spent the beginning of the night with this really hot girl who let me do things to her I'd only ever fantasized about doing."

I felt her body shudder at my words, but she ignored her body's reaction and sighed instead. "I'm serious. What happened with your dad?"

I pulled in a deep breath, wanting nothing more than to tell her something resembling the truth. "He has high expectations of me."

"That's a bad thing?"

I grunted. "When his expectations don't mesh with mine, yeah."

"Oh." I could tell she wasn't following. How could she? I was being anything but forthcoming. "He must see your potential and just wants you to reach it."

I snorted at her positive spin on it. It actually sounded good in theory. "He definitely sees my potential…"

"Well, I'm here. Whatever you need. You know that, right?" Her voice was so sincere. I was sure if I could've seen her eyes, they would've been the same.

I nodded, knowing there wasn't a chance in hell I could tell her my secrets. Especially now that she'd picked my drunk-ass up from a bar. Now that she let me into her home. Now that I knew what I needed to do. Now that I had feelings for her I was too chicken shit to admit.

* * *

"I've never caught a home run ball before," Hadley said after my game.

"And I've never been this far off the ground before." I couldn't disguise the slight quiver in my voice as I looked out at the town aglow in orange at dusk from the top of a water tower. My arms were locked tightly around the bar that circled the top for fear of falling to my death.

Hadley laughed, her arms linked around the same bar as mine, her legs dangling off the side like the distance to the bottom was no big deal. "You scared?" Her hair whipped about her head, tangling around her face as her smile stretched a mile wide.

If there was something I hated more than the shit my dad made me do, it was heights. But how could I tell a beautiful girl I didn't want to follow her up a steep ladder, feet from her perfect ass? Not to mention her cutoffs that awarded me numerous glimpses of her panties underneath. Yeah. That was definite motivation to climb higher. My eyes cut to hers. "Not much scares me."

"*Sure*," she teased.

"I'm serious."

"Not your big tournament tomorrow?" she asked.

I scoffed. "I'm only scared of taking off an outfielder's head with one of my missiles."

Hadley burst out laughing. "Your arrogance knows no bounds."

I shrugged. "It's a gift. No, but seriously, I might be a little scared leaving you alone for the next three days. I wouldn't want you falling to pieces. I know it can be tough without me to look at all the time."

She rolled her eyes. "*Right.* Well, I'm not embarrassed to admit a lot of things scare me."

My head recoiled. I hadn't expected this strong girl to have any fears, because she certainly didn't have any flaws. "Like what?"

She shrugged.

"No, I'm serious. Tell me."

I watched her eyes focus on something in the distance as she considered my question. "I've never told anyone this before." Her eyes cut to mine. "But I worry about losing my dad."

I nodded, understanding firsthand the pain that accompanied that loss. "Yeah. It sucks."

She cringed, realizing what she'd said. "I'm sorry. That was thoughtless."

I shook my head, hoping to ease her guilt. "No, it was honest. You're always honest with me. It's refreshing."

A silence stretched between us before she continued. "I worry when he's on duty."

I'd never considered the family of a cop before. They had every reason to worry. But I couldn't let Hadley believe that. "He's trained. He knows what he's doing."

She scoffed. "He may know what *he's* doing. I'm worried about the criminals who are consumed with getting what they want. Like the thieves robbing my neighbors. If my dad got in their way, they wouldn't think twice about hurting him."

Her words gutted me, sucking the air right from my lungs. She was like this angel on my shoulder, reminding me what was right and good in the world. The problem was the devil on the other side. The one harping in my ear and forcing my hand. The one I couldn't shake no matter how badly I wanted to. And forget his accomplice. She was just as powerful with her constant reminders.

You're all each other have.

I shook off the voice. "I think you're right about one thing. Those thieves are wrapped up in getting what they want. But I don't think they want to hurt anyone. Not purposely anyhow."

She nodded, though I doubted my words comforted her. They sure as fuck didn't comfort me.

"Tell me something else," I urged, needing a subject change.

Hadley smiled. "I'm scared of snakes."

"I think most girls are."

"Yeah, but I'm scared of finding one in my toilet."

I laughed. "Your toilet?"

"I saw a television show on it once. It scared me to death. I check every time I go into the bathroom."

"You check to see if there's a snake in your toilet?"

She nodded. "Every time."

I shook my head, loving that she was letting me in on the small things other people probably didn't know. "Tell me more."

She pulled in a deep breath, letting it out slowly. "I guess I'm scared of not succeeding."

My brows furrowed. "With art?"

She shrugged. "Just in general."

"Hadley. You're determined. There's not a doubt in my mind that you'll get whatever you want in life."

"Yeah, well, I was determined to stay away from you. Look how well that turned out."

My head fell forward and I laughed because it was the truth. I hadn't given her much choice. And I never would've never taken no for an answer. I'd weakened her defenses. And I had no regrets. I felt larger than life when she was with me—and guilty as sin.

"I'm scared of never feeling the way I do right now."

My laughter subsided. She looked so vulnerable. So honest. I couldn't peel my eyes away from her, even if I wanted to.

"You don't have to say anything," she said. "I just realized it was something I was scared of."

Without thinking of anything but the girl beside me, the girl who feared losing me, I leaned over and sealed my lips over hers. She hadn't expected it, I could tell by her sharp intake of breath before my lips touched down.

And for the first time all morning, I could care less about the hundred plus feet that separated me from the ground. Or the job I had to do. It was Hadley and me in that moment. *Just* Hadley and me. And the fact that her feelings for me were so strong that they scared her, made me both elated and a complete asshole.

Hadley

Any snakes in your toilet today?

I smiled as I typed a reply to Caynan's text on Thursday afternoon—one of many he'd sent since leaving for Atlanta's Mid-Week Classic baseball tournament on Tuesday. **None today. Three last night. If you were here, you could've helped.**

Why is it that all girls need me? I could practically hear his arrogance from across the state.

My thumbs went to work. **Don't make me go back to hating you.**

You never hated me.

I wondered if the other guys harassed him for the amount of time he'd spent texting me over the last three days. **Believe what you will, player.**

We're back to player, huh?

Just playing. Pun totally intended. I laughed at my own wittiness.

Can I see you when I get back?

I wondered if his excessive texts had anything to do with what I'd said on the water tower. *Ugh*. Me and my big mouth. I sent him one last text.

"Hell-o. Best friend still here," Cass' voice echoed through my kitchen.

My eyes lifted from the phone, glancing to her sitting at the center island. "Sorry." I tossed it down on the island.

"No need. It's about time you were happy."

I laughed. "I've never been unhappy."

She shrugged. "I just meant he's good for you...I still can't believe what you told him."

I'd held off telling her what I'd said on the water tower for fear of feeling even more embarrassed than I already did. "Unfortunately, I did."

"Well, who knows? Maybe you played it right."

The oven buzzed, stealing my attention. "It's not a game, Cass."

"Tell that to the guy you made chase you."

I laughed as I slipped on an oven mitt and walked to the oven, opening the door and pulling out a cookie sheet filled with pastry. "What do you think tonight's all about?" I placed the cookie sheet on a cooling rack on the counter.

"I give you props, girl. Bold move."

I slipped off the oven mitt and tossed it at her. "Yeah, well it's out there."

"I'll say."

Caynan

I stared down at Hadley's last text. I hadn't been able to look at much else since it arrived during the bus ride home. Even as I climbed the steep driveway to her dark house, my eyes were glued to my phone. **Tonight. 7. My house. Alarm code 4-8-6-9.**

It wasn't the implication of the text and what I hoped it meant. It was what she'd given me. A way into her home. A way into her family's safe where I assumed a million-dollar pistol would be kept. A way to destroy everything between us.

My growing guilt gnawed away at my sanity as I climbed the concrete steps to the front door. I had no idea what would happen inside. Being away at the tournament made it easy to forget the pistol. But now that I was back, and her parents were still away *and* my father had been up my ass to get it done, it seemed like the best time to do it. But I had a feeling waiting until she left with them the following night, made a lot more sense.

I punched in the four-number code on the alarm keypad. A green light shined. I almost wished it hadn't. I turned the knob on the front door and pushed it open.

Stepping inside the foyer, my eyes jumped around, trying to adjust to the darkness. "Hadley?" I expected her to greet me—expected her to at least be nearby. When she wasn't, I closed my eyes tightly, gathering the nerve to proceed. I pulled in a long shaky breath then released it, opening my eyes. The soft rustling of the light breeze outside surrounded me. "Hadley?" I tried again.

"In here," her voice trailed in from the back of the house.

I expelled a deep breath—relief, disappointment, and excitement all wrapped up in one. *Please let her be naked.*

Yup, so I wasn't just an asshole, I was a horny asshole.

I walked down the marble hallway, my sneakers squeaking a little with each step. Soft music played in the back of the house. Was that a British boy band? I stepped into the industrial-sized kitchen. Her voice had definitely echoed from the cavernous room, with its perfect lighting and massive island, which was unexpectedly empty. "Hadley?"

"What's wrong, player?" she taunted with a smile in her voice. "Having a little trouble?"

My head shot around. She wasn't behind me. I knew she wouldn't be. Her voice came from too far away. "You do know what I'm gonna do when I find you, don't you?"

Her giggles trailed in from yet another direction. "I sure hope so."

The words from the song filtered in from outside, drawing my attention to the open French doors off the kitchen. I stepped into the doorway. My body froze. I blinked several times, forcing the amazing sight to stay in focus.

Throughout her sprawling back yard sat London Bridge constructed with Styrofoam and rope. Big Ben made from stacked cardboard boxes with a clock face painted at the top. A standup cardboard cutout of the same boy band whose voices played softly as suspected. A huge plate of some kind of pastry—crumpets if Hadley was keeping with the theme—sat on the patio table, along with tiny teacups surrounding a tea kettle.

It must've taken her days to come up with the idea and construct it all.

For me.

Slender arms slipped around my hips from behind and linked across my stomach. "Welcome home."

God, I was such a rotten person. She'd done all of this for me. Someone who'd never even been to England. Someone who continually lied to her. Someone who wasn't fit to wash her car, let alone be a part of her life.

When this ended between us—which it would—it was going to be bad. Really bad. The worst one yet.

But still, even in the midst of my confusion and remorse, my guilt infused with something warm in the pit of my stomach. Something completely foreign to me.

Hadley had done this for *me*. She kept doing things for me. And while some might argue she didn't know the real me, I knew the truth. She knew me better than anyone else. And though I couldn't be completely honest about every aspect of my life, I'd been myself with her. I'd let her in as much as I could.

I turned to face her, making sure she didn't drop her arms from my hips. I stared down into her beautiful blue eyes that gazed up at me. "I love it."

Her lips twisted regrettably to the side. "I figured after the other night, you needed some reminders of home."

The irony that her arms were one of the few places I'd ever felt at home had not been lost on me.

So how could I lie to her? How could I *keep* lying to her? Keep up this elaborate charade when she looked at me like I held her future? I'll tell you how. I was a fake. A phony. Someone who entered people's lives only to vanish, never to be seen or heard from again. Someone who took advantage of other's weaknesses. Took advantage of other's wealth. I was conditioned not to care if they'd earned their money or inherited it. I just knew they were a pawn in an elaborate game.

Hell. I was a pawn in an elaborate game. One where I didn't make decisions, except how I took advantage of the people I'd been sent to target.

"When did you do all this?"

"While you were away—come see." She grabbed my hand and pulled me outside toward the table, pushing me gently into a patio chair. I couldn't let go of her. I wouldn't. Not after what she'd done for me. I tugged her down into my lap earning me an adorable giggle as I hooked my arm around her and pulled her against me.

This right here…this is all I need. No matter how wrong I knew it was to want it. To prolong the inevitable. I wanted it. I *needed* it.

Hadley smiled. Smiled in a way that told me I was it for her. There wasn't a doubt in my mind that if I offered to fuck her senseless right there and then, she would've accepted.

I'd fooled her. Fooled her like everyone else. And in that moment, I wished more than anything that I hadn't brought her into my world. My life. My fucking heart.

I shook off the notion, hearing the final verse of the song floating through the speakers. "Seriously?"

She threw back her head and laughed. So carefree. So happy. So damn pretty words didn't do it justice. She grabbed a small remote from the table and pointed it at the iPhone dock. A Beatles song began.

I grabbed her cheeks between my hands. Mine were so much bigger than her delicate face. I loved the way she made me feel so much stronger. "You planned that all along, didn't you?"

"I didn't take you for a boy-band kind of guy. I can't believe you made it through the entire song."

"I can't believe I made it through life without you." The damn words tore out of me like a bat out of hell.

The truth wiped the smile right off her face. The playfulness in her eyes quickly transformed to shock.

You fucking idiot.

I dropped my hands.

Hadley tilted her head, assessing my face through narrowed eyes for a long time. "Really?"

This was my chance to take it back. Backpedal. Get myself out of an awkward situation. "Absolutely."

The smile that lit up her face erased any trepidation I'd felt. Hell, it made me hard. "I know what you mean," she admitted.

"That's it?"

She shook her head. "Nope." She hopped off my lap and held out her hand. "I think they're playing our song." I stared down at her extended hand. Even if my inclination was to think dancing in the middle of Hadley's backyard was the lamest thing going, with her, it felt right. *She* felt right.

I grabbed her hand and stood. She turned into me and wrapped her arms around my neck as I slipped my arms around her back, pulling her tightly into me. I loved the way the soft swells of her breasts pressed into me when we were close. A feeling I could seriously get used to. This time I didn't have to keep it formal with a room full of people dressed to the nines. It was just Hadley and me. I could hold her however I wanted. We moved in time to the slow song in the middle of her patio surrounded by structures from England. The full moon illuminated them so I could see the time and effort she put into making each one lifelike and precise. "Your parents still away?"

She nodded.

Did that mean what I hoped it meant?

"Why's your heart racing?" One of her hands trailed from my neck down the front of my shirt. The gentle pressure of her fingers sent a chill through me. "I can feel it." Her hand rested over my heart. "Are you nervous about having me all to yourself in this big empty house?"

I swallowed around the giant lump in my throat. "Nervous is definitely not the word I'd use."

Her face beamed up at me. "Excited?"

I pushed my hips into her, letting the bulge in my jeans speak for itself.

Her eyes rounded. "Oh. Excited it is."

I'd been with lots of girls. But at that moment, with Hadley in my arms, I had absolutely no idea how to proceed. My eyes flicked toward the table, settling on the teapot. "Did you really make tea?"

She grinned as her head moved from side to side. "Long Island ice tea."

I laughed. "You really went all out."

"I figured if you didn't want to stay, I'd get you sloppy drunk so you had no other choice."

My smile stretched to my eyes, excitement grabbing hold of every part of my body. This girl would be the death of me. "So, you want me to stay?"

She nodded, her eyes showing a nervousness her words hadn't indicated.

I wanted to reassure her. No. I needed to reassure her. I leaned down to meet her lips, stopping an inch away. "Good. Because I really want to kiss you in the morning."

She closed the distance between us, opening and allowing me in. My tongue swept out, exploring her mouth with gentle strokes that left me needing more. *A lot* more. And given her tight grip on me, I had a feeling I had a very good shot of getting more than just a kiss.

Hadley

Caynan seemed to like everything I'd done for him, but he was such an enigma at times, I couldn't be sure. Before I knew what was happening, he stopped dancing and picked me up, lifting me over his shoulder.

I yelped. "What are you doing?"

"Baby, I need you upstairs all to myself."

"But you've got me right here all to yourself."

He stilled, quickly lowering me back to my feet. "I'm sorry. I guess I'm just a little eager."

I dropped my head and laughed, his honesty a breath of fresh air. "I like that you're eager."

That dimple in his right cheek dug in. "Is that so?"

I nodded. "I just want tonight to be perfect."

He cupped my cheeks and lowered his forehead to mine. "Hadley. You doing all this for me. You wanting me here with you. It's all perfect."

I nodded, or at least tried to with his forehead holding mine still.

He pulled back enough to see into my eyes. "*You're* perfect. Don't you see that? From the second we crashed into each other, I needed to be near you. Needed you to want to be near me. When you didn't, it wasn't my ego that hurt." He reached down for one of my hands and brought it to his chest. I could feel the vibration of his heart still racing underneath. "This hurt."

It would've been a freaking miracle if I didn't collapse into a pathetic pile of mush. No guy had ever said anything like that to me before. And while it might've been the remnants of his player ways, what girl wouldn't want a romantic declaration underneath the stars from a hot guy who wanted to take her upstairs and get her naked? "Sold."

His brows pinched between his eyes. "What?"

Anxiety and excitement fought for control of my body. "I believe you. Now take me upstairs."

Caynan howled with excitement as he grabbed hold of me again, this time lifting me under my butt so I had no other option than to wrap my legs around his hips. He hurried toward the house with the Beatles serenading us as we went. "I seriously didn't think you could get any hotter. But here you are."

"Here I am," I laughed.

Once we stepped into my dark bedroom, things became real. Fast. He walked us inside until his knees hit my bed in the center of the room. He lowered me down on my back and followed me, settling between my legs. I closed my eyes as my head fell back, my entire body relaxing into the down comforter while the weight of his body pressed into me. His lips lowered to my neck, moving gently over the sensitive skin below my ear, licking a delicious path down my collarbone. "God, Hadley, you taste amazing."

"*Mmmm*," was the only sound I could manage.

His lips disappeared, moving to the opposite side of my neck as one of his hands trailed down the side of my body igniting tremors everywhere. "I want to make this last," he breathed into my ear.

Was he talking about sex or this thing between us? I couldn't be sure. Especially with my body buzzing like a live wire.

He pulled back from his assault on my skin and stared down into my eyes. The playfulness I expected quickly morphed into something else. Something predatory. Something raw. Something so damn real it stole my breath away. "I need to remember this moment. Right here. Right now."

His words came out hushed, knotting my stomach in two. I reached up and cupped his cheek, a light dusting of stubble scratching my palms. I wanted him to kiss me. No, I *needed* him to. "We could always take a picture."

The smile on his lips deepened the creases around his eyes. "Nah. I won't forget. Not something like this."

My stomach unfurled, flipping over itself. "Kiss me."

His smile grew, but he shook his head. He sat back on his knees and gripped the hem of my shirt, slowly peeling it up my chest. I lifted my arms and the material cleared my head. He tossed it to my floor. "Keep your arms like that." His voice was raspy and demanding.

And I loved it.

Loved that he took charge. Loved that he knew what he was doing.

He bent down, his hands grasping my bare sides as he circled my bellybutton with his tongue. My eyes rounded at the unexpected sensation tingling in every direction. Thoughts of us in my art studio came barreling back, his talented tongue front and center sending shivers scurrying up my arms. He dragged his tongue up the center of my stomach, his hands reaching behind my back and unclasping my bra. I had no time to be self-conscious. He tugged it up my arms and tossed it off the bed. His eyes stayed on mine for a long time, like he knew the second they ventured to my breasts, he was done.

Once his eyes dropped, a slow sexy smile lifted one side of his lips and he lowered down to me, sucking one of my nipples into his mouth. His tongue swirled around it, causing my eyes to roll into the back of my head before fluttering shut. His tongue proceeded relentlessly, around and around. Without warning, he bit down gently. I gasped as a shot of pleasure shot between my thighs. He tempered the sting with another swirl of his tongue as his hands ran up and down the sides of my body.

"Caynan," I moaned softly. Needing to touch him. Needing him to touch me where I ached for him. Just. Needing. *More.*

My breast popped free from his lips. "Keep your hands where they are, Hadley," he hummed into my skin.

God, I loved the way my name sounded on his lips. Against my bare skin. In my bedroom.

He pulled back, his eyes drifting over my body, the mere look causing goosebumps to erupt everywhere. He leaned back down, this time finding my mouth. His tongue plunged inside as his hands massaged my breasts, the pads of his thumbs dragging over my nipples then circling them in slow torturous circles. I moaned into his mouth. He tugged playfully causing me to gasp, the sensation rocking right through me.

That was all I could take. I lowered my arms, sliding them around his back and running them underneath his shirt. As my nails skated over his smooth skin, he froze, his lips and hands stopping altogether.

He pulled back slightly, his eyes dangerously sexy. "Did you forget something?"

I shook my head, biting my bottom lip to stop from giggling.

He grabbed hold of both my wrists and lifted them over my head. "Keep them there."

"Take off your shirt." If he could be demanding, so could I.

His lips kicked up in the corners as he reached behind his neck, tugging his shirt over his head.

Seriously? I'd seen him shirtless before. And he was incredibly hot. And built. And all perfect. But being on top of me with his erection pressed right between my legs, I knew I wasn't going to be able to keep my arms in place and my body from self-combusting for much longer. "And your pants," I added, my eyes locked on his.

With his cocky grin in place, he rolled off to the side of me, reaching into his back pocket and digging out a condom. He tossed it onto the pillow beside my head as he pulled down his zipper and tugged off his jeans. Yup. He rocked it commando.

I tried to keep my eyes on his, but his confident smile urged me on. "You know you want to look." He grabbed the condom and tore into the package.

Feeling brave, my eyes dropped to what the good Lord gave him, in all its erect state. My eyes remained locked as he placed the condom on the head, his deft fingers rolling it down the length.

"You do this to me," he said, causing my eyes to jump to his. "No one else."

I wanted to believe him. Wanted to believe that this thing between us would stand the test of time. But I wasn't stupid. I knew high school romances didn't last. So, as I lay there—with Caynan naked beside me and my arms stretched above my own naked chest, I made sure to commit every feeling, every sound, every smell to memory.

His eyes tightened as I reached down. But instead of purposely disobeying him for no other reason than to piss him off, I unbuttoned my shorts and pushed them down my legs, making sure to tug my lacy panties along with them. Caynan watched as I discarded them on the floor and then lifted my arms back over my head.

He smiled a pleased grin as he rolled on top of me, pressing me into the bed. "I can't stay away from you." His lips descended on mine.

My stomach dipped, my heart dancing like mad as he kissed me deeper. Harder.

When we finally broke apart, coming up for much-needed air, he pulled back just enough to see my eyes. "I don't want anyone else to ever see you like this."

The elation sweeping over me was almost too much to take. And, in that moment, with his erection pressing into the wetness he'd created, Caynan pushed into me with one hard thrust. My entire body arched, my head pushing back into my pillow and my breasts pressing against his solid chest. Our groans mirrored each other. "I'm not hurting you, am I?"

I shook my head, never wanting him to stop.

"God, Hadley. You feel so fucking amazing." Caynan's hips lazily thrust into me. He wasn't in a rush. Wasn't racing to his release. This was just the beginning. And he made sure he took his time.

My body buzzed each time he hit that spot between my thighs, nearly liquefying my limbs. And he did it. Over and over again. Relentless in his pursuit to bring me pleasure. "Don't stop," I moaned. How could I not with this massive guy hitting spots inside me I didn't really believe existed?

Caynan's lips were on my mouth, my neck, my ear, his tongue its own entity. I felt him everywhere. His hands kneading into my skin. His rotating hips, shockingly unyielding. His powerful thrusts driving him deeper inside me.

I wondered how long he'd prolong it.

How long he'd keep me teetering on the brink.

And just like that, I felt trembling building between my thighs. Then my core. Gradually, an eruption of sensations exploded to every nerve in my body. My back arched into him as my body stilled and a deep hum overtook me. Caynan stared down at me as I fought to catch my breath, a satisfied smile on his face. But his hips didn't stop. He continued moving above me as my body relaxed, pressing back down into the bed. He leaned down, his lips capturing mine while his hips pounded into me. The sweat on his forehead dripped onto my face while he ravaged my mouth. This kiss was sloppy and wet and everything I wanted. He thrust a few more times, harder and more eager, before he pulled away from my lips. His eyes closed and he groaned through his final thrust. His body stilled, quivering from the inside out.

I watched the euphoria sweep over his tightened features, loving that I'd done that to him. Loving that we'd done that to each other.

A silence—filled only by our breathing—descended upon us.

When Caynan's eyes opened, he relaxed the weight of his body on top of me, burying his face in my neck. I'd never felt anything more comforting than his entire body draped over me. Heavy. Sweaty. Mine.

"My, God," he rumbled into my skin. "That was…"

"Amazing."

He lifted his head, his heavy-lidded eyes finding mine. "Yeah?"

I nodded.

He pulled out of me and rolled onto his side, pulling off the condom and discarding it in its wrapper on the nightstand. "That it?"

I snickered as I rolled onto my side so I could see him. All of him. "Mind-numbing."

That cocky grin slipped into place. "Go on."

"Earth-shattering."

He reached out, placing his hand on my hip and pulling me into his chest. "Now you're just trying to be funny."

I shook my head. "I'm trying for round two."

His eyes widened as he rolled me onto my back and devoured my lips for a very long time. At least until we went for round two.

CHAPTER TWELVE

Caynan

Somehow, Hadley and I made it to school on time the following morning, neither of us getting much sleep.

I spent the majority of English class staring at her, wondering how the hell I got so lucky.

She glanced over, finding my eyes on her yet again. "Pay attention," she whispered before a smirk quirked her lips.

"Oh, I'm paying attention all right."

Amused, she shook her head.

I loved pushing her buttons. Actually, I liked making her smile more. "I'm just wondering what it'll take to kiss you tomorrow morning, too."

"You know I'll be away." She glanced back to the front of the classroom where Ms. Atwood droned on about British literature.

After the previous night, I wasn't thinking about British Lit. I was thinking about Hadley. What she'd done for me. What she'd said to me. What she'd let me do to her. *God.* She was every guy's living, breathing fantasy—whether she realized it or not. And she was all mine. At least until I wasn't there anymore.

I couldn't even begin to imagine what that day would be like. Would I just leave without a goodbye, like I'd done so many times before? But then, I hadn't been leaving anyone important behind. Sure, I left friends, but not a girl I had feelings for. Before Hadley, I kept it casual. No strings attached. Because seriously? Strings wouldn't have stretched as far as the miles I'd traveled.

But things were different now. Hadley was different. I was different. Or at least part of me was.

At the end of the day, I leaned against Hadley's car, knowing I wanted to catch her before my game since I wouldn't be seeing her all weekend. She walked out of the building shaking her ass, purposely giving me a little show. I smiled as she approached.

"Waiting for someone?" she asked.

My eyes gave her body a slow perusal. "Yup."

"Anyone I know?" She stopped in front of me.

I nodded as I slipped my arms around her and pulled her into me. Instantly, she buried her head below my chin.

"Gonna miss me this weekend?"

She chuckled. "I'm sure your texts will keep me occupied. Especially the naughty ones."

"Will I be getting any in return?"

"Is there any other kind?" she asked.

I held her tighter, wishing she could somehow tell how much I cared about her. How much I didn't want to hurt her. "I don't deserve you." I couldn't even be bothered to disguise the seriousness in my voice.

Hadley pulled back and looked up at me, shielding her eyes from the bright afternoon sun. "Why would you say that?"

I shrugged. "I just know you could do so much better than me."

She tilted her head, her eyes assessing my face. "Well, that's too bad. Because I want you."

Fuuuuck.

* * *

Since leaving Hadley, I'd been battling a pit in my stomach. Knowing she'd be away, made everything real. I parked in front of my trailer and noticed the picture Hadley had drawn of my mom rolled up in my passenger seat. If that wasn't a fucking sign, I didn't know what was. I grabbed it and headed to the door, wanting the picture to have a place in my room.

"Where is it?" My father's gruff voice stopped me dead in my tracks the second I stepped inside.

I cringed, the picture clutched tightly in my hand. "I don't have it yet."

He slammed his fists down on the kitchen table rattling the walls of our trailer as he jumped to his feet. "Then get it!"

"Back off!"

His eyes blazed with rage. I'd never seen anything so cold. He flew across the room, shoving his forearm into my neck and slamming me against the wall. My head bounced off it, clouding my vision. "What'd you say to me?"

I stared into his eyes. And for the first time, I saw them for what they were. Eyes of a monster. A monster who'd controlled me for far too long. He might've wanted to hurt me as he glared at me mere inches from my face, but I didn't want to hurt him. I wanted to be *free* of him. And getting that pistol was the only way to do it.

As if he'd just realized what he'd done, he shook his head and stepped away from me. He'd been physical in the past. But nothing I couldn't handle. Knowing we both needed to calm the fuck down, I tore off into my room and slammed the door behind me. Nothing like a near beat-down to get the adrenaline pumping. My limbs quivered as I walked to my closet, searching for a spot to store the drawing until I could hang it.

My door flew open, slamming into the wall behind him. "Don't walk away from me, boy!"

I spun around, shocked he'd followed me into my room. With him that angry, I needed to be the voice of reason. "You need to trust me. I need more time."

He stared at me like I'd spoken some foreign language. "These aren't the type of men you make wait. I told them it'd be ready for shipment this weekend. It will be." His eyes dropped to the picture in my hand.

Fuck.

I tried moving it behind my back, but he yanked it from my hand before I could. His face tightened coldly as he unrolled it. "What the hell is this?"

"Mom." I didn't even try to disguise the hate I felt for him in that moment. "Remember her?"

He stared down at her likeness for a long time. I actually thought it might've brought out his humanity. Might've displayed some shred of sorrow. "We don't need reminders." He tore the picture in half.

I watched in horror as the pieces fell to the floor. Pieces of my mom. Pieces of Hadley's art. Pieces of me.

Rage gripped hold of every part of my body. I wanted to hit him. Throw him through the wall. Leave and never see his face again.

You're all each other have.

My mother's words pushed through my thoughts, but they were distant. Softer. Weaker. As if they were fading. As if they didn't hold the weight they once held. It suddenly struck me. They *didn't* hold the weight they once held. They weren't the truth anymore.

I had Hadley.

I pulled it together long enough to walk straight out the front door. My heart raced something fierce as the door closed behind me. I jumped into my Jeep, my hands digging through my hair. Digging into my scalp. Needing the pain. The self-inflicted type. Not the type he doled out. If he wanted the damned pistol. I'd get him the damn pistol.

Then to hell with him.

I was done.

Hadley

"Hadley? Is your luggage in the car?" my mother called from her bedroom.

I rushed out of my room, wearing a red strapless dress that fit my body in all the right places. Too bad Caynan wouldn't get a chance to see it. Chances were it wouldn't have stayed on for long. "Yeah. I'm all set."

My mother stepped out of her room fastening a diamond chandelier earring into her ear. "Your father's going to have to meet us there in the morning."

"If I have to go, why doesn't he?"

"They've got him working an overnight. I think a lead's come in on those robberies."

I contemplated asking if I could stay too, but didn't want to leave her there alone. Normally, I wouldn't have minded going to one of my grandfather's fundraisers. But things were going so well with Caynan, I just didn't want to leave.

I made my way outside, hopping into the waiting car. My mother followed in a shimmering gold dress. Once her door closed and our driver slid into the driver's seat, we were off. It was only an hour away, but it was far enough away from Caynan.

"Care to tell me why you wanted to skip tonight's fundraiser?" My mother held out her wrist so I could fasten her tennis bracelet for her. "You usually enjoy this one."

"I just wanted to spend time with Caynan."

She lifted a perfect brow. "Oh? So, things are back on track after the mix-up?"

"Yeah." I'd told my parents about his dad dragging him out of town. They were more understanding than me. They were the ones who ultimately pushed me to get over it and forgive him. "I know we're young, and high school romances don't usually work out, but I like him. I *really* like him."

One of those nostalgic smiles danced across my mother's face.

"I guess I just want him to feel the same way I do."

"How do you know he doesn't?"

I shrugged. "Guys are different. No matter what they say, they don't *feel* the way we do."

"They don't *think* like us either," she laughed. "Have you told him how you're feeling?"

I shook my head. "It's still kind of soon to be discussing our relationship. I wouldn't want to scare him."

She gave me a maternal look. One that came with years of practice and worldly experiences. "Maybe you should."

"Being away for the weekend doesn't really lend itself to a deep discussion."

"I'll tell you what. You stick around tonight, and I'll let you skip tomorrow's itinerary."

My mouth parted. "Seriously?"

She winked. "Who am I to keep young love apart?"

CHAPTER THIRTEEN

Caynan

Except for a few scattered street lights, Hadley's neighborhood sat shrouded in darkness. I looked right then left, ensuring no one saw me in the shadows. My gloved hand shook as I punched in the alarm code, luckily the covered entryway and darkness concealed me. The green light on the alarm pad flashed and the *click* of the front door unlocking filled the silence.

I turned the knob and slipped inside the foyer. Like the rest of the house, it was completely dark. I hated being there. Being in that big, empty house without Hadley.

I pulled in a deep breath, knowing with much certainty that I was an asshole.

The girl who'd shown me love, acceptance, compassion, and given all of herself to me, was just like the rest of them. She had something I needed.

It was all so fucked up. On the drive over, I'd actually convinced myself Hadley would've understood what I had to do if she'd known the truth. If I'd told her about my dad and his associates. If I'd let her in on my plan to be done with it all.

It would've been the hugest risk I'd ever taken. I would've been putting it all on the line.

And for what?

To disappoint her? To ruin everything we'd shared? To implicate her in a crime?

And what if the risk didn't pay off? Would she have turned her back on me and ratted me out to her dad?

I just needed to get it over and done with.

That's why I stood there. All alone in her empty house, en route to her parents' study. I was fairly confident it's where they kept their safe since hiding spots for safes were practically a staple in floor plans for homes like theirs. And if the pistol wasn't in the safe, I assumed they had a gun cellar in the basement. And those were even easier to crack than safes.

I crept upstairs, my weight creaking the steps beneath me. My mind flashed back to carrying Hadley up the same stairs on the way to her bedroom. She'd squealed when I lifted her, having no idea how excited I was to see her completely naked for the first time. To touch her body in places I hadn't been able to. To wrap her in my arms and do whatever I wanted to do, knowing she'd let me. To sleep with her wrapped in my arms. To wake up and see her face and kiss her lips.

I reached the second floor and crept down the hallway, my pulse pounding in my temples. I passed Hadley's dark bedroom. Visions flooded my mind of the first time I woke up in there and found her curled up in the chair. Of last night. The way everything was just so damn perfect.

I passed her art studio. Visions of our time in there slammed into me, begging me to turn around and forget the pistol. The amazing drawing she'd done for me. The nervous look in her eyes once I saw it. Her striptease and desire to take our relationship further. The way she tasted. I shook my head, literally forcing away the thoughts.

I stopped in front of the one closed door in the hallway. I reached out, trying the knob. It turned in my gloved hand. I almost wished it hadn't. I wanted to work for it. I didn't want it to be so easy. So effortless to take something from someone I never wanted to hurt.

I stepped inside the room, not bothering to close the door behind me. I'd be quick. I pulled out my tiny flashlight and assessed my surroundings. Satin curtains hung to the floor, blocking the windows and darkening the already dark room. The standard mahogany desk, matching armoire, and decorative sofa were placed precisely around the room.

I walked behind the desk. Hadley's picture sat front and center. Her smiling face was a glaring reminder of everything I'd be losing if I got caught. I turned to the painting on the wall behind the desk and slipped my fingers under the frame, peering with the flashlight underneath, only to find a bare wall.

My eyes flashed to the armoire and I made my way over, wondering if that's where I'd find the safe hidden. I'd researched the 1847 Colt Walker pistol I needed to retrieve. Hadley's mother had obtained it at an auction for over a million dollars. I wished it hadn't been publicized. I wished no one knew who had it. Then I wouldn't have been there. I wouldn't have had to take something from someone whose daughter cared about me. Trusted me.

But I did what I always did. I rationalized it.

I assured myself Hadley's mother didn't need the pistol. It wasn't like she planned to fire it. It was a status symbol to people like her. Something to say she owned. Something to keep locked away in her safe.

Guilt crept into every crevice of my body, overwhelming me with its force. I was delusional. Her mother wasn't about status. Sure, she was rich. But she also helped others. Others in need.

Unfortunately, guilt wasn't enough to stop me. Because in the end, I did what I had to do—especially if I planned to use it as leverage to be free from my father once and for all. I tugged on the armoire's handle and opened it. The safe sat right inside, like it had been waiting for me to arrive.

I stuck my earbuds in my ears, held my phone to the door of the safe, and spun the knob. *Click. Click. Click-click.* That's all I needed to hear.

Hadley

I'd plastered on a smile, mingled with the benefactors, and stayed by my mother's side the entire night. Everything she needed me to do. Now my work was done.

My leg bounced anxiously as my mother's driver drove me home. I needed to change out of my dress and get in touch with Caynan. I'd waited to call since I really wanted to surprise him. He hadn't texted me all night. I wondered if he hadn't wanted to bother me during the fundraiser or his game ran long and he went out celebrating with the guys. Either way, it played perfectly into my plan to surprise him.

Once I was minutes away from my house, I tried his cell. My call was sent to voicemail. I left him a quick message to let him know I was almost home and wanted to see him. There was no way I wasn't going to see him.

Once the car pulled into my driveway, I gathered my shoes and clutch and hopped out, taking two steps at a time. I punched in the code, but the green light didn't shine. *Shit.* My mother forgot to set it. I grabbed the front doorknob and stepped into the foyer. I flipped on the light on the table beside the door, dropping my shoes and clutch down on it. Since Caynan wasn't answering his phone, my thumbs went to work, typing a quick text.

A sound from the second floor stilled my thumbs. Hell, it stilled my entire body. My eyes shot to the top of the stairs. I waited, silencing my breathing, my eyes locked on the second floor landing. I didn't see any shadows. I didn't hear any other sounds. Had I left my window open? Had something fallen? Had it just been my imagination?

I crept toward the stairs, taking one at a time, my phone clutched tightly in my hand. But seriously? The house belonged to a cop. No one in their right mind would be stupid enough to break in.

I reached the platform at the top of the second floor and moved slowly to the decorative bench there. I raised the top of the bench, hoping it didn't squeak when I opened it. I reached inside, digging under the neatly-folded throw blankets. My hand found what I sought. Something cold and metal. And all I needed to feel safe. A .22 semi-automatic handgun. The first gun my father ever let me shoot at the shooting range.

Most teenage girls would've felt uncomfortable handling a gun, but my dad made sure it was second nature to me. Unfortunately, being in our big house all alone with a potential intruder made it a lot less second nature.

I replaced the bench's cover and waited. If someone *was* in my house, there was only one way down. I listened, focusing for a long time on nothing but silence.

As the silent minutes stretched on, I felt ridiculous standing there with a gun. In a formal dress. In my own home. I lifted my phone and sent Caynan the text. As soon as I hit send, a noise traveled from the other end of the hall.

My stomach dropped. *Fuuuuuuck.*

I don't know what gave me the nerve, maybe adrenaline, maybe foolishness, but I stepped toward the noise. This was my house and someone had the nerve to enter it. Okay, even that seemed like a lame justification. But I trekked on. Gun in hand. Heart beating out of my chest. My knees wobbled as I inched down the hallway, passing my dark bedroom. I released a small breath as I continued past my art studio. I wished Caynan were there with me. He would've been the brave one, or the one to talk me out of doing one of the craziest things I'd ever done.

I could see the open door to my parents' study up ahead. My heart sputtered. They never left it open. *Holy shit.* I'd lost my freaking mind.

I inched slowly along the wall, my knees knocking wildly. A light flickered into the hallway.

Holy shit. This is real. This is fucking real.

I extended the gun in front of me, my hands trembling fiercely and my heart pounding in my ears. I turned into the doorway with my gun extended into the room.

My eyes collided with the brown eyes I dreamt about at night. The eyes that smoldered when his body covered mine. The eyes of the guy I trusted. The guy who stood with my mother's pistol in one hand and his cell phone in the other. The guy who was ripping my heart out with his bare hands.

Caynan didn't move as everything rushed at me at once. The realization. The shock. The betrayal. It had been him. He'd been evading the police. He'd been lurking in the darkness. He'd been taking advantage of the people in my neighborhood. He'd been taking advantage of *me*.

The notion sent my anger to the brink and my sanity to pieces.

I released the gun's safety. The *click* echoed throughout the room. Caynan's eyes expanded.

"Hadley." He didn't say it in warning, more like fear.

"Don't," I ground out through gritted teeth. "Don't say anything."

He expelled a deep breath. "I never wanted to hurt you."

"I said '*don't!*'"

I kept the gun aimed in my right hand and pressed my number one contact on my phone in my left. I lifted the phone to my ear, my eyes locked on Caynan, whose shoulders dropped in defeat. "The thief's in our house," I said into the phone.

Caynan closed his eyes, as if in pain. As if *he* were in pain. The freaking irony.

"I'm okay. He won't hurt me," I assured my father, who demanded I get out of the house immediately.

"Of course I won't hurt you," Caynan interjected, though his voice was hushed and detached.

I clicked off my phone, cutting off my father's pleas.

"You don't need that gun. I'm not going anywhere."

I stared across the room at the liar. The fake. The *thief*. "I don't believe you." I nodded toward the pistol in his hand. "Was that worth it?"

He glanced to the pistol—the one my mother had recently bought for my father. The one he was going to display at the local museum to help her bring in big benefactors for her next fundraiser—an auction to raise money for a new children's wing at the hospital. Caynan tucked the pistol back into the safe. "Nope."

Sirens in the distance sent both our eyes shooting toward the window. "I can't believe I was so stupid."

"Don't," he demanded. "None of this is your fault."

The sirens outside grew louder, though they couldn't compete with the ringing in my ears.

"I'm good at what I do," he continued. "You couldn't have known."

I closed my eyes and shook my head. "I thought it was real." I held back the tears fighting to break loose. I'd be damned if I let him see how badly he'd hurt me. Not in this lifetime. When I opened my eyes, Caynan stared at me, unmoving, silent.

A moment passed. A long torturous moment as we stared across the huge divide that now existed between us.

I'd never known him. Not even a little bit.

The front door downstairs slammed open and a brigade of heavy footsteps dispersed, some checking the main floor while the others plodded upstairs. Within seconds, police officers appeared in the open doorway, guns aimed at Caynan.

My father immediately rushed to me, lowering my gun and wrapping me in an embrace. Over his shoulder, I watched the men surround Caynan, shoving him down on the desk while yanking his arms behind his back, cuffing him roughly.

I turned away as my father continued to hold me in his arms while the police read Caynan his Rights, moving him quickly out of the study and out of my life forever.

PART TWO
THREE YEARS LATER

CHAPTER FOURTEEN

The door to my cell rattled open, echoing through cell block C. Guys from the surrounding cells stepped out of theirs, all freshly groomed in their matching tan shirts and pants, heading to the visitation room for their weekly visits. They passed by my cell, none bothering to look inside.

I wondered if visiting with their loved ones gave them a sense of normalcy. A taste of the outside. A reminder they weren't actually animals herded from place to place, ordered to eat, sleep, and shut up. They were actual human beings. Something I hadn't felt like in a very long time. Unlike them, I'd never had a visitor. It wasn't like I had any family members or friends who missed me. I'd denied my baseball coach's request to visit. He'd taken a chance on me and I'd lied to him. Lied to him and used him to get what I wanted, just like I'd done to everyone else I'd encountered. I didn't need a reminder. I was in prison. I was reminded every damn day.

After copping a plea that earned me a lighter sentence and threw my father under the bus, I'd done my time alongside thieves and businessmen who'd committed fraud. It wasn't like I got thrown in with serial killers and gangbangers. But being surrounded by liars and cheats every second of every day did little for my sanity. So, for three years, I'd mostly kept to myself.

It had been a long three years. A reflective three years but a fucking lonely three years.

Once everyone disappeared for visitation, I lay on my bed and absorbed the silence. I'd never realized how much I craved the peace and quiet until I didn't have it anymore. With a pencil in hand, I began my final letter. The last one I'd send before I was released. For someone who had to conceal the truth for so long, it was shocking how good I'd become at spilling my guts. The letters gave me an outlet.

For my guilt.

For my sadness.

For my loneliness.

Besides honing my writing skills, I'd earned my GED while on the inside. But that wasn't good enough. I wouldn't let my incarceration stop me from earning a college degree, so through a privately-funded night class program, and additional online distance learning courses, I was halfway through my Bachelor's degree. Days were definitely long inside. Studying gave me a purpose. Writing brought me some peace. And lifting in the gym kept me in shape so on the off chance I ever got to play baseball again, I'd be ready.

* * *

"So, our time together has come to an end," Marie said, her thick-rimmed glasses sitting low on her nose.

I nodded from my slouched position in the chair across from her, my eyes taking in her office for the last time. I could still remember the first day I walked in there. Nothing had changed. It still had the same sterile smell. The same bare walls. The same empty desk.

An unfortunate condition of my plea bargain had been weekly counseling sessions. And though I agreed to go, I never agreed to talk. So, for the first year and a half, I sat there and said nothing. I just listened to her drone on about releasing myself of guilt and acknowledging my father's emotional abuse. She said what he'd done to me had a medical term: psychological maltreatment. She spent each session explaining how his manipulation had inhibited my psychological growth, causing my grasp on right and wrong to become distorted. I didn't need a shrink to tell me that. I lived it.

A year and a half into listening to her psycho-babble, I couldn't take it anymore. I unloaded on her. And when I say unloaded, I unloaded everything I'd been keeping inside. And not just for the year and a half…for as long as I could remember.

I talked about my mom and her words that haunted me. I talked about my dad and my need to hold us together. And I talked about Hadley and the regrets I had not being honest with her. Once I got started, I couldn't stop. I talked about the shit I'd done. The shit I'd seen. My regret. My pain. My fear for the future.

Marie didn't try to fix my problems. She listened and encouraged me to come up with my own solutions. She gave me ways to ease my conscience and to live a normal life once I was released.

It felt strange having encouragement from an adult who wanted nothing but to help me. I told her about the letters. After praising me for taking the initiative, she explained it was my subconscious trying to retrieve a piece of myself—at least who I presumed my true self to be. I'd worn a mask for so long I didn't really know *who* I was.

Marie assured me, once it came time for me to walk out the front gates of the prison, I'd have the tools necessary to live a normal life. I just wished I was as sure as she was.

"Wow," she marveled. "When we first met, I never thought you'd even speak. Now look at you. Speaking and almost smiling."

Almost smiling.

I learned early on that no one smiled in prison. There was nothing to smile about. You'd lost everything. And whatever brought you there in the first place—and the guilt that carried with it—ate away at you, prohibiting you from any form of happiness. But meeting with Marie had become a safe haven for me. A place to almost feel normal again. And Marie had grown on me. She truly wanted the best for me. "Yeah, well time heals all wounds. Right, Doc?"

She smiled. "I think I might've heard that once before."

"Once?" I grunted. "Try every damn time I've been in here."

She laughed. "So, what now for you?"

I shrugged. "Get a job. Sign up for classes."

"Make amends?" she asked.

My eyes shot to the sole window in her office. The bars did nothing to block the sunlight that gleamed outside. Sunlight on my face. That was something else I didn't realize I'd miss. But having limited time outside made me appreciate every second I was out there even more. The warmth on my skin. The positive energy it added to a day. It was crazy how I missed the most basic things. Rain. Traffic. Eating when I wanted to. But soon, I'd be able to appreciate everything—no matter how big or small—so much more than I'd done before.

And as much as I longed for my freedom, it also scared me. What would I do with so much independence? From prison. From my dad. From the lies. I had no idea how to just be me. What a crazy thing for a twenty-one-year-old guy to admit. But it was the truth. I'd never actually done "me" before. And that scared the shit out of me.

"Do you plan on seeing your dad?"

I shook my head. The thought had never even crossed my mind. "Nope."

She nodded. "It's probably for the best. You'll do it when you're ready."

I balked as I dragged my hands over my prison-mandated shaved head, knowing I'd never be ready to face him.

"Do you know where you're going to live?" She pushed her glasses up her nose.

"I'll figure something out."

"Are you still planning to do what we talked about?"

I nodded. It's all I'd thought about, night and day, for three years.

She assessed my face, her unspoken thoughts flashing behind her glasses. I wondered what insight she'd impart on me as our final session came to a close. "Will you promise me something?"

"What's that?"

"Be patient. Some things are easier said than done."

I shrugged. "I've lost everything, Doc. I've got nothing left to lose."

"True. But I just don't want you to set your expectations too high."

"No worries. I'm a patient man. And I've got all the time in the world." And for the first time since being there, I *almost* smiled.

Hadley

"Why don't you come up here, babe?"

Books lay spread out before me on the floor of my room as I chewed on a piece of licorice. I glanced to my bed where Jake lay, staring down at me. Those blue eyes of his had lured me in. So deep in their depths yet so different from the ebony ones that haunted my dreams. "I'm studying."

"Yeah. I can see that. But I'm done and want you up here with me." He patted his hand down beside him on my fuchsia comforter.

I smirked. "That's where you always want me."

He laughed. "Have you looked in a mirror? You're hot."

I laughed, fully aware that Jake dished out compliments like waitresses served meals. We'd been dating for six months, taking a break over the summer before returning for senior year a month before.

Jake crawled off the bed and onto the floor, crouching beside me, his shaggy blond hair falling over his forehead. "Fine. If you're gonna be studying all day, I'm gonna go meet up with the guys. Do you mind?"

I shook my head. "No. Go have fun. I just really need to ace this test." His lips landed on my shoulder trailing a soft path up my neck where he nuzzled in, knowing it would make me giggle. And it did. "Get out of here before I don't let you go."

Laughter rumbled in his chest. "Don't toy with me like that, tease."

I grinned as he stood up, towering over me like the rugged hockey player he was. "I'll pick you up at eight."

I nodded as he turned and walked out of my room.

All the guys I'd dated in college had been safe. They'd been guys I knew wouldn't hide things from me. Deceive me. Take advantage of me. I'd created walls with barbed-wire on top to keep those types out. Jake had been my biggest risk. He was good looking and a hell of a hockey player. I knew I'd never completely trust him, not with all the puck bunnies looming. But he'd pursued me relentlessly. On his ninth attempt, I finally agreed to go out with him—just to get him off my back. But he turned out to be fun and there'd been a spark—something that had been missing with every other guy I dated.

My phone buzzed beside me on the floor. I grabbed it, checking the screen before hitting the speaker. "Hey."

"Hey, back at ya," Cass's voice greeted me from sunny California. We'd spent all summer together on the Georgia shore, renting a cute little beach house far from the town we'd grown up in. Neither of us wanted to return to the drama there. But in all honesty, being with her for three straight months made returning to school difficult. "I miss you already."

"I miss you, too."

"So, where's mister hockey stud?"

"I needed to study. He took off."

Her sigh carried through the phone. "It wouldn't kill you to let him in. He clearly likes you. Give him a chance."

"Who said I wasn't?"

She scoffed. "I know you, remember?"

"We've been together six months," I reminded her, though I felt like I was reminding myself.

"Do you want an award because he's lasted longer than the rest? And where was he this summer? Oh, yeah, that's right. Not with you."

This time *I* scoffed. "Come on. Cut me some slack."

"I've been cutting you slack. And now I just want you to have a great senior year."

She'd given me the same speech every year since leaving for college. This time I wanted it to stick. I *needed* it to. And maybe it would. It's not like I'd become a nun since high school. I'd had fun. Did the whole reckless-college-girl-thing other girls did. Went to parties and bars. Hooked up with guys. I just guarded my heart. A lot of people lived that way. And someday it would serve me well.

* * *

Jake rounded the hood of his car and opened my door. He took my hand and helped me onto the sidewalk, stealing a quick kiss before leading me to the cobblestone building where I lived. Unlike other seniors who ventured to off-campus housing, I lived on campus. The suite-style apartments were nice and primarily occupied by upperclassmen, so parties were kept to a minimum. Not that I minded a good party. It just kind of lost its charm after too many nights praying to the porcelain gods.

Once we reached the top step, Jake spun me toward him, wrapping his arms around me so I had no choice but to stare up into his blue eyes. "You sure you don't want me to come in? I'll make it worth your while."

I wished more than anything that his good looks and amazing body had the power to tempt me. "I don't doubt that for a second."

He leaned down and pressed his lips to mine, soft and gentle. The exact opposite of how he kissed me when we were naked. He pulled out of the kiss with a smirk, the way good-looking guys always did—like they knew something you didn't. "Once you ace this test Monday, I get you all to myself for as long as I want you."

I grinned. "That was the deal."

"Oh, babe. I've been holding onto that for the past week."

I laughed, placing my hands on his chest. "I promise. You'll have my complete and undivided attention."

His eyes searched my face. "Oh, the things I plan to do to you."

I pushed him back, knowing he'd never leave if I didn't give him a push. "Go. Leave me to the ever-exciting world of philosophy."

"See you tomorrow?"

"If you're lucky, and you let me go in so I can study."

He lifted his palms in surrender. "All right, all right. I'm going." He made his way down the front steps. I watched until he'd slipped into his car and disappeared at the end of the road.

I turned to the door and scanned my keycard. It was an old sensor, so you needed to move it around until it eventually unlocked the door.

"What kind of guy doesn't walk his girl inside?" a deep voice asked.

Every part of my body froze. The hair on the back of my neck stood on end.

Holy. Shit.

CHAPTER FIFTEEN

Hadley

A shiver tore through my body at the sound of that voice. I didn't dare move for fear of losing my balance. And my freaking mind.

"If you ask me," he continued. "The guy doesn't know how to kiss you the way you deserve to be kissed."

My heart pounded like a drum line solo as my eyes snapped shut. Was I hearing things? Had it been a twisted figment of my imagination? If it was him, where was his accent? I spun around, squinting into the darkness.

Caynan stepped out from behind one of the cherry trees lining the street with his hands buried deep in the pockets of his jeans.

My stomach plummeted as I stood speechless, my arms falling to my sides. My chest heaved at the sight of him as my breath pushed in and out through my nose like I'd just finished a marathon. The last time I'd seen him he was being led from my house in handcuffs. Now he stood in front of me with a light-colored shirt stretched across his broad chest. The thick stubble covering his chin made him look older. And the tightness around his eyes indicated a seriousness I'd rarely seen on his face.

My eyes shot around, fear suddenly grabbing hold of my body. Had he come alone? Had he tracked me down to hurt me?

He made an attempt to step closer.

"Stop right there." My voice came out deep and self-assured, though the rest of my body was nowhere near. Who knew what he planned to do to me—the person who turned him in. The person who made sure he was arrested and sentenced to time in prison. The person who hated him more than anything in this world.

His eyes flared. "Jesus, Hadley. I'm not going to hurt you. I'd never hurt you."

Tears pricked my eyes. That's *exactly* what he'd said in my parents' study and *exactly* what he'd done to me.

The pain in his features indicated he'd read my thoughts. We'd always been good at reading each other. Or at least I thought we'd been. In the end, I guess he'd been the only one doing the reading. Reading me so he could play me. Find a way into my life. Into my home. Into my parents' safe.

He took another small step, perhaps wanting to console me. But he was the last person in the world I wanted to do that. Especially since he was the reason I needed consoling.

"I'm serious." I cleared my throat, determined not to sound as tortured as I felt. "Not another step." I grabbed my phone from my back pocket.

"Hadley wait…I just want to…I just need to talk to you."

My face scrunched. Where the hell was his freaking accent?

"I just got released."

"Today?"

He nodded.

"And you came to see *me*?"

"Yeah. Of course." He sounded as though it had been arranged. As if we'd spoken over the past three years and decided we'd meet up when he was released.

I needed to be smart. Play this right or there was no way I was getting safely into my building. "I'm happy for you, Cayn—"

"Conner."

My head recoiled. "What?"

"My name. It's Conner." He said it like I should've already known. "And I'm not British."

A huge breath whooshed through my lips, compressing my chest as if an invisible weight pressed against it. I grabbed the banister at my side as a shrill sound rang in my ears. Was I about to hyperventilate? Pass out? It was the second time in three years that I'd felt that off-kilter. My world was spiraling and I was at the core. Again. "Why are you doing this?"

"Doing what?" His eyes riveted wildly between mine. Could he sense something was wrong?

My body trembled. It was as if all the anger, resentment, and humiliation I'd held inside for three long years had bubbled to the surface. "Making me feel more stupid than I already do." I couldn't hold back any longer. "Wasn't it enough you wormed your way into my life and turned it upside down? What could you possibly want from me now?"

His eyes cast down, his head following. "You didn't read my letters." It wasn't a question, more like the truth registering. "I mean, I know you never responded. But none of them were returned. I figured you had to have read them." He glanced up, his dark eyes narrowed. "I can't believe you didn't."

I said nothing, just stared back at him. At this guy I'd never known. Everything I thought I'd known about him, everything he'd told me, had been one big lie. He'd been right about one thing. I hadn't read his letters. Not one. There was nothing he could've said that would've made up for the hurt he'd caused me.

"But I know you." His voice was pained. "You're so curious. I banked on you reading at least one."

I shook my head.

He took two steps closer. "Then let me tell you what they said."

I fought the urge to cover my ears like a spoiled child. "There's nothing you can say that will make this better."

He dragged his hands over his shaved head. "I know that! Don't you think I fucking know that?"

My body jerked back. *Wait a freaking minute.* He did *not* have the right to get angry at *me*. If anyone had the right to be angry, it was me. I planted my feet and crossed my arms, like his rage unfazed me. He didn't need to know

I needed my arms to somehow protect me from him. "You need to leave."

"Scared your boyfriend might come back?"

A growl erupted from deep within me. "Fuck you."

"Now we're getting somewhere."

My eyes flared and my arm shot out, my index finger pointing fiercely at him. "*You.* You did this. Not me."

"And I regretted it every second!"

I scoffed. "It didn't stop you."

His eyes splayed. "Didn't stop me? Didn't *stop* me? I could've run, Hadley. I could've kept running. But I stayed. I stayed for you."

"Bullshit. Everything you did—everything you've done—you've done for *you*." My last word echoed through the silent night as I stared across the space between us. His chest heaved just as harshly as mine. His eyes were just as wild. "Go away, Cay—" I winced at my mistake. "Whatever your name is. We're done here."

I turned on shaky legs and scanned my key card. Thankfully, it unlocked the door on the first try. I shoved open the door and stepped inside my building. Having said what I needed to say for the past three years, I slammed the door on my past once and for all.

Conner

I took off down the sidewalk toward the bus stop where I'd been dropped off, still reeling from seeing Hadley again after three long years. I didn't expect so many emotions to rush at me at once. So many unresolved feelings. I also didn't expect her to still hate me so much.

But even with the venom she spewed at me, I could still see I affected her. If I didn't, she wouldn't have been so heated over my presence.

I couldn't believe she hadn't read my letters. I sent one every damn week since I'd been arrested. How could she not have read even one? But the cold glare in her eyes and her surprise at my name and missing accent confirmed she hadn't. It sucked knowing all that time spent spilling my guts to her was for naught. She'd never received my apologies. She'd never heard the reasons for my betrayal. She'd never forgiven me.

She'd spent the last three years hating me.

I crossed the quiet street to the covered bus stop and dropped down onto the metal bench. I needed to find a place to crash until I had my own place secured. Luckily, my father had always been a step ahead, emptying most of our cash into off-shore accounts. I just needed to bide my time before I started sniffing around those accounts. I couldn't end up back in prison—where my father was still rotting away in maximum security. I just couldn't.

Three years had given me plenty of time to come to terms with a lot of things. His manipulation was not one of them. What Hadley had done...that was a different story. I'd accepted her decision to turn me in. I understood what that night meant for me. What it meant for *us*. She had to do it. Had she not, there was no telling where I would've been. I liked to believe that night would've been the end of that life for me. But in reality, maybe I would've been too scared to leave. Maybe I would've been unable to make it on my own. Maybe Hadley wouldn't have followed me.

I wasn't stupid. I knew what she and I shared was rare. We may have been young, but what we had was real. She was the first person I ever felt connected to. She was the first person I wanted to be around all day and night. She was the first person I wanted to confide in—to tell my darkest secrets to. I knew, even back then, I needed her in my life.

And now, I just needed her forgiveness.

There really wasn't any other way I'd survive.

Hadley

Ohmigod. Ohmigod. Ohmigod.

My phone shook in my hand as I leaned against my door and slid down to the floor. My heart walloped in my chest as I pressed Cass's name and lifted the phone shakily to my ear.

"Hey."

"He showed up." My voice came out a mere whisper.

"Who showed up?" I could hear her confusion.

"Caynan."

She gasped. "What? Where? I thought he was in jail?"

I squeezed the bridge of my nose, trying to stop the incessant throbbing. "Yeah. Me, too."

"Did he hurt you?"

I shook my head, though she obviously couldn't see me. "No."

"Did you call your dad?"

My dad. God. He would've freaked if he knew he'd shown up. "Should I?"

"If you want him thrown back in prison, yes."

He'd been in prison for three years. Sure, I hated him for what he'd done to me, but did I want to be the reason he was sent back? And for what? Coming near me? It wasn't like I had a restraining order. But was I sure he didn't plan to hurt me? *And* could I keep something that big from my dad? Did I even want to?

"What'd he say?" Cass interrupted my inner struggle.

"He brought up the letters."

"I told you to read them. I told you *I'd* read them."

"I know. But apparently, he was under the impression I'd know he was coming. And that I'd forgiven him."

"Well, then he's more bat-shit crazy than we ever thought."

I scoffed, still unable to wrap my head around the fact that he'd reappeared in my life. After three long years. And for what? To apologize? Could I even believe that?

"How'd he look?" Cass asked.

I couldn't shake the image of him standing in the darkness outside my door. It was practically engraved. Like a vivid dream. Or better yet, a nightmare. "Older…"

"Hardened?"

I shrugged to the empty room. "More serious. Tired. Sad maybe."

"Je. Sus."

I blew out a much-needed breath. "And his name's Conner. He's as American as you and me."

"No shit?"

I had no response. I was still trying to process it all.

"I bet your dad knew. I bet if you'd let him breathe that name around you, you probably would've known everything. Including the fact that he was released."

She was right. After that night, I wouldn't let anyone talk about him in front of me. Not my parents, not Cass, not anyone from school. Not that they dared bring him up. Sure, there were whispers every time I entered a room, but no one said anything directly to me. I thought I'd handled it pretty well, but the whole thing sucked more than I let on. I'd fallen hard for him. I'd given him all of me. And to turn around and use me like I was nothing to him, how could I ever forgive him?

"Is he coming back?"

I shrugged. "I don't know."

There was a long pause on her end. "Hadley?" I hated when she used that concerned tone on me. Like she was my mother and not my best friend.

"I'm here."

"Do you think maybe you'd be able to move on if you had some closure? There has to be a reason why you haven't been in love with anyone since him."

"I've—"

"Let me finish. I know you blame him for your trust issues, and you have every reason to. But I think you not really moving on has more to do with the lack of closure between the two of you. There's no denying he was your first love. That leaves a mark on someone, no matter how it ends."

After hanging up with Cass, I sat for a long time considering what she'd said. Had he been my first love? Had I not moved on? I felt like I had. I dated guys. I'd been with Jake for six months. That had to mean something. But maybe Cass had been right. Maybe I did need closure. Maybe Cay—Conner's deception had rendered me incapable of fully trusting anyone again. Maybe I did need to hear whatever it was he needed to say. Maybe that's exactly what I'd needed for the last three years.

The doorknob behind my back rattled and the door pushed slightly, my weight stopping it. "Hadley? Is that you?" Lorelei asked.

I pushed myself to my feet, moving away from the door so my roommate could step inside. "Sorry."

She eyed me curiously from under her thick black bangs. "You okay?"

I shrugged.

She dropped her handbag onto her desk in the opposite corner of the room. "Did the hockey star break your heart?"

I shook my head. "No. But my past showed up shocking the hell out of me."

"An ex?"

I shrugged, not in the mood to share the sordid details. "Kind of."

She pulled open her drawers and grabbed her pajamas. "Well if you need me, I'm here. If not, I'm gonna go take a shower."

I shook my head, appreciating her offer. "I'll be fine."

She smiled before taking off for the shower we shared with the suite next door. Lorelei had been a great roommate since we were paired up freshman year. The good thing was we had our own friends. We weren't constantly together which made living together easier. We also didn't confide in each other the way girlfriends did. That's why our conversation about Cay—Conner had been so vague. I'd never unloaded that drama on her.

I grabbed my own pajamas from my dresser and threw them on, nestling into my warm bed. Once darkness and silence surrounded me, I was left with nothing but my thoughts—the events of the night were front and center. Tears glazed my eyes. There was nothing stopping me at that point. Not my pride. Not my resolve to remain strong. Not my surprise or anger. I let it all go. Tears slipped down my cheeks and onto my pillow as I cried myself to sleep.

CHAPTER SIXTEEN

Hadley

I woke the next morning to unrelenting birds chirping outside my window like their lives were so fan-freaking-tastic. Mine currently sucked. I'd barely slept after my unexpected visitor, and Lorelei hadn't stopped snoring all night. The sunlight shot daggers at my eyes as I struggled to open them. Twenty-four hours remained before my philosophy test, so I needed to get my head screwed back on straight and recapture my focus.

Being Sunday, I knew the café down the block would be empty, so I threw on some sweats and a worn band T-shirt. I grabbed my phone and debit card and dashed into the hallway, needing to grab a latte before hitting the books. I'd barely stepped outside when I lost my footing, nearly tripping over the person unexpectedly seated on the front steps. I squealed as my hands shot out, trying to stop myself from taking the steps face-first.

Two strong hands gripped my arms, stopping me from going down. My head whipped up. As if electrocuted, I jumped back, freeing myself from Conner's grasp. "What the hell are you doing here?"

He stood there, brushing pebbles off the back of his basketball shorts. On even ground, he was taller than he'd been. I needed to look up even more to see his eyes. He also looked like someone who lifted weights. I guess that's what criminals did with all their time.

"I'm serious. Have you been out here all night?"

He shook his head.

"Then what are you doing here now?" I glanced at my phone. It wasn't even seven.

"I wanted to see you."

My eyes jumped around. If he did in fact attempt to hurt me, there was no one around. "You need to stop showing up. This isn't normal behavior."

"Says who?"

"Says the person you're scaring."

The shock in his eyes stretched them wide. "Scaring?" He stepped back. "Why would you be scared of me? *Me*, Hadley. It's just *me*."

My hands balled into fists at my side, my nails digging into my palms. "And who are you?" I couldn't stop my voice from rising with my anger. "Because I have no idea. I *never* knew."

"Of course you knew me. You still know me."

My head dropped back as I closed my eyes, searching for the strength I desperately needed to get through this conversation. When my eyes popped open, I decided if nothing else, I could fake it. "Tell me. What do I know? Because from where I'm standing, I *knew* a guy named Caynan from England who played baseball and wanted to go pro. Not a thief named Conner with a fake accent from somewhere in the United States."

He stared at me with those same dark eyes, though they lacked the playful youthfulness they once had. Prison had hardened him. It had changed him. At least who I thought him to be. I could sense him acknowledging the fact that my argument held weight. That he was never who he claimed to be. That he had in fact deceived me to an unforgivable extent. That I never knew him. "I don't really know," Conner said.

I cocked my head. "You don't know?"

"I've played a part for so long. I honestly don't know who I am anymore." His somber tone turned hopeful. "But I want *you* to help me figure it out."

I sucked in a sharp breath. Part of me wanted to feel sorry for him. For the lost look in his eyes. But the other part wanted to strangle him for having the nerve to ask me for *anything* after what he'd done to me. I shook my head. "That's not something you can ask me to do. That's something you've gotta figure out for yourself."

"Being with you was the only time I ever felt the most like me," he said. "At least the me I wanted to be."

"I can't be some safety net for you because I'm familiar. That doesn't work for me. I need to be someone's everything."

I watched my words strike a chord behind his eyes.

Three years of solitude had apparently made him reflective. He didn't immediately spout out a comeback. He thought through what he wanted to say. "Nebraska."

My eyes narrowed. "What?"

"You said somewhere in the United States. I'm from Nebraska. At least that's what my dad told me."

A shaky breath parted my lips. Why did the revelation of more lies crush me even more?

"Say it, Hadley. Say whatever you need to say. I can take it."

"It was all a lie. Every last detail was fabricated and I fell for it." My arms spread wide. "Congratulations. You got me."

"It wasn't all a lie. I swear to you."

"Hadley?" a voice called from behind me.

I whirled around.

Lorelei's head poked out the front door, her hair a bed-headed mess. "Are you okay? I heard yelling."

I shook my head. "I haven't been okay in a long time." Without turning back to him, I made my way toward the steps.

"Hadley, wait?" he implored. "Talk to me."

I ignored his pleas and jogged up the front steps, hurrying through the door Lorelei held open for me. I didn't get my latte. But then again, I'd lost my craving right along with my sanity.

Lorelei closed the front door, following me down the first floor hallway and into our room. "Want to tell me what that was about?"

"That was my past barreling right back into my life the same way he entered it."

"I wish my past looked like that."

I dropped down onto my bed and fell back, draping my arm over my eyes. "Don't let the good looks fool you. I made that mistake once. It left me with nothing but a broken heart."

Conner

I spent the hours following Hadley's brush-off walking around campus, trying to get my thoughts in check. Maybe I'd been too rash to approach her the way I had. Maybe I'd said too much too soon. Maybe she was right. Maybe I needed to figure things out on my own. Maybe she wasn't my safety net. But I knew damn well she was my compass.

I approached the campus quad. Old cobblestone buildings surrounded it. Students sat on the freshly-cut lawn talking and eating. Some played Frisbee, some played football. It seemed like a great place to be—surrounded by people with the same interests and goals. All destined for a promising future. Not the criminals I'd spent the last three years of my life stuck with. Not the frauds all convinced they'd done nothing wrong.

That was the difference between us. I knew I'd done the crime. Maybe I hadn't wanted to, but I'd done it nonetheless.

And I'd be a liar just like them if I said Hadley's words didn't sting. Not because they'd been said to hurt me, but because they'd been the truth. All she knew of me was a lie. I just wished she knew everything I said to her—everything we shared—was the truth. The God's honest truth. But seeing her now, all grown up and strong, it was clear that getting *this* Hadley to accept me after the pain I caused her, wouldn't be easy.

I spent too many days in prison wondering what my life would've been like had my father played catch with me instead of teaching me to case houses and crack safes.

I think I always realized my life wasn't normal. My father fucked up my childhood. But I was a man now. I couldn't blame him forever. I'd taken responsibility for my actions, now I needed to make something of myself. That's why I got my GED. It's why I took college classes. I considered enrolling part-time at Hadley's school, taking classes during the day and working at night. But I had no cash. I needed a job before I could enroll.

I glanced to the small garbage truck that pulled up to a trash can concealed by a decorative cover at the corner of the quad. Maybe I could get a job on campus. Maybe if I stuck close to Hadley, I'd keep my sanity. If that meant taking any job I could get, then I'd take any job I could get. I mean, come on. Collecting trash was better than folding other guys' stained underwear liked I'd been doing.

I jogged over to the kid dumping trash into his truck. "Hey."

He looked up from the can in his hands.

"Question for you." I stopped a few feet away. "What do I need to do to get a job on campus?"

His eyes narrowed like he thought I was busting his chops.

"I'm serious. I'm in need of cash sooner rather than later."

He searched my face, probably determining if my words were sincere or not. "What are you looking for?"

I shrugged. "Anything, man. I just need to make some cash."

"Check out the student union." He pointed to a modern building just past the quad. "They've got postings for on-campus and off-campus jobs. A lot of students are on work study, so they snag all the good ones first. As you can see, none of them wanted my gig."

"Yeah. Kind of sucks to be you, huh?"

He laughed, pointing me in the right direction.

I headed for the student union, finding the board filled with job opportunities. I spent a good ten minutes scanning the postings ranging from dining servers and office help to security guards and construction workers for a new science facility. But what were the chances any of them would hire someone like me? Someone with a criminal record?

"Looking for something in particular?"

I turned to find a petite girl with blond pixie hair and a bright pink hair bow standing behind me. I towered over her but she met my eyes. "Not really."

She smiled. "Yeah. Me neither. I'm just sick of being a tour guide for potential students and their families. If I hear another joke about the freshman fifteen, I'm gonna poke my eyes out with a fork."

"Ouch. That bad?"

"You have no idea." She stuck out her hand. "Vik."

I shook her tiny hand, needing the contact more than I realized. It had been a long fucking time since someone touched me. I was hoping Hadley would be the first, but that was definitely a work in progress. "Conner." It felt weird actually using my real name. The prison guards called us by our last names, so I still wasn't used to it.

"Well, Conner. What do you say you and I scour this board until we've found ourselves the perfect jobs, and then we go grab some lunch?"

I patted my pockets, knowing I needed to be more careful with the insignificant amount of cash I'd earned on the inside.

"No worries. It's on me," Vik assured me, pulling out a dining card and waving it around. "My parents put more money on this thing than I could eat in a lifetime."

"Thanks, but I—"

"*Tush.* It's not every day I can take a hot guy to lunch."

I liked her honesty. But that was the problem with chicks. They saw the outside and automatically thought they knew me. If they knew the truth about me—knew the truth about what I'd done—what would they see then? "Well, I'm not exactly enrolled here yet."

"I kind of figured. I would've seen you around by now if you were."

CHAPTER SEVENTEEN

Hadley

"What's wrong?" Jake stared at me as I mindlessly stirred my cold latte.

"Huh?" I said.

He lifted his chin at my filled cup. "I picked you up to give you a break from studying. But all you've done is stare at that coffee. You haven't even taken a sip."

I shook my head, trying to snap out of the daze I'd been in all day. Jake was right. I needed a break from studying, if, in fact, I'd been studying all day. Don't get me wrong. The books were out. My mind was just elsewhere. It had been, since Cay—Conner showed up. "Sorry. I've just been a little distracted."

"Ya think?" He said it with a smile, but I could see the frustration in his eyes.

"Why do you want to date me?"

His eyes flashed around the quiet café. "What?"

I don't know where the question came from, but in that moment, when my head felt so screwed up, I just needed to know the answer. "Why me?"

He laughed. "Why *not* you?"

"Come on. I'm distracted. I'm always studying. I'm not like the girls who fall all over themselves to get near you."

"If I wanted those girls, I'd be with those girls. I want you, Hadley. Whether you're studying for weeks at a time or just being your cute self, I want you."

Most girls would've loved hearing those words from such a great guy, but I needed more.

"But I feel like you barely know the real me."

He reached across the table and took my hands in his. "I know everything I need to know."

"What do I like to do in my free time?"

He stared back at me like I was crazy. Maybe I was.

"I'm serious."

"Then that's easy." He grinned. "Watch your boyfriend play hockey."

I shook my head.

He looked a little insulted but tried again. "Watch chick flicks."

I wrinkled my nose.

"Hang out with Cass."

I exhaled. "I draw."

His brows arched. "You do?"

"I used to."

"Come on, Hadley, just because I don't know something small like that, doesn't mean anything."

I averted my gaze, staring out the window. Darkness had descended. "Yeah, but you never ask about my past."

"Why would I? I don't care about your past. Besides, you get uncomfortable anytime I even come close to bringing it up. So I don't."

I nodded, knowing my life would've been so much easier if I'd never met Cay—Conner. *God dammit!* I wished he'd never come into my life. Never destroyed my concept of trust. Never messed up my head. Because as I sat across the table from a guy who didn't care about my past, who only wanted to be part of my future, the only thing I could think about *was* my past.

* * *

"I think I'm having a mental breakdown."

"You're not having a breakdown," Cass assured me, her face filling my laptop screen. "But does that mean you haven't taken my advice?"

I scrubbed my hands over my face. "I don't want to see him again. I've seen him twice and both times it's made me…made me feel like this."

"Maybe it's just gonna take time."

I lowered my hands and stared into the screen. "How much time? Because I already feel like I'm losing my mind."

She shook her head. "That I can't say. But in the meantime, just do what you always do."

"What's that?"

She held up her fists, fainting right then left like a boxer. "Roll with the punches."

I scoffed. "Punching someone sounds like a great idea."

"I thought the daughter of a cop knew better. *You* don't do it. You have someone else do it for you."

I grunted. "If it were only that easy."

"But punching him in that pretty face would be so much more gratifying, wouldn't it?"

I nodded, picturing said face and wondering where he was and what he'd been doing since I'd sent him away. Did he even have a home to return to?

"Have you told your parents yet?"

I shook my head. "My dad actually called today. He wanted to let me know Conner had been released."

Cass laughed. "That was the perfect time to work it in the conversation."

"Yeah, but I just don't want him worrying. Besides, as soon as he finds out, I'll have campus police parked outside my building twenty-four-seven."

"Yeah, the rest of your building would love you for that."

I scoffed. "Yeah."

Conner

"I can't crash here."

"Why not?" Vik asked, sitting cross-legged on her bed in her dorm room.

I crossed my arms, leaning my ass against her desk. "Well, I'm not even a student here."

"So?"

"You're a chick," I pointed out.

"Who's into girls," she countered.

I shook my head, her feistiness reminding me of the beautiful blonde who currently hated me.

"I've got this huge single and an air mattress in my closet," she added.

"What do you get out of having me here?"

Her drawn-out blinks were deliberate. "Seriously? Have you looked in a mirror? I'm banking on you taking lots of showers and coming back in nothing but a towel. I may like girls, but it doesn't mean I won't enjoy ogling you."

I laughed to myself. "I appreciate it. I really do. But I told you where I've been the past three years. I'm not what you would call a good gamble."

"Dude. I've got nothing of any value hanging around here. If you choose to pocket my panties, have at it."

I smiled, appreciating how she could make a joke out of my past. I needed someone like Vik in my life. If the time I'd spent with her all day applying for jobs had been any indication, she was a great person to have in my corner. And I desperately needed that.

Hadley

I hurried into the student union before class the next day, searching for a quick breakfast. In an hour, my test would be a distant memory. And if I got to class early, I'd be able to get a little more studying in. Before I could reach for the blueberry muffin with the perfectly crusted top, my body froze, my eyes locking in place.

What the hell was he doing there? And who was the tiny blonde seated across from him?

I had difficulty pulling my eyes away from Conner. Even across the busy cafeteria, and with a shaved head I assumed prison required, his good looks were still very much present. Yet I could see how prison changed him. In the way his shoulders pulled back, broader, stronger, ready to turn on anyone who approached him. His stare was more intense, staying focused on the girl across from him as if gauging her words carefully.

Then, as if sensing me watching him, his head lifted, his eyes zeroing in on mine. Even with the distance between us, I could still see the darkness of his irises piercing through me. I could still feel the pull. The static in the air that happened whenever we were in close proximity. But this time, for me, it was yanking me toward the door—away from him.

The tiny blonde twisted around, spotting me. Her lips asked, "Who's that?"

Had he not told her the reason he was on campus? *Was* I even the reason he was on campus anymore? Or did he just plan to make his way through all the female coeds now that he realized the supply was plenty?

He jumped to his feet. Just as quickly, I turned and hurried out. I had a test I needed to focus on. A test I needed to pass in order to graduate at the end of the year. And I didn't plan on letting anyone—especially someone who'd turned my life upside down—stand in the way of me achieving my goal.

My empty stomach growled, but I wasn't going to stick around to hear more of Conner's excuses. I made it across campus in record time and hurried down the third floor hallway to my classroom. My phone vibrated in my pocket. I pulled it out finding a text. **Please stop running. I'm not.**

What was I supposed to do with that? He couldn't just reappear after everything he'd put me through. After every bit of pain he'd caused me. After everything he'd done. Yes, he knew where I lived. Yes, he clearly still had my phone number. But, no. He couldn't have me.

* * *

Jake's lips moved from my neck to my ear, soft groans coming from him as he ravaged my skin. "God, Hadley. You don't know how much I've missed you." He'd stripped me down to my black bra and matching boy-shorts underwear, so his hands had free-range, traveling up my bare sides as I squirmed beneath him on my bed.

I curved my neck, giving him better access. There was something sexy about being almost naked with him fully dressed, his clothes rubbing over my sensitized skin. I loved the way he made me feel when we were all alone. The special attention he paid to me. The special attention he paid to my body. I'd made him wait the past week, and he'd been patient. Tonight, though, he was being anything but patient. And for once, I got lost in the sensations. Lost in the idea of being so thoroughly wanted. Being so thoroughly worshipped.

Buzzing came from my nightstand. I shifted my gaze. My phone lit up with a text. Jake ignored it, pressing his erection into me, making sure there was nowhere else I'd rather be. No one else I'd rather be with. And, in that moment, there wasn't. Jake knew what he wanted, and he was making damn sure he took it.

There was something satisfying about letting him have his way. Letting him distract me.

But to say I wasn't curious who'd texted would've been a lie. Conner hadn't texted since earlier. And, of course, I hadn't replied. Why provoke him? Why give him reason to believe I'd forgiven him?

My phone buzzed again. Jake's hands dug into my hips, his lips still moving over my skin. "Ignore it," he murmured.

I nodded, grasping the back of his head and pulling his lips to mine. I lost myself in the feel of his lips, the motion of his tongue, and his very large erection fighting to break loose from his jeans. I reached down, stroking it over the denim. He groaned into my mouth. I loved that. Loved knowing the slightest brush of my hand could make him feel so good.

"I want you out of these," he whispered against my lips.

A bout of déjà vu swept over me. Caynan and me by the night train. *Gahhhh.* I shook it off, wanting to be in the present. And presently I planned to have sex with a hockey god. And I was gonna enjoy it if it was the last thing I did.

My phone buzzed again. This time, Jake reached over and grabbed it, checking the screen. "I want to see you." His brows raised as he read the text. "Please stop pushing me away."

I grabbed for the phone which he held away from me. Since he had me pinned beneath him, there wasn't anything I could do but plead my case. "It's nothing."

He continued reading. "I can't stop thinking about you." His eyes shifted to mine. "Anything you want to tell me?"

My head fell back on the pillow. "He's making my life miserable."

He tossed the phone back down, his eyes gentle as he lay down beside me, his hand brushing my cheek. "Who is? Talk to me."

I shook my head. "It's a long story."

"Try me."

I looked into his eyes. He was serious. He wanted to know. Whether for selfish reasons or because he truly cared about me, he really wanted to know. But I didn't want to tell him. Scratch that. I didn't want to revisit it. Didn't want to feel the pain. The humiliation. The betrayal. "Can we not do this now?"

"Oh, I think it's the only thing we're doing now. I can't believe I'm gonna admit this, but I kind of lost momentum when I saw some other guy texting my girl."

"It's not what you think."

"Well, that's good because what I'm thinking right now is I need to go find this asshole and show him whose territory he's infringing on."

I rested my palm on his chest. I could feel his heart slamming against it. "Relax. He's an old mistake. He just showed back up and is having a difficult time understanding why I don't want to see him."

"Does he know about me?"

I nodded. "It isn't stopping him. We left things very…unresolved. And he just needs closure."

"Do you?"

"What?"

"Do *you* need closure?"

I thought about Cass' words. I thought about my own reaction to seeing him again. Seeing him in my new reality. Why had he gone through the trouble of seeking me out? Why was it so important to have my forgiveness after all this time? Why couldn't I get him off my mind? "I think I might."

He dropped his head and nodded like I hadn't given him the response he'd hoped for.

"But not the kind you're thinking," I assured him, cupping his cheek with my palm. "I just think I need to let it all out. Everything I've been feeling these past three years. And then maybe, just maybe, I'll be okay."

"So, you're not okay?"

I shrugged. "Cass says he's the reason I have trouble letting people in. Do you think I have trouble letting people in?"

His face revealed what his words weren't likely to admit. "I don't know. Sometimes I feel like you're closed off to the possibility of a future with me. It's like, you like hanging out now, but now is now, and later…who knows?"

"I do like hanging out with you. But I think maybe I have trouble seeing a future with anyone because of what happened with this guy."

"That bad?"

"He destroyed me. He made me believe nothing's what it seems."

"This is exactly what it seems." Jake leaned in and kissed me, like really kissed me, wiping Conner's face from my brain. When he pulled back, he looked directly into my eyes. "I can wait. Go exorcize this dick from your brain and then we can pick up where we left off."

My forehead creased. "You're joking."

He shook his head and sat up. "Nope. I only want two of us in this room when I sleep with my girl. If that means you need this guy out of your head, then get him out of your head. Or, if you want, me and my boys can make sure he's not only out of your head but also out of your life."

I laughed, a warmth spreading over me. Jake made me happy. He was someone I could see in my future. But first I needed to do something about my past.

Conner

Now what?

I stared down at my phone. I'd wanted this, but now what? My fingers went to work. **Meet me.**

I barely blinked before Hadley replied. **Fifteen minutes. Quad.**

An anxious shudder rocked through my body. She agreed to meet me which meant she planned to listen to me. Or if she was the same Feisty I'd known, she planned to put me in my place.

I grabbed my white T-shirt from the floor beside the air mattress I'd been sleeping on in Vik's dorm room. The girl was hysterical, and as promised, gaped at me when I came back from the shower. I made sure to leave water droplets on my chest just to give her a show. Why not? I'd been showering with dudes for three years. Having a little female attention didn't hurt my ego. And even if it wasn't the female I wanted looking at me, it was a female nonetheless who'd taken me in after knowing my situation.

I threw on my T-shirt and some loose gray sweat pants and slipped quietly out of Vik's room. The cool night air greeted me as I stepped outside, heading uphill toward the quad. I knew it would be deserted since it was nearing midnight, so the thought of Hadley walking alone unnerved me.

I wondered if her boyfriend knew she was meeting me. The whole idea of her even having a boyfriend turned my veins to ice. I wasn't stupid enough to think she hadn't been with other guys since I'd been gone. She was hot and guys were bound to come sniffing around. It wasn't like I gave her a reason to wait for me. Especially since she hadn't read my letters. If she had, maybe I could've prevented it. Man. I'd spent so many hours with a pencil and paper spilling my guts to her. More and more of me exposed in each one. If only she'd read them. If only she hadn't given up on me. If only she hadn't given up on us.

I stepped onto the quad. The surrounding buildings cast dark shadows onto the grassy area. I walked out into the center, knowing it was the best place to wait since I'd see her approach from any direction. Three years was a long time. There so many things I wanted to say—wanted to explain to her. But there were also things I wanted to know about her.

I didn't have to wait long. Hadley emerged from the darkness, her small frame concealed by a hoodie and jeans. She walked slowly toward me, each tentative step drawing us closer and closer together. Exactly how it should've been. She stopped once she stood in front of me in the center of the square, her eyes locking on mine and her arms crossed, an impenetrable shield from the monster she thought me to be. "So?"

Having her in front of me brought back all the same feelings. The ones I felt when we first met. The attraction. The fascination. The happiness. "Hi." I almost smiled.

"You didn't text me three times and interrupt my night just to say hello. So speak."

I stared at her. This girl I thought about every day I was behind bars. The one who inhabited my greatest memories and filled my dreams. The one I envisioned when my right hand was my only form of pleasure. She looked older. And tired. And so incredibly unhappy to see me. I hated the disgust in her eyes—the disgust at my presence. "Why don't we grab a bench," I asked.

Her head whirled around, her eyes settling on one to our right. Without a word, she walked toward it. I hastened my steps, trying to keep up. She sat down and I followed, my leg brushing hers as I settled onto the bench. Her entire body jerked away as if repulsed by my touch.

I wouldn't lie. It sucked.

"Speak."

I winced at the harshness in her voice. At the thought that I'd caused it. "What do you want me to say?"

"Whatever was so important that you ruined my night."

My body tensed. What had I ruined? Was she with her boyfriend? What were they doing that she was so pissed I interrupted it? I wouldn't let my mind wander there. Not now. Not when I was there and determined to win her back. I averted my gaze, my eyes staring out at the empty quad. "I'm sorry I ruined your night."

She huffed out a breath. "You ruined a lot more than just my night."

I nodded. "I deserve that."

"Deserve *that*? You deserve a lot more than that."

I nodded, though I wished somehow the debt I paid society over the past three years had been enough for her.

"I think I loved you."

Her words sucked the air from my lungs as my eyes shot to her. She wasn't looking at me. It didn't matter, though. It was the first time she'd said it. The first time I knew for sure that what I'd felt for her hadn't been one-sided. It had been as real for her as it had been for me. "I didn't know that," I said.

She shrugged. "Would it have mattered?"

I shook my head. "Probably not."

"Why?" Her eyes finally cut to mine. "Why'd you do it?"

"I didn't have a choice."

She scoffed. "We all have choices. You just chose wrong."

"You don't understand. That was my life. Moving place to place looking for the next big score. I didn't ask to be part of it. I was made to be part of it. I was made to do things people like you just couldn't understand."

"People like me? People you used and stole from?"

I dragged my hands down my face, frustrated she didn't get it. She didn't understand. "I swear to you, I didn't use you."

She balked.

"And I never stole anything from you."

Her mouth opened into a giant O. "Are you serious right now? Because had you not gotten caught, you had every intention of stealing from me."

I exhaled my frustration. "I wish you read my letters. It was easier to explain when you weren't sitting inches away from me looking so beautiful and smelling the way you always did." She opened her mouth to respond. But I continued. "I remember just burying my nose in your hair when I had you in my arms so I could smell you. So I could take your scent back home with me. Take it back to the lifeless trailer where I lived. And I could sleep well knowing you were safe from my world while you were tucked away in that big house of yours."

She sat quietly for a long time. I'd given her something to think about. Or at least a reminder of how much I cared about her. "Well, I didn't read your letters. And now I'm here. But I'm not inches away. I'm freaking miles away. You're a stranger to me."

"I loved you, too, Hadley. I still love you."

She sucked in a sharp breath. "Don't. Not after everything that happened. Everything you did."

"God dammit, woman," I growled. "Don't tell me what I can say. Or feel. Or think. I. Still. Love. You."

She shook her head, unable to believe my words. Unable to believe the truth. I wondered if those were tears glistening in her eyes or just a reflection of the moonlight. "You don't even know me anymore."

"Why do you think I'm here?"

Her eyes narrowed. Her forehead scrunched. "What do you want from me, Cay—Conner? *God dammit*," she cursed herself for forgetting my name. But why would she remember? That's how she knew me. That's the guy who pushed his way into her life. The guy she fought like hell to keep out, caving only after he showed a true glimpse of who he desperately wanted to be.

"I told you." I jumped to my feet, unable to be that close to her without touching her.

She rolled her eyes. "Yeah, convenient. You've got nowhere else to go, so you look for the one sucker who'd fall for your lies. Telling me you love me was a nice touch, by the way. But I'm not that girl anymore. I'm not that sucker."

A stab of pain pierced my chest at her hardened tone. At the way she put herself down. At the way she viewed me. "You were never a sucker, Hadley. Stop saying that."

"Did you see me that night when we first met and think, *her*? She looks like someone I can get close to. Someone I can fool."

You'd have thought sirens blasted the silence the way my ears rang. "Stop it."

She jumped to her feet, moving toward me with angry steps. "No, you stop it. Stop contacting me. Stop showing up at my place. Stop trying to play me. Wasn't once enough?"

Unable to stay away any longer, I grabbed hold of her shoulders. "Stop saying that. Stop believing that. I never wanted to hurt you. I only wanted to know you. And hold you. And fucking love you."

We stared each other down, our chests heaving. I was so close to her, it would've taken nothing to lean down and kiss her. It's what I wanted—what I'd thought about—more than anything else over the last three years. But given the harsh look in her big blue eyes, it would've been a huge mistake.

She jerked her shoulders back, pulling free from my grasp. "Then why? Why blow it? Why throw it away for something I could've gotten for you if you just asked me? If you just told me what was going on. If you just told me the truth."

My head dropped forward, realizing in that moment—just like I'd known three years before—she would've had my back. She would've helped me if she'd known what I had to do. What I'd been up against. But I hadn't told her. And now I had to deal with the repercussions. The aftermath of me not being honest with her. Not trusting her to stand by me. "I'm sorry. I should've trusted you enough to tell you. Believe me. I wanted to. I *so* fucking wanted to. But I weighed my options. Lose you or do what I had to do and hopefully hold on to you."

She stared at me, her face blank and her eyes depthless holes. "Well, you lost me anyway."

I stared back. "I'll be damned if I make that mistake again."

Her hands shot out to her sides. "Can't you see? It's too late."

"It's never too late."

She shook her head. "Don't you get it? I'll never trust you again."

Her words seized my heart, squeezing it so hard I'd have sworn it ceased my pulse. It was the moment. The moment I realized what I'd been too afraid to even consider.

She might never forgive me.

And that fucking sucked.

We stood with our eyes locked. Silence filled the space around us. With each passing second, I was losing her all over again. That was never supposed to happen. I knew that. She needed to know it, too. "I'm thinking of enrolling here."

Her eyebrows shot up, probably at both my news and the subject change. "Oh."

"Yeah. I have over fifty credits. I did some work while I was away."

She buried her hands in the pockets of her hoodie, her sneakers kicking away at the grass beneath her feet. "That's good."

"You think this campus is big enough for the both of us?" I smiled, trying to give off the impression that I was all right with the outcome of our conversation. I wasn't. I was nowhere *near* all right with it. I couldn't even begin to envision my life with her at a distance when all I'd done over the past three years was envision her in it.

She shrugged. "I'm graduating in May, so it's only for a short time."

I ignored the possibility that time was running out. "You still doing art?"

She shook her head. "Not so much."

My head withdrew. "Why not?"

"There aren't many jobs in the field."

Needing to be closer, I stepped forward. "That's a shame."

Hadley slowly stepped back, obviously wanting to distance herself from me.

"You're really talented," I said.

Her lips twisted as her shoulders shrugged. "Goodnight, Conner." She turned and started back in the direction of her place.

Shit.

"I wanna see you in the morning."

She stopped, glancing over her shoulder. "I knew a guy once who promised to kiss me in the morning."

I smiled. She hadn't forgotten my words. "Smart guy."

She shook her head. "Not really. He didn't end up with the girl."

"I bet he's not one to give up."

She scoffed, turning again and heading away from me.

"Hey, Hadley."

I wasn't sure she'd stop. I thought it was the moment she walked out of my life for good. But she did stop, under the blue security light, glancing back over her shoulder.

"Even if I have to walk ten paces behind you, there's no way in hell I'm not walking you home."

She stared back at me, the blue glow emanating around her. I wasn't sure what she was thinking. But I prayed it wasn't the last thing I'd get to say to her. Without warning, her lips slipped into a small smile. "Make it twenty."

I nodded as a shred of hope filled in a small space in the hole in my heart. "Will do."

And I did. I followed her to her place, waiting until she stepped safely inside her building before taking off across campus and slipping back into Vik's room.

Hadley

I walked across campus in the same daze I'd been in since meeting up with Conner the previous night. I thought speaking to him would've made me feel better. Given me closure. Stopped me from being sidetracked by thoughts of him and memories of us together throughout the day.

It hadn't.

It only made me think about him more. The touch of his hands on my shoulders. The way he looked me in the eyes like what I said meant everything to him. The way he spoke with that same possessiveness over me he once had. The way he followed me home to be sure I was safe.

Damn him.

The truth was I wanted the person I thought he was. The guy who'd done thoughtful things for me. Who'd uttered sweet things into my ear. Who'd made me feel things I'd never felt before. I'd given myself to someone who didn't exist. Someone who never existed. And that was one of the hardest things I'd had to come to grips with.

Jake left messages, but I'd been too afraid to return his calls. In all honesty, I didn't know what to say. Telling him I couldn't shake my past wouldn't have gone over well. But Conner's words had been so sincere. So heartfelt. So honest. And while part of me hated myself for wanting to believe the liar, the other part felt there had to be some truth to his words. He'd shown up the day he'd been released from prison and had yet to disappear again. That had to say something.

But how could I be sure? How could I allow myself to believe him?

I returned to my room after dinner, walking straight to my closet and standing there, not moving, not thinking, mentally willing myself to walk away. Walk far away. But I couldn't. I knew what I needed to do. I knew what would help me understand. What would help me determine what was the truth. What would give me closure. What would put an end to it all.

It's what I should've done—should've had the strength to do—when they arrived.

I kneeled down, pulling the bottom shoebox out from under the stack of boxes. I walked over to my bed with my heart racing and my hands shaking. I sat down, pausing to take a breath before lifting the cover. Over a hundred unopened envelopes filled the box.

I'd held off doing it. I'd held off opening a single one. They'd been delivered to my parents' house and my mother had kept them. I couldn't understand why she'd kept them. I couldn't understand why she hadn't burned the damn things knowing who they'd come from. Knowing the pain, humiliation, and heartache he'd caused her daughter. Yet, there they sat. All in one place. All in order. She stored the box in my closet, and for some reason—call it curiosity, call it stupidity, call it finally being ready to get rid of them once and for all— I'd grabbed them on my way back to school. And now, after he'd thrust his way back into my world—after he'd made his presence loud and clear—I considered reading them.

But could anything good come from reading his words? Hearing his excuses? Allowing him back into my head? What closure could I gain from written words that the actual person couldn't give me?

I pulled the first envelope out of the box, noting the postmark stamped a week after he'd been arrested. I stared at the right slant of his handwriting. The block lettering he used to write my name. The return address. I found it difficult not to envision the old concrete building I passed by on the highway. The one where he'd lived behind bars for three years. I flipped over the envelope, noting it was still sealed.

I can do this.

I slipped my finger under the flap and tore open the envelope. I could see the folded white-lined paper inside.

A shudder rushed through me.

Before talking myself out of it, I yanked out the paper and unfolded it, reading what he'd assumed I'd read three years before.

Hadley,

I'm so sorry. I can't write it enough times to convey how much I mean it. I'm sorry this happened. I'm sorry you believed in me. I'm sorry I hurt you. But you must know, none of this was about you. You didn't cause this. You didn't make me do this. You didn't know I was capable of this. And you shouldn't have known. I was groomed to be a thief since the moment my mother died and my father convinced me he needed cash to pay for doctors' bills. I had no choice. He controlled everything I did. Where I lived. Who I stole from. When I up and left a town. The only thing he didn't control were my feelings for you. Those were mine. Those were real. And as much as you believe it wasn't real between us, it was. All of it. The more time we spent together, the more I cared about you. The more I wanted to be around you. The more I wanted your goodness to wear off on me.

But while I may have been falling for you, I still wanted to push you away. No, I needed to push you away. Not because of you, but because I knew it was just a matter of time before I hurt you by leaving. I never imagined my father would make me steal from you. Never imagined everything would end the way it did. Before you, Hadley, I didn't see a future of my own. I know to someone like you that might not seem like much because you have such a bright future ahead of you, but to someone like me, someone who had no shot at his own future, seeing one was monumental. And that scared the hell out of me. Because at times, I actually believed it could happen. Believed it could happen with you.

But then there were times that I knew I was fooling myself because there was no way in hell it could happen. No way in hell I could pull you into my life. It had heartache written all over it and you deserved better. I'm not happy how things ended between us, but I'm happy things ended. Happy Caynan could be out of your life. Happy you could be free of the duplicity he brought into your life. Happy the lies would stop. So, I guess what I'm trying to say is thank you. Thank you for turning him in. Thank you for putting a stop to his terrible existence.

I can serve three years of my life if it means when I get out, I can start over. And when I say start over, I mean start over with you. I will prove to you that I can be the guy you need me to be. The guy who wants nothing more than to introduce himself—his real self—to you. A guy who wants to spend time with you. A guy who wants to get to know you again. A guy who wants to kiss you every morning for the rest of your life. Believe me, Hadley. Believe the truth and forgive me.

Yours,

Conner Cartwright

AKA Caynan, Micha, Steven, Allister…to name a few

I dropped the letter to my lap and heaved a breath. Would the letter have been enough for me to forgive him three years before? Would I have been convinced by his apology? Would I have been convinced by his desperation to prove himself worthy of me? Would I have caved?

CHAPTER EIGHTEEN

Conner

I trudged through the worksite, lifting one two-by-four after another and depositing them into piles, sending up clouds of dust from the dirt-covered ground. Construction work was no joke, and though it kicked my ass, I smiled as I did the jobs no one else wanted to do. It meant I was getting my life back on track. I also didn't need a gym when the job required me to lift heavy lumber and equipment. And if I ever wanted to see a baseball field again, I needed to stay in shape.

Besides working my ass off, Vik had dragged me to some of her classes, introducing me to her professors in hopes they'd let me audit their classes. That way when I enrolled part-time during the second semester, I'd already be ahead of the rest. I could obviously use all the help I could get. Moving around when I was younger wasn't easy. I left one school in the middle of a unit and got to the next where I was expected to have already learned it. It sucked. And my education suffered.

After work, I met Vik down at the school's sports facility. Her new gig at the field house gave her access to the indoor batting cage. She got me in most nights right before closing when the area was deserted so I could get in some swings. Since I hadn't swung in three years, hitting a ball had never felt more invigorating.

"Did you see her today?" Vik asked from behind the backstop as I pounded away at the balls shooting out of the batting machine.

"Nah. I think I need to give her some space."

"Is it wrong to hate her?"

I glanced over my shoulder before the next pitch came. "Hate her?"

"Yeah. The girl's got you wrapped around her little finger and has the nerve not to forgive you. How long does she plan to wait?"

I laughed to myself as I blasted a ball deep into the far net. "I hurt her. I didn't expect it to be easy. Besides, she's always played hard to get. Didn't I tell you how long it took for her to agree to go out with me when we met?"

"I get that. But when will you reach a point that it's just not worth it anymore?"

The balls stopped coming and I turned to look at Vik through the metal fence. "I don't know."

She leveled me with her eyes. "Well, if she doesn't forgive you soon, she's gonna have to deal with me."

I smiled at this tiny girl who'd known me for such a short time and was still willing to go to bat for me. "Thanks."

Hadley

Tears ran down my cheeks and letters surrounded me on the floor of my room. It was a bad scene. Thankfully, Lorelei had just left me to do my thing. There really wasn't much she could have done to stop the madness anyhow.

...I like dogs. Did I ever tell you that? We've got one in here. I get to help train it to be a service dog. The dog's awesome to have around. Her name's Sheba. When I get out of here, I think we should get one...

I knew the moment I'd done it. The moment I'd picked up the second letter that I shouldn't have.

...I want a big family. Like a huge one since I didn't have one. My place was always so quiet and depressing, so I want a home that's loud and full of life...

The second letter just led to a third and a fourth. Then I couldn't stop.

...I like living in the south. The warm weather always seems to make people happier. Have you ever noticed that? Like when it's cold and dreary people all seem angry. But when the sun's shining, people are all laughing and having fun. In case it's a deal breaker for you, I can deal with the cold, too. I've spent plenty of time up north and can chill in the snow with the best of them. So, I guess what I'm saying is I'm willing to move wherever your art takes us...

It had been a week since I'd seen Conner. A week since I'd read the first letter. I wondered if he'd purposely been off the radar. Purposely left me alone. Or if I'd just gotten good at avoiding him knowing it was better for both of us.

...Oh, here's an interesting fact. I don't know how to ride a bike. Did I ever tell you that? I was never taught. Go figure. Maybe you can teach me. I can just see it. You running down the street

behind me until you let go of the bike and yell, "You're doing it."
I'm almost laughing at the vision in my head right now…

With every word, Conner made sure I remained part of his life. Part of his heart. Part of him. He'd spent the last three years making sure I didn't miss a moment. Made sure I was very much present in his thoughts. In what he did. In what he was trying to accomplish on the inside. In what he had planned for the future. I, on the other hand, had shut him out, ensuring he stayed far from my thoughts. Far from my memories. Far from my heart.

At least I tried to.

I grabbed my phone and hit send, lifting it to my ear. I didn't wait for a hello. "Why'd you do it?"

"Do what?" my mother asked.

"Save the letters?"

There was a long pause. I wondered if she could hear the slight quiver in my voice or sense my tears. "I take it you read them?"

"You could say that."

She sighed. "Hadley, everyone roots for the underdog."

I wiped at my wet cheeks with the back of my hand.

"When the first one arrived, I wanted to burn it," she explained. "He'd hurt my baby. And no one hurts my girl. But then I figured it was better to let you decide. Since you wouldn't talk about him, I tucked it away. But then the next one arrived and then the next. I realized you may have given up on him, but he wasn't giving up on you. I liked that about him. I liked that he was willing to fight for you. I also knew with time, your pain would ease and then you could decide what to do with the letters."

"Dad would kill you if he knew you kept them."

She snickered. "I'm not scared of him. Are you going to tell me what they said?"

"He talks about his past. And being in prison. And he apologized. A lot."

"He had a lot to apologize for. But Hadley, he didn't miss a week. Not once."

My eyes drifted to the window, the darkness outside reminding me of the dark hole I'd been in after his betrayal—after realizing everything had been a lie. But now, the lines had blurred. "Sounds like you want me to forgive him."

"You've just become so guarded—more like your father, questioning everything and everyone. I just want you to be able to trust again. If that means you forgive him, then yes, I want you to forgive him."

"It's not that easy."

"Most things in life aren't." She paused. "Just know. No one will judge you if you do."

I didn't even try to disguise my doubt. "Not even dad?"

"It's your life. Your decision. And, honey, he didn't kill anyone. He made a mistake. Don't let that define him."

I scoffed, wondering if she would've been giving me the same advice had she known he showed up on campus.

A knock on the door sent me scrambling to my feet. "I gotta go," I said, disconnecting the call without even waiting for her response. I scooped up the letters and shoved them along with the box under my bed. I blotted my face with my sleeve, ridding my cheeks of the tear stains—or at least trying to, then approached the door cautiously. "Who is it?" I held my breath, knowing I wasn't ready to face Conner yet. Not with so much indecision running through me.

"Jake."

I let out a slow breath. Jake I could handle. Since he'd been scrimmaging schools up north for the past week, it had given me the time I needed to clear my head. Until I'd confused myself even more by reading the letters. Though he'd called, I hadn't spoken to him. I found it easier to text. That way I could keep my responses brief and clear of the topic of Conner.

My time was clearly up.

I pulled open my door. Jake stood there, his hair damp from a shower. "Hi."

He didn't smile. "You haven't returned my calls." His eyes ventured over my shoulder as if expecting me to have company.

"I'm sorry. I've just had a lot going on."

"Yeah. I figured. Can I come in?"

I stepped away from the door and he brushed by me. His eyes jumped around my room. So did mine, hoping I'd hidden all the letters. That's all I needed him to see. He dropped down onto my bed, his elbows resting on his knees. "I'd like you to get dressed."

I looked down at my sweats and T-shirt. "What?"

"I wanna take you out."

"I'm not really—"

"I've been patient, Hadley. I want to take my girl out. And I want her to *want* to go out with me. Want to be with me. You've been avoiding me and I feel like if we have this conversation here, I might not handle it well."

I stared down at him, not really knowing what to say. Did he think I planned to break up with him? Did he think I'd reached some clarity over the past week? I wanted to explain myself. Explain my confusion. Explain the mental torment I'd been enduring with the letters. So, I did what I thought was right. I agreed to go.

* * *

The bar was packed for a Wednesday night, with loads of familiar faces filling the room. Jake chose a corner table, away from all the eyes of his fans. I scanned the room over his shoulder, finding it difficult to meet his eyes. He ordered us two beers and then looked at me, making sure I was looking at him before he spoke. "Tell me what happened?"

"What happened?"

"Come on, Hadley. You're not a stupid girl. What happened with the guy?"

"You mean the other night or three years ago?"

He took a deep breath, exhaling it slowly. "Start from the beginning."

I did. I explained everything. It wasn't easy to revisit the humiliation, but I did it. And Jake listened. He nodded. He showed anger. He showed compassion.

"So, now he wants forgiveness," I explained.

"Forgiveness? You sure that's all he wants? I saw the texts."

I shook my head, feeling guilty I'd read the letters. Guilty they made me feel. Guilty I was unsure how I felt about anything anymore. I'd spent three years believing I knew the truth. Believing Conner was a calculating villain who'd preyed on me. But the letters shot all that to hell. Because, in reality, he'd fallen for me and we'd become unfortunate victims of circumstance. "He wants me back."

"No kidding. He had an awesome girl and blew it." I exhaled my frustration. "I know this sucks. It's why I didn't want to involve you. It's why I never talked about it. But then he showed up and everything got so confusing."

"Confusing? He hurt you, Hadley. Purposely. Seems pretty cut and dry to me."

I cringed as the words left my mouth. "He wrote letters."

His face scrunched in disgust. "What kind of letters?"

"The kind he sent while he was away."

"He wasn't away, Hadley," he reminded me, his voice cold and harsh. "He was in prison. Are you forgetting that?"

"Forgetting? How could I forget? I live with it every day. He tried to steal from my parents. He used me. He broke my heart. Of course I remember."

"Do you still have the letters?"

I nodded. "I didn't open them until recently. I thought I'd closed that chapter of my life a long time ago."

"So?"

I sighed, feeling so defeated. "So what?"

"Are they enough?"

"Enough?"

His lips tightened into a straight line, his frustration with me very much evident. "Enough to win you back."

I cocked my head. "I'm with you."

His head shook from side to side. "No, you're not. As much as I want you to be with me, you have to want it too. And I think we can both admit, I'm the only one invested here."

An overzealous crowd walked through the door, snatching my attention away from Jake. The little pixie from the cafeteria led the way. A knot jumped to my throat as I watched closely as guys and girls followed her in. My heart stuttered when the last one stepped through the door. Conner.

Shit.

My eyes flashed back to Jake.

"See, even in a crowded bar I can't keep your attention for a few minutes at a time. It's like you're always somewhere else."

How could I disagree with him? How could I argue the truth? "I know I haven't been fair to you. But I've never lied to you."

"Oh, that's reassuring." Sarcasm laced his tone.

"I just mean, you're the one who started this."

"This is my fault?"

My eyes drifted away, feeling like complete shit now that he'd called me out. I watched as Conner's eyes scanned the bar, making a slow sweep over the room as if searching for someone. His head jolted back when his eyes collided with mine. A sad smile conveyed his hello. I mirrored it with my own before my eyes focused back on Jake. "No. It's not your fault."

In a perfect world, I wouldn't have been there. With my head feeling like it had been shoved in a blender and spit back out. With my heart being pulled in two completely different directions. With my present across the table begging me to give him my all and my past across the room inciting me with his mere presence—not to mention his words swirling around inside my head.

"I'll be back." Jake hopped down from his stool and took off for the men's room.

I watched him go, wondering why I was so torn. Wondering what I'd say when he returned to make it better. Wondering how I'd be able to get myself out of such a mess.

My phone vibrated on the table. I didn't need to check the screen. My eyes shot across the crowded room to Conner who stared at me with his phone to his ear. I stared into the same dark eyes I'd been unable to shake for three years. Eyes that looked at me like I held his future. Eyes that knew me better than most. Eyes that when they held indecision and kept me at arm's length three years before, it had all been to protect me. All been an attempt to push me away so I didn't end up hurt.

My phone continued to vibrate on the table. I didn't answer it. I couldn't. I didn't know what he expected me to say. What he expected me to do. Luckily, he didn't know I'd read his letters. Then he wouldn't be calling. He'd be hounding me.

When he realized I had no intention of answering, he nodded subtly and slipped his phone into his pocket. His attention moved away from me as he joined his group at the bar. The little pixie handed him a shot that he threw back without hesitation.

That's what he meant when he asked if the campus was big enough for the two of us. I was beginning to think the state wasn't big enough.

Jake returned, but I found myself drawn to Conner's group and their increasing volume and laughter. Was he creating new memories with different people? People I'd never know? I watched girls around the bar eyeing him, while others boldly approached him. It was Katie McGraw's party all over again. The first time I saw him. The confidence. The ease. The pull that drew others to him. And as usual, he did what he always did. He made them comfortable. Greeting them with a warm smile and patiently answering their questions. I hadn't seen that smile in three years. And as hard as it was to admit, it hurt seeing him wasting it on girls he didn't know.

Was that what it would be like to see him moving on? Was the attention he received reminding him what it felt like to be free? To be available? I'd given him no indication that anything had changed between us. He was a single guy who'd been surrounded by guys for three years. Would he consider going home with one of those girls? Or was the pixie more his style now?

Would it affect me if he moved on? Would I be jealous? Hurt?

Yes.

I jumped to my feet, suggesting to Jake that we leave—before I confused myself even more.

I tried not to look at Conner as I walked to the door, but I couldn't stop myself. His eyes were focused on the little brunette on her tiptoes whispering something into his ear. Something that garnered a smile. The smile that used to be meant for me and only me. I don't know what I expected. But his eyes on another girl who was rubbing up against him was not it.

Jake and I walked in silence through the dark parking lot toward his car in the rear of the lot. My emotions were all over the place. Were Jake and I over? Was I pissed at Conner? Was I meant to be alone? Was I—

"Hadley."

Shit.

Jake stopped and spun toward the voice. I wanted nothing more than to keep walking, but I had no choice. I stopped, cringing as I turned.

Conner jogged out of the bar. "Weren't you gonna say goodbye?"

My eyes expanded. *Fuck, fuck, fuck.* What was he doing?

"Hadley?" Jake stared at me, confusion clouding his eyes.

I looked back to Conner who stopped in front of me. "Goodnight, Conner."

"Conner?" Hate dripped from Jake's lips as he assessed Conner for the first time, now standing directly in front of us exuding that frustrating confidence.

"Um…" My eyes jumped frantically between them, both just a couple of feet apart. My past and my present.

"You knew he was here?" Jake's eyes stayed on Conner.

"I…um…"

"Speak, Hadley," Jake demanded. "I asked you a fucking question."

Conner's eyes narrowed as he stepped toward him. "Speak to her again like that and I'll level you."

Jake's head jerked back, a scary snarl on his lips. "You think I'm gonna let some punk ass criminal tell me how to speak to my girlfriend?" Jake stepped right up in Conner's face, bumping him hard with his chest.

"Jake," I warned, my heart hammering inside me.

"If you think this punk ass criminal's gonna sit back and let some college boy talk to her that way, you're delusional." Conner bumped him back, his eyes glaring into Jake's.

Shit. I sprang forward, pushing myself between them. I was surprised that with all the testosterone in the air, they actually let me. I faced Jake, my hands braced on his chest. Normally, he seemed so big and broad. But opposite Conner, he seemed smaller. "Come on. We're leaving." I pushed my hands with as much force as I could, but he didn't budge. His eyes weren't even on me. They were over my shoulder as he shoved up his sleeves.

Conner leaned down, brushing his lips against my ear. A ripple rolled through my stomach at the contact. "Hadley, I'm gonna need you to move out of the way." He grasped my shoulders gently, walking me backward a couple of steps.

"This is ridiculous." I tried appealing to him, the seemingly saner one.

He gazed down at me, his eyes holding that same gentleness he'd always shown me. "Promise me you'll stay right here."

My eyes begged him. "This is stupid."

He tucked a stray piece of hair behind my ear, stealing my breath away. "When have I ever backed away from a stupid decision?"

"You, asshole," Jake growled, charging toward us.

Conner whirled around moving me out of the way just as Jake lowered his shoulder and plowed into his stomach, propelling them both to the ground with loud *oomphs*. Jake jumped to his feet, towering over Conner. "Stay the fuck away from her."

Conner's head slowly lifted. I expected to find rage in his eyes. Expected him to jump to his feet and lunge at Jake. Expected something. But he just climbed to his feet with a knowing grin. "That all you got, pretty boy?"

I stood helplessly. They doubled me in size. And neither seemed to be listening to reason.

Jake lunged for Conner again, but Conner moved, shoving him by the shoulders down on the pavement. Jake landed hard, but he jumped up swiftly, anger etched in the lines of his face. He lunged at Conner again, shoving him in the chest with all his might. Conner stumbled back a couple of feet, his chest more of a brick wall than the punching bag Jake expected.

"Last time you caught me off guard. That won't happen again," Conner assured him, that same stinking arrogance I fell for years ago still very much present. "Now, we can do this all night, but that wouldn't be fair to Hadley." Conner's eyes cut to mine, a lopsided grin fixed in place. "It'll only prove what a pussy she's dating."

Oh, shit.

Jake growled, charging at him with his fist flying out from behind his back. It connected brutally with Conner's face. *That* caused Conner to reel back, grasping his nose.

"*Jake*," I screeched, my eyes daggers. "What the hell?" I rushed to Conner, his nose already bleeding profusely. I dug in my handbag and pulled out some crumpled tissues. "Here." His fingers brushed mine as he took them. "Are you all right?"

He sopped up the blood with the tissue. "Your man's a wuss."

I hurried over to Jake who shook out his sore hand, clenching and unclenching it like he'd broken something. Served him right for being an ass. "Let's go." Though he resisted at first, I pushed him toward the driver's side of his car. "Get inside. I don't want to do this here. You got a piece of him. That's what you wanted, right?"

"I wanted more than a piece," he shouted loud enough for Conner to hear. "I wanted to kill him for what he put you through."

My heart ached at the idea that he'd done it for me. He'd tried to defend me. He'd wanted revenge for me. I opened the door and urged him inside.

He paused, looking behind the car at Conner. "That's just the beginning of what I intend to do to your face, criminal." I shoved him in the car, and this time he let me.

"I'll call you later, Hadley," Conner called, no longer holding the blood-soaked tissue to his nose, though blood dripped down to his mouth.

I braced my hands on Jake, stopping him from jumping out of the car like he looked like he wanted to. "He's trying to provoke you. Please, let's just go." I closed his door, rounding the car quickly so he didn't do something stupid like jump out. I looked to Conner standing there all smug and confident. "Was that necessary?"

He smiled. "Just wanted to be sure we all knew where I stood."

I shook my head, unequipped to deal with him at that point. I slid into Jake's car without bothering to look back.

Jake sped out of the parking lot using his left hand while clenching and unclenching his right hand in his lap.

Idiot.

"You didn't have to hit him."

"So this is my fault?" His eyes jumped between the road and me.

I shook my head. "No, but he wasn't going to fight you."

"Can't you see? That's exactly what he was doing."

I closed my eyes, wishing I didn't feel so angry at both of them. Wishing I didn't have to deal with my past and present in one night. Wishing my life was easy. "What do you want from me?"

"Make a decision. Choose one of us and be done with it."

I contemplated Jake's words as we drove in silence back to my place. Contemplated the whole ridiculous scene. Contemplated the way Conner wanted to provoke him. I couldn't have them both in my life, regardless of the capacity. Jake saw Conner for what he'd done to me. And Conner saw Jake as the guy in his way. Currently, I saw both of them as two guys who let their frustration with me turn them into complete fools.

Jake parked in front of my building, not even bothering to get out to walk me to my door. I turned to him. "You were one of the best things that happened to me since getting here."

He scoffed, the coldness I'd witnessed in the parking lot rearing its ugly head. "That's your decision? Seriously?"

"If you're giving me an ultimatum—"

"Something needs to push you to make a choice."

I stared at him, baffled by his rationale. "So you thought punching a guy who had no intention of punching you back would make my mind up for me?"

"No." He grinned. "But it felt damn good."

I sat there at a loss for words. At least the right words. It wasn't funny. Nothing about the situation was funny. I had two completely different guys fighting for me. Most girls would've loved to be in my place.

"It doesn't have to be like this, Hadley."

I nodded. "Right now, I think it does."

"So there's nothing I can say to change your mind?" It was then, with his blue eyes on me and his heart on his sleeve, I saw that regardless of how emotionally unavailable I'd been throughout our relationship, Jake had been fully committed to me.

My lips twisted regrettably as I shook my head slowly. "At least now you'll have your pick of the puck bunnies." I lifted a shoulder, a weak consolation.

"Yeah. Too bad the one girl I want, doesn't want me."

"Don't take it personally. That girl has no idea *what* she wants."

He scoffed, a hint of a smile on his lips.

I pushed open the door and stepped out into the brisk night. Leaves wafted around my feet as I looked back into the car. "Goodnight, Jake."

"Goodnight, Hadley."

I closed the car door and made my way inside my building. I couldn't shake the bloody image of Conner from my mind as I walked inside my empty room. I switched on the light and spotted an envelope peeking out from under my bed, remembering my haste to hide the letters when Jake showed up. I gathered the letters from under my bed then crawled onto it.

Why hadn't Conner swung back? Why had he let Jake hit him? Did he think it would prove something? Because it only made me angry. And confused. And…I pushed Jake away because of it.

That bastard.

My phone vibrated beside me. I grabbed it, my eyes flaring at the message. **Is he gone yet?**

My thumbs pounded away at the screen. **Is that why you let him hit you?**

Absolutely.

I sucked in a sharp breath. I'd played right into his plan. I'd done exactly what he wanted me to do by cutting Jake loose. I was still the same sucker. The one who fell for every-freaking-thing the guy did to me. I dropped my head, subsequently dropping the box of letters to the floor. Envelopes fluttered everywhere.

"God dammit!"

I dropped to my knees, gathering them once again. This time I haphazardly shoved them back in the box until sobs tore through me and I could no longer see through my tears. I'd worked too hard to put it all behind me. And to think I almost gave in after reading the letters. Now I'd been played by him again. And for the second time, I hadn't realized it until it was too late.

I felt myself spiraling. Spiraling into an abyss. One that wouldn't release me with both my head and heart intact. I lay down on my floor and closed my eyes, praying sleep would pull me under so I didn't need to feel anymore.

CHAPTER NINETEEN

Hadley

Lorelei barged into our room a week later. "That's it."

I didn't bother pulling my attention away from the glow-in-the-dark stars on the ceiling above my bed. The same ones I'd been staring at for God knows how long.

"Get up. We're going out."

"Out? It's after eleven."

"Exactly." She walked over to her closet and shuffled through her clothes. "The good stuff never happens until after midnight."

"I'm not really in the mood."

She ripped a tight green top from a hanger and tossed it on my bed. "I'm sick of watching you walk around here like a zombie." She moved to my dresser and pulled a pair of torn skinny jeans from my bottom drawer.

"Maybe I like zombies."

She tossed the jeans right at my head, so I had no choice but to grab them. "Sure, and like zombies, you haven't showered in days."

I thought about it for a minute. She was right.

"When my beautiful, confident roommate starts letting herself go, I need to step in."

"How do you plan on doing that?"

"By getting you showered. Then getting you drunk."

* * *

Lorelei had been right. Good things did happen after midnight. Beer pong. Cups. Quarters. And, apparently, I was the master. And stinking drunk for the fifth night in a row. And while I didn't normally hang out with Lorelei outside our room, the girl could drink, draw a whole lot of attention from hot guys, and keep me distracted.

The houses we'd been partying at had been a revolving door of frat guys, jocks, local rockers; you name the type, they'd been through. Thankfully, I hadn't seen or heard from Jake or Conner since the night of the fight. I hadn't really expected to hear from Jake after we parted ways. But Conner…I wondered if his disappearance was part of his plan—another one of his strategies.

I'd forgotten how nice it felt to get lost in a crowd. But being the reigning beer pong queen, I was drawing more attention than I was used to.

"Throw it back to us," Lorelei shouted over the music to our opponents, two frat guys who'd waited in line for half an hour to play against us. Now that they'd gotten their chance, we were two cups away from beating their asses.

They tossed the ping pong ball across the table. Lorelei grabbed it. She aimed it at the cup at the point of the triangle in front of them and lobbed it right in. One of the guys retrieved the ball and downed the beer. The other tossed his ball into the corner cup closest to me. I picked out the ball and threw back the beer like the champ I'd become. It had been going down like water—I had the slurred voice and squinty eyes to prove it. I aimed my ball at the back center cup, the only one of ours left with beer in it. With as much precision as I could muster at one in the morning, I released the ball. It sailed through the air and hit off the rim of one of the other cups, bouncing high into the air and landing back down, somehow managing to bounce into the last filled cup.

Our opponents cursed while Lorelei and I screamed, grabbing each other into a hug like we'd won the state championship in an actual sport.

"Why haven't we ever hung out like this before?" I asked, feeling drunk and wistful.

She pulled back, looking me right in the eyes. "Oh, Hadley." She didn't even try to disguise her sympathy. "You're a great roommate, but you make it so damn hard to get close to you."

I felt my face fall.

"Freshman year I tried to include you in everything I did. Don't you remember?"

I shrugged. Most of the year had been a blur.

"You always just kept to yourself."

"It wasn't you. I'd just been through a tough time."

She nodded. "I figured that. But I also figured you'd eventually talk to me about it or get over it on your own."

"I didn't."

She shook her head. "But this week's been a start."

I smiled. "Better late than never."

She laughed.

Over her shoulder the front door opened, carrying in a gust of cool air and my worst nightmare. Conner and his crew. I was not ready to see him—especially while I was drunk. Though I couldn't miss the turning heads and whispers as he trailed into the party. Something about his confidence commanded attention. And attention is what he got. His eyes did their usual sweep, but I wasn't about to be caught in his gaze.

I stepped back from Lorelei and walked over to our opponents. "Great game." The guy closest to me held up his hand for a high-five, but I threw my arms around his neck instead, surprising him. I didn't normally play games. I liked to believe I was straightforward and honest. But, apparently, I'd learned from the pro.

At that moment, my presence registered on Conner's face. His eyes flared and he stalked across the room. His steps determined. His eyes focused on mine. As if hypnotized, I couldn't look away.

I held onto the frat guy a little tighter. He took that as encouragement and wrapped his arms around my waist. Conner didn't need to know I'd just met the guy. He didn't need to know anything.

"What's going on, Hadley?" Conner asked when he stopped beside us.

I released the guy and turned to Conner. I felt my body sway on my knee-high boots, but I recovered. "It's called having fun. You should try it sometime." I leaned closer, lowering my voice like I had a secret to share. "Or can you not find time while you're busy looking for your next victim to play?"

He eyed the frat guy with what could only be described as his prison glare. The wimp took off in the opposite direction. Conner leveled me with the same scary glare. "Where's your boyfriend?"

I didn't bother with a response. He knew I'd done what he planned for me to do, sending Jake packing after the fight. Why affirm it?

He stepped toward me. I stepped back. I remembered his game and was in no mood to play. Unfortunately, my boots made it difficult to maneuver backward while drunk. "Is there a reason you don't know?"

I glared at him, looking for the lies in his eyes. "Stop acting like you don't know," I slurred, more than what was acceptable. *Actually, was slurring ever acceptable?*

He took another step. So did I. "Did it have anything to do with him *trying* to kick my ass at the bar?"

"Trying? I saw the blood. Serves you right for provoking him."

His lips twitched. "I bet you liked watching me fight for you."

I cocked my head to the side. "Getting punched in the face was you fighting?"

He shook his head, a slight smile now tipping his lips. "That was me letting him know I'm not going anywhere." His nearness was daunting and he smelled so freaking good.

"I must've missed that while I was worried about him kicking your ass."

"No need to worry." There was a bite to his words. "That would never happen." His eyes roamed over my tight clothes and boots. "The girl I knew rocked cut-offs and band T-shirts like no one's business."

"The girl you knew is gone."

"Yeah, I guess I should've figured. She wouldn't have been caught dead hanging all over some random guy. She hated girls like that."

I pulled in a breath as my eyes blazed with fury. "First of all, I can hang all over whomever I choose." *Good one, Hadley.*

"Then choose me." He didn't smile. He was completely serious.

I swallowed my surprise. I would not be distracted by him. "And second, it's none of your business what I do."

"Everything involving you is my business."

I laughed sardonically. "Oh, that's right. You still love me. That's why you keep playing me."

"Playing you?" His voice was incredulous.

"Just when I think maybe there's hope for us, you go and blow it."

His eyes were frenzied, caught off guard by my admission. "Hope for us? What does that mean?"

Shit. "Nothing. Stop changing the subject. You knew if he punched you, I'd send him away."

"I hoped, but I didn't know," he assured me quickly, clearly hoping I explained what my big mouth just admitted.

"You don't care who you hurt, do you?" I glared at him, hating him for getting it wrong. For not understanding. For sending me the damn letters. For making me want to forgive him after reading them. "As long as you get what you want, to hell with everyone else. Is that who the real Conner is?"

He flinched. "I never wanted to hurt you."

I ignored the sincerity in his eyes. "But that's what you keep doing." My head began to spin with all the alcohol I'd consumed, so I looped my arm through Lorelei's, who'd remained close by. "Let's get outta here." I pulled her toward the door and away from Conner. As drunk as I was, I knew the longer I stayed there, the greater the risk of me saying something I would've regretted in the morning.

* * *

The next morning my head throbbed like the second hand on a clock. I rolled over and reached for the glass of water on my nightstand. I gulped it, hoping it stayed down. Given my queasiness, it was fifty-fifty. I grabbed my phone from the spot beside my now empty glass. I had one text. I pressed it. My heart stuttered as the photo Conner had taken of us at my mother's fundraiser filled the screen. The message below it read: **The real me loves dancing with you**.

I stared at the photo. At our younger selves. At our smiles. We looked so happy. At the time, I'd tried so hard to keep him away for fear of being hurt by the school's newest player. But in the end, I was only hurting myself by staying away. I stared at the picture for a long time. I could see, even now, he'd been happy to be there with me. He gained nothing from it, only the opportunity to spend time with me. And from what his letters claimed, he didn't even know about the pistol until the week of his arrest.

"Looks like you throwing down the gauntlet, set a fire under him," Lorelei said as she walked into our room later that week. She moved to my desk, where a box filled with packages of licorice—enough to feed my entire building—sat on my chair. She grabbed a package and tore into it. Her eyes shot to me studying on my bed.

My eyes moved around the room, stopping on all the things I'd received. The box of licorice with the note: *The real me likes girls who eat licorice.* A huge bouquet of pink flowers sat in a vase beside my bed with a card sticking out the top. The message read: *The real me might send flowers.* A box of art supplies sat untouched on the floor beside my desk with a brief note on top: *The real me loves your art and wants to see more of it.*

"He's all about proving who the real Conner is, isn't he?" she asked, though it wasn't a question. She'd been there when I asked him the question. It was my fault he took me at my word and made it his mission to show me.

I released a sigh.

"Have you called to thank him?" She dropped down onto her bed, gnawing away at the licorice.

I shook my head. "I'm happy he's trying to figure out who he is, but it doesn't mean I have to be part of it."

"But he's making you part of it." She leveled me with the same eyes Cass used when I was being stubborn. "Look, I'm not trying to tell you what to do. But the guy wants you back. If you don't want him, be upfront. The way you dealt with him at that party, I couldn't tell if you wanted to kick him in the balls with those killer boots or jump into his arms and kiss his face off."

I stared across the room at her, my mind jumping to all our interactions. Had I been giving him mixed signals? Had my confusion translated to playing hard to get? It was difficult knowing how to act with him, especially after reading the letters. Part of me wanted to forgive him and the other wanted to hate him for deceiving me *again*.

When Lorelei left the room for a shower a little while later, I pulled out my phone and sent him a text. **This has to stop.**

And just like that, radio silence. No texts. No gifts. No run-ins for the next week. Thankfully, hanging out with Lorelei each night afforded me little time to even think about him. She purposely kept me distracted. Purposely avoided mentioning him. Purposely kept me focused on the future and not the past. Saturday night, we sat a high-top table at a crowded bar near campus. Lorelei had met a guy, and I got stuck talking to his best friend.

"So, what's your major?" he asked.

Ugh. "Undecided."

"Oh, cool. You live around here?"

"On campus." I smiled, trying to act interested. But I wasn't. Getting drunk, meeting new guys, and staying out until all hours of the night wasn't me. It never had been.

"Oh, yeah? Maybe we can go back there later and party."

"Maybe," I lied, before excusing myself and walking to the line at the bathroom. Usually, I wished the line moved quickly. Not tonight. My eyes scanned the congested bar. Nothing about it made me want to stay. Not the loud music. Not the crowded dance floor. Not the constant elbows from people walking by. Not the small talk with people I didn't have anything in common with. I needed to leave. I needed the quiet of my room. I needed something else.

I returned to the table a little while later, letting Lorelei know I'd already called an Uber and was ready to head out. She hugged me hard and whispered that she wouldn't be coming home. The girl was definitely taking advantage of the college experience. Good for her.

I smiled at the guy whose name I couldn't even remember and made an excuse about not feeling well so he knew he had no shot at coming home with me. After my quick goodbye, I bolted to my awaiting car and settled inside the backseat. As we pulled away from the curb, I eyed the line of people outside the bar waiting to get in. The groups of girls laughing with their friends. The guys behind them checking out their skimpy outfits. The couples in tight embraces keeping each other warm on the cool night.

Was this what my life had come to? Rides home alone? Talking to guys in bars I had no interest in talking to? Feeling alone in a room full of people?

Before long, my driver pulled onto campus and the familiar cobblestone buildings materialized. When he pulled up at the curb in front of my place, I stepped out of the car, pulling my coat snuggly around me to ward off the crisp fall air that had descended without warning.

I walked toward the front door, jarring when I spotted Conner sitting on the steps with his elbows dug into his knees and his hands clutched tightly together. "Conner?"

He glanced up, his eyes squinting at me.

I exhaled a deep breath, blowing wisps of hair up as I did. "What are you doing here?"

He patted the spot on the step beside him. "Sit with me."

I contemplated standing for no other reason than to be difficult, but my boots were killing my feet and my curiosity proved too much to stand. I took a step forward and sat on the cold concrete beside him. His presence still overwhelmed me. His crisp scent still invaded my senses, burrowing in like a sweet memory. His imposing form still gave me a sense of security, like no one could hurt me when he was around. Ironic, given the fact that he was the one who kept hurting me.

"What's going on?" I asked.

"For three years I've held on to you. My memories of you. My feelings for you. My need for you in my life." His voice carried a slight quiver. "My feelings never wavered. Not even a little."

My guilty eyes cut to his.

"But being here has made me realize I need to give up."

I swallowed back my surprise. I guess I never imagined he'd back down.

"Chasing you around. Trying to remind you of what we shared. It's not me. The real me anyway. I want you, Hadley. Make no mistake about it. But I can't force you to want me. And I can't force you to forget what happened. I guess what I'm saying is…*I need to be someone's everything, too."*

My heart constricted, leaving a dull ache in my chest.

"Just because I made mistakes in the past, doesn't mean I don't deserve a future with someone who wants me for me. I deserve to be wanted, too." He shrugged, brushing unexpectedly against me as he did. "Maybe this is what was supposed to happen. Maybe I needed you to teach me that lesson."

The finality of his words made me uneasy. Made me search for the right thing to say. Made me wonder if him leaving would make my life easier—better.

He stood up and faced me. "All I know is I can't keep doing this. I can't keep feeling this way. I was supposed to be happy once I was released. But all I feel is…"

My eyes dropped to my knees, uncomfortable with my hand in his unhappiness.

"I don't blame you, Hadley. What happened with us sucked. And I shouldn't have been pressuring you to forget it." He shook his head. "I should've never come here."

I looked up at him. Like really looked at him. His hair had begun to grow back. The stubble on his chin was thicker. The light dusting of freckles still graced his nose. His long eyelashes still fanned over the tops of his cheeks. His full lips, the ones I'd spent hours kissing when I was younger, were still just as inviting.

So much time had passed. And though parts of our younger selves still remained, we'd grown. Life had taught us both valuable lessons. Lessons I'd been too naïve to know existed in the real world. But now I knew. Good things did eventually come to an end. And Conner and I were no different.

"Hadley?"

I blinked, realizing he'd spoken. "Yeah?"

"Thank you for all the memories. Regardless of how this turned out, I'll still cherish them and think of them as some of the best times of my life."

If words had the power to destroy, his words—his honesty—crushed me.

"I don't think I'm gonna stick around." His eyes focused on anything but me. "I can take classes anywhere. I was only here for…well, you know."

I nodded, my heart cracking like a spider web of glass.

"I'll let you know before I take off. Just in case you want to know."

Unexpectedly, my eyes pricked with tears. This was happening. He was actually leaving. Leaving for good.

He buried his hands in his pockets. "Bye, Hadley."

I watched as he turned away, each step taking him further away from me. Inside, I was screaming for him to stop. For him to give me more time. For him to fight harder. But the words wouldn't come out of my mouth. I couldn't stop him. I couldn't give him a reason to stay.

Once he'd disappeared into the darkness, I sat for a long time wondering if I'd just made the biggest mistake of my life.

CHAPTER TWENTY

Hadley

A week had passed since Conner walked out of my life for the second time. He hadn't called to let me know he'd left, but he probably decided not to bother. It wasn't like he owed me anything. I'd been the one who wouldn't accept his apologies. The one who ignored his attempts to prove himself. The one who let him go.

I'd stopped partying with Lorelei. Instead, I'd spent a lot of time alone with my thoughts. I realized that while partying distracted me, it hadn't fixed my issues. That took time. Time without Jake. Without Conner— showing up or sending gifts. Without letters bombarding my every thought. Time alone. Time to process everything that had happened since Conner showed up on campus.

My phone rang as I made my way across the quad after my afternoon chemistry class. Once I saw the name on the screen, I paused nervously before lifting it to my ear. "Hi, Dad."

"Hey. Just checking in on my girl. I haven't talked to you in a while." I could hear how much he missed me, and it killed me to know I still hadn't been honest with him.

"Yeah, I figured you were avoiding me," I teased.

His hearty laughter carried over the line. "Never."

"Actually…you may want to after I tell you something I've been holding off telling you."

"What's wrong?" He immediately went into serious detective mode.

I approached a bench and dropped down onto it. "Well, I haven't been expelled, arrested, and I'm not pregnant."

"Hadley," he warned in that tone that said he was in no mood for jokes.

"I just need for you to not flip out."

"I can't promise that."

"Then I'm not telling you." I stared out at the other students rushing across the quad to their next classes, wondering if what I was about to do would relieve some of my guilt. I hadn't realized how much keeping a secret from my parents would wear on me.

"Fine," he relented. "I promise."

I pulled in a deep breath. "Conner—Caynan showed up on campus the day he was released."

"I'll kill him." The anger in his voice told me he would.

"Dad, you promised."

He sighed, staying silent for a long time. So long I wondered if he'd texted campus police while still on the phone with me. "Continue."

"He wanted to apologize. Wanted to make amends."

"Did he hurt you?"

Had he hurt me? Or had I done it to myself this time? "No, he didn't hurt me. I actually sent him away."

"That's my girl."

A breeze carried some leaves in front of me, swirling them at my feet. "But I've been giving it a lot of thought and…would it be wrong to forgive him?"

"Oh, Hadley." He morphed back into dad mode. "It's never wrong to forgive someone. Forgiveness is really about you. It releases you of anger."

"Wow. I did not expect that."

He laughed. "See. I can be reasonable. Now if you said you wanted to date him again, it would be a different story."

I laughed to myself.

"Would you be upset if I called campus police—just to let them know he's been around?" he asked.

"Of course I'd be upset. He's not going to hurt me. He's not even here anymore."

"Can I ask why you decided to tell me now?" my dad asked.

"It just felt wrong keeping it a secret from you and Mom."

"You never want to keep things from the people who matter to you," he assured me. "They're the ones who always deserve the truth."

* * *

I hurried into the cafeteria to grab a quick breakfast after philosophy the following morning. I reached for the last cranberry muffin in the bakery section as another hand reached for the same one. "Oh, sorry." I pulled my hand back, turning to the person who'd grabbed it. Conner's pixie friend with a bright red bow in her hair stood there with the muffin in her hand and a death-glare on her face.

"Bitch."

I jerked a glance over my shoulder, but no one stood there. I looked back at her scowling face. "Tell me how you really feel."

"Nah. That would take all day," she said, the hate in her eyes transparent.

"Well, hey, enjoy the muffin," I said as I turned away from her. "Be sure to choke on it." Her quiet laughter stopped me and I spun back around.

She stood there looking slightly amused. "He said you were feisty."

I cocked my head. "I thought I was a bitch?"

"Yeah, that, too" She turned and handed her dining card to the cashier.

"Did he leave yet?"

She snorted, her head glancing over her shoulder. "Careful. Someone might think you actually care."

"I never said I didn't care about him."

She walked over to me. "You have a screwed up way of showing it."

I narrowed my eyes. Who was *she* to tell me how to handle Conner?

"Come sit with me," she said, turning and grabbing a handful of napkins.

I glanced over my shoulder again. Still no one but me.

"I hate eating alone," she continued, walking to one of the empty tables in the corner of the room and sitting down.

Was this girl for real? My curiosity carried me toward the table.

"Sit."

I slipped into the seat across from her as she split the muffin and handed me half. I stared down at it. "Did you poison it when I wasn't looking?"

She laughed. Like really laughed. "He said you were funny too."

Our interaction was getting stranger by the minute. "Look, I don't know what else he told you, but—"

"He loves you." She lifted her bony shoulder. "That's what he told me. What else is there to know?"

"There's more to it than that." I broke off a piece of muffin and popped it in my mouth.

"The way I see it, a hot guy spent three years paying for his crimes. He got out a changed man and headed right here because he wants *you*. What more do you want?"

I popped another piece of muffin into my mouth, knowing I didn't have an answer. I didn't doubt Conner loved me. And to be honest, I was tired of not trusting him.

"Just so you know, he's got his pick of girls."

"Yeah. Nothing I haven't seen before."

"For what it's worth, he hasn't touched a single one." Her lips twitched. "The guy could be a priest."

"He's not really into forward girls. He's more into the chase."

Her sad eyes stared across the table at me for a long time before she spoke. "Until he's not anymore."

I averted my gaze, snagging the eyes of a girl in my chemistry class who smiled at me from across the room. I tried to smile back, but my eyes shifted back to the girl in front of me. "So, is he still around?"

* * *

I sat on the concrete steps in front of my building. My body trembled nervously as I watched people pass by on their way to their dorms. It was after nine and wispy clouds from my breath floated in front of my face as I pushed out a deep breath.

The sound of more footsteps trailed over from the right of my building. My heart surged as Vik and Conner approached, walking down the sidewalk engrossed in a conversation. Conner didn't notice me sitting there—or at least he tried like hell not to notice—as they made their way by. Vik stopped abruptly in front of my building.

Conner took a couple more steps before stopping and turning toward her. "What are you doing?"

She didn't answer, but I assumed her eyes cut to me because his head whirled around and he found me sitting on the steps. Vik walked over to him. She said something as she patted his chest and walked away, leaving him standing alone.

I took another deep breath and let it out slowly. I hadn't really considered what I'd say once Vik got him near my place. "You're still here."

He nodded. "I told you I'd let you know before I took off."

The tapping inside my chest kept a steady tempo. "I was hoping I'd run into you."

His eyes narrowed. "Why's that?"

I swallowed down the nervous lump in my throat. "I've never done it before, but I could probably teach you to ride a bike."

His face filled with a mix of confusion and disbelief as he took a step toward me.

There was no stopping now. "And my mom does some fundraising for animal shelters. So, if you're looking to get a dog, we might look there first."

His eyes were locked on mine as he continued walking slowly toward me "You read my letters?"

I nodded.

A look of hope swept over his features as he took the remaining steps, stopping directly in front of me. "And?"

I shrugged. "I'm confused."

He dropped to his haunches in front of me, his big hands cupping my cheeks and forcing my eyes on his. The feel of his hands on my skin warmed them, numbing them in a way I hadn't felt in three years. "I'm not stupid enough to think it won't take time, but I will prove to you I'm the guy you want. The guy you need." He sounded so sincere—so convinced he could do it.

"How can you think it'll be easy?"

He dropped his forehead to mine, the action taking me back in time. "Because I love you. I love that you challenge me. I love that we argue but it doesn't change my feelings for you. I love that I've never felt more alive than when I'm with you. Whether we're on the top of a water tower or watching a train pass by, I just want to do everything with you by my side."

I pulled in a shaky breath as my eyes glazed with tears. It was one thing to read his feelings on paper, but hearing them right from his lips overwhelmed me.

"I love you enough for the both of us right now," he assured me. "I've had three years to think about my feelings for you. You've spent those years hating me. I know you must be confused, but I promise, I'll do everything in my power to gain your trust. I'll stay by your side or keep my distance while you figure it out. Whatever you need. The ball is in your court. You call the shots."

Gahhhh.

His candor and desperation blindsided me. I felt lightheaded, dizzy from the depth of his words. "I know I don't want to lose you—"

His smile spread so wide you'd think I told him I'd forgiven him.

"But I don't know if I'll ever be able to fully trust you."

He nodded. "The only way to gain your trust is to prove you can trust me. I know that. I just need you to give me time to do it."

I stared into his eyes. Being that close, it was as if I'd been transported back three years. "How can you be sure it wasn't your loneliness talking in the letters? How do you know you weren't wrapped up in me because I was familiar?"

"You are the only person who has ever given me hope. The only person who has ever shown me love. The only person who has ever given me all of herself and made me want to do the same. I won't let you down again. I promise. I *will* kiss you every morning for the rest of your life. If you let me."

It was all too good to be true. The poignancy of his words. The sincerity in his eyes. I'd been in that spot before and look where I ended up. "I don't know if I believe you."

That slow-spreading cocky smirk lifted his lips right before they crashed down on mine. His tongue plunged inside my mouth. There was nothing gentle about it. This was three years' worth of pent-up frustration. He was proving his words. Proving his apology. Proving his love for me. His hands stayed on my face, turning it to fit with his before they dropped to lift me up like I weighed nothing at all. My legs locked around his hips as he climbed the steps and slammed my back into the front door. My hands slid behind his neck rough and desperate.

I wanted to hate what he was doing. Hate the feel of his lips as they consumed mine. Hate the feel of his hands clutching my ass. Hate the force of his body pressing up against mine. But the truth was, for me this kiss was three years' worth of resentment. I was punishing him for the pain he caused me—the unnecessary pain. For the love I once had for him. For making me feel again.

I dropped one hand and pulled my key card from my pocket. He ripped it from my hand and somehow managed to use it to unlock the door with my back pressed against it and his lips devouring mine.

Once the front door opened, Conner tore down the hallway. "Room twelve," I said against his lips. He pinned me against the door to my room, using my key card to unlock it. He shoved it open, causing us to practically fall inside. Once he'd kicked the door shut, he carried me to my bed. He lowered me onto my back and followed me down, his weight heavy on top of me.

We didn't break contact. We were grabbing and pushing and maniacal. Everything felt so right in that moment. It was as if, with our tongues melding and our teeth clashing, I'd forgotten the pain. The anger. The humiliation. I just wanted his hands on me. His mouth on me. His body one with mine.

He reached for the hem of my shirt, only releasing my lips to tug it over my head. I grabbed at his shirt yanking it over his head. Then both of us were tugging off our own bottoms unable to get back to the other fast enough. I was turned on and needy. Needy for him to possess me. Possess me in a way his eighteen-year-old self hadn't. Possess me in a way only his twenty-one-year-old self was capable of.

I pulled him down to me, my hands wrapping around the bulges in his biceps. He was jacked, so much more so than before. There wasn't an ounce of fat on his body.

He was defined, cut, and perfect. And currently turning me on.

He unlatched my hands from his arms, lifting my arms above my head. "Keep them up, Hadley. Let me look at you." He sat back on his knees, his eyes burning into every inch of my skin, sweeping slowly and methodically. Like he was memorizing my body, in case he didn't have another opportunity to see it.

Devoid of his body heat, the room chilled my skin. Goosebumps erupted all over. Conner seemed to notice, leaning down and rubbing his hands up from my ankles all the way to my thighs, his hands igniting a fire inside me. He trailed them up my hips, his fingers digging in, moving slowly up my sides. His thumbs purposely brushed the sides of my breasts.

A moan erupted from me.

"Oh, you like when I do this?"

I willed myself not to beg him for more. Not to cry at the absence of his touch for the past three years.

"Let's see what else you like." He leaned down, his mouth closing over my nipple, the gentle suction crossing my eyes. "Oh, you still like when I do this."

My breathing became labored as I fought to keep my hands above my head.

My breast popped free from his mouth. "I want you so bad," he murmured into my chest before sucking the other nipple into his mouth. One of his hands slid down my stomach to between my legs. I groaned as his fingers skated over my wet skin. I lost all sense of reason as he slipped two fingers inside.

"Tell me you forgive me?" he murmured as his fingers pumped slowly in and out.

I whimpered softly, unable to say a word.

"That wasn't an answer. I need you to tell me you forgive me. I need to hear you say it." His fingers stopped moving, taking with them the ripples of pleasure he'd sparked.

My eyes popped open, flashing down to him staring up at me. "Is that all you want?"

His lips tipped up in the corners. "Do I look like that's all I want?"

I didn't even blink. "Yes."

He grabbed me by the legs and twisted me onto my belly, covering my back with the weight of his body. His lips moved up the side of my neck as he sucked his way up to my ear. "I want all of you, you crazy girl. I want this beautiful body." His left hand slid down the length of my side. "I want this beautiful mind." He buried his lips in my hair and kissed me hard. "And I want every moment from here on out to be spent making you love me and only me. So, I'll ask you again. Do you forgive me?"

I vibration of his heartbeat ricocheted against my back as his weight pushed me into the bed, his erection steel against my butt. "I want to. Every part of me wants to. But I can't be that girl again."

He dropped feather-light kisses all over my bare shoulders. "I just want you to be you."

"Then don't ask me if I *do* forgive you. Ask me if I *could*."

He paused, giving my question the seriousness it deserved. "Could you forgive me, Hadley?"

"Yes," I whispered, knowing without a doubt, it would take time. More time than we had before both of us shattered with need.

Conner flipped me over so quickly, I had no time to hold on. He smiled down at me, clearly pleased by my response. He reached for his jeans hanging off the side of the bed and dug into the pocket, pulling out a condom and slipping it on. "I need to look into your eyes." He lowered his weight onto me, his knees on either side of my hips, his elbows by my head. "I need to see the second I'm inside of you again."

I stared up into his eyes. The eyes of the guy I wanted in that moment. The guy I could very well love again one day. The guy I missed more than I realized—more than I thought possible.

As if he heard my thoughts, his lips crashed down on mine. My arms slipped around him, holding him to me, my knees bending and cradling him.

He pulled back. "I've thought about this for three years. What it would feel like. What I'd say. What you'd be like."

"And?" I gasped.

"I fucking love you more than life itself, Hadley." With one forceful thrust, he pushed inside me for the first time in three years. He groaned, low and feral.

I arched into him, his bare body gliding against mine, the friction electric. His anxious thrusts mirrored the desperation in his voice. I pulled him toward me, my lips taking control as my hips met his thrust for thrust. He filled me, stretching me wide. It was glorious, like no time had passed. Like nothing had changed between us. Like we hadn't changed. His kisses became sloppy and wet, devouring my lips whole.

Needing a breath, I eventually pulled back, my head pushing into the pillow as my eyes rolled into the back of my head. He nuzzled into the crook of my neck, his tongue licking and his teeth nipping a path to my ear. He reached down and circled my right wrist with his hand, lifting it above my head. He held it there, lacing our fingers and bracing himself with it. I reached down with my left hand, my fingernails digging into his bare ass as he pounded into me over and over again, hitting spots inside me no one since him had been able to reach.

"You are my everything, Hadley," he murmured into my neck, the rasp in his voice and the certainty of his words firing sensations through me. "I've missed you so damn much."

"I've missed you, too."

My words ignited a fire in him. His hips thrust faster. Harder. Our anxious panting parted the silence in the room. Then the trembles deep inside me started, slow then fiercer as his thrusts became unyielding. An explosion of vibrations rocked through me jetting out to every neglected part of my soul. I gasped, as my body hummed and a blanket of calm fell over me. A stillness I'd only ever felt with him in my life.

He didn't stop. He kept moving, grunting into my neck as his body glided over mine. Then, as if my release had pushed him over the edge, his hips pumped one last time, deep and hard, and his body froze, quivers taking hold of him. His weight slowly lowered down on me, crushing me into the bed.

I'd never felt so complete in my entire life.

"I'm never letting you go again," he breathed.

"Prove it."

Conner

The early morning sun peeked through the blinds in Hadley's room as I turned over in her twin bed, wrapping my arms around her small body. I buried my nose into her hair, inhaling that strawberry scent I'd missed so damn much. At some point during the night, I'd let go of her, something I never thought I'd be capable of doing once I had her back in my life. She shifted, burrowing into my chest. I lay with her in my arms for a long time absorbing the moment, the reality of what had happened, and the possibilities that lay ahead for us.

In prison, I realized my life was best described as two chapters. Before Hadley and After Hadley. Before Hadley, I was a shell of a guy. Sure, I had confidence and girls, but I lived my life controlled by my father. Controlled by the fact that I was incapable of making it on my own. Incapable of cutting ties.

After I met Hadley, everything changed for me. I started thinking about a future. About the opportunities ahead of me. And in the end, I'd made it out to the other side unscathed. I moved through each day knowing I had a future and I was convinced Hadley would be part of it.

My phone vibrated on the nightstand, snapping me out of my head. Besides Hadley, only two people had my number. Vik and my PO. I released one arm carefully and grabbed the phone before it woke Hadley. I glimpsed the screen and accepted the call, whispering into the phone. "Hold on please, Sir."

I slipped out from Hadley's arms and dug my feet into my sneakers. I grabbed my clothes from the floor, slipping them on as I moved to the door and ducked into the hallway. "Sorry about that." I kept my voice lowered so I didn't wake Hadley or her entire floor. "What can I do for you?"

"You staying out of trouble?"

I leaned against the wall, dropping my head back against it. "Absolutely."

"Good." He paused. He never paused. He was straight-forward and most of our calls lasted no more than thirty seconds. "So, listen. The reason for my call is a little unorthodox."

"Okay."

"Your father contacted me."

I stood in the empty hallway with that same familiar pit in the bottom of my stomach. The one I'd lived with growing up. The one that disappeared the moment I'd been behind bars—ironically enough.

"You still there?"

"I'm here," I assured him, my pulse thumping in my ears.

"He wants to see you."

What the ever-living-fuck? A brigade of unwelcome emotions rushed me at once. The anger that consumed my youth. The deep-rooted hate I had for him. The guilt I carried for my part in his arrest. What could he possibly have to say to me?

"Conner?"

"Still here."

"Look, I'm no counselor. But it's been three years since you've talked to him. You're both grown men. Holding a grudge doesn't do anyone any good."

Yeah. That's what he thought.

* * *

My hands twisted together on the worn wooden table in front of me. My eyes shot around, taking in the inmates meeting with their family members around the cold room. Their families looked upbeat and excited to be there. The inmates all looked the way I felt when I was in their place. Alone in a room full of people.

A heavy door in the far corner of the room clattered open. My eyes shot up. An older version of my father walked through the door in his matching khaki shirt and pants. His hair had turned entirely gray. His steps slower.

He stepped up to the seat across from me. We both took a minute, observing the physical changes we'd both undergone. Acknowledging the passing of time. Recognizing the huge divide that existed between us— the same one that *always* existed between us. "Hi." He lowered slowly into the seat. "Thanks for meeting me."

I shrugged. As much as I didn't want to see him, I knew I didn't have a choice.

"You look good."

"Thanks."

He linked his fingers on the table, his eyes fixed on them. "How'd they treat you in there?"

"I held my own."

He nodded. I wondered if he'd had similar experiences. Wondered if his longer sentence—even just the thought of it—had taken a toll on him. I didn't dare ask. I didn't want that shit in my head.

"Got my GED."

He finally glanced up at me. "I always wanted that for you."

"I know." I found it difficult to meet his gaze. He *had* always wanted that for me. Just nothing more. He didn't want me to reach my full potential. In school or on the baseball diamond. "I started work on my Bachelor's degree."

"That's good." He tried to smile, but I could see it was difficult for him. It was the first thing I'd done on my own. Without him pulling the strings.

My eyes shifted, landing on a young girl and her mother visiting an older inmate who stared at the girl like she hung the moon. I wondered if she had any shot at a bright future with a criminal as a dad. Maybe that's why I felt the need to keep talking to mine. To keep proving to him that I'd done it. I'd broken free from a life of crime. I'd broken free from the future he laid out for me. "I'm not sure what I'll major in, but now that I can actually attend real classes, I think I'll be able to figure it out."

"Sounds like you've got a plan."

I nodded.

His voice lowered like he didn't want any of the other inmates or their families to overhear. "I didn't do you any favors, did I?"

I stared across the table at this man who had lost everything. The majority because of his poor decisions, but some through no fault of his own. "You just got caught up in the wrong shit."

He dropped his head, his voice lowering even more. "Your mom would've been so disappointed in me."

I definitely had not expected that. "Yeah…she would've been. But she'd also be happy to know I made it out okay. My life is now on the straight and narrow. I've got a girl who I plan to marry someday. A degree that's within reach. And if I play my cards right, I might even be able to earn a walk-on spot on the baseball team."

His eyes held regret. And I kind of liked that they did. It meant he was human. And he could feel things again. "Do you ever think you could forgive me?"

I averted my gaze, watching the kid interact with her father. If Hadley could forgive me, then I knew I could forgive my father. Would I ever have a real relationship with him? Probably not any time soon. But I didn't want to live a life filled with anger and regret. Holding onto it didn't get anyone anywhere. When I glanced back to him, his eyes were hopeful. "Some day."

* * *

The sun had slipped beyond the horizon as I ducked in the front door of Hadley's building as a guy stepped outside. I approached her closed door unsure how to proceed. I'd sent her a text on my way to the prison and on my way home, but she never replied to either. I worried that meant she was having regrets. Me not being there when she woke up might've given her time to reconsider her promise to try to forgive me.

I tapped the door with my knuckles and waited. I couldn't hear any rustling on the other side, but I tapped on the door again.

The door unlocked and swung opened. But it wasn't Hadley who stood there. It was her roommate, staring me down like she wanted to kill me. She dug two fingers into my chest. "Hurt her and I will kill you." She stepped around me and took off down the hallway.

I stood in the open doorway staring at Hadley who sat on her bed with a shoebox on her lap. "Hi." I stepped inside, closing the door behind me.

She stared at me, her eyes dropping to my empty hands. "I expected a coffee. Or at least some licorice."

I walked over and sat down beside her, the mattress dipping under my weight. "I gave you a lifetime supply. Are you already out?"

She shook her head.

"Did you get my texts?"

She nodded. "How was it seeing your dad?"

I thought of the creases around his eyes. His graying hair. His attempt to smile. "Sad."

Sorrow filled Hadley's eyes. "You haven't spoken to him since…"

"Since before I got arrested? No."

She chewed on her bottom lip, contemplating her words. "Did he want to apologize?"

"Yeah."

"Did you forgive him?"

I nodded. "You showed me it was possible."

She smiled sadly. "I'm sorry you got gypped in the dad department."

I laughed. "Well, there's always your dad."

Hadley burst out laughing. "Yeah. I'd hold off getting him a Father's Day card any time soon."

The thought that Hadley would eventually have to tell her parents about us turned my gut. "He hates me that much?"

She patted my knee. "I'm sure you'll grow on him…in like fifty years."

I laughed, knowing making amends in all areas of Hadley's life wouldn't be easy. But I needed to do it for her. I nodded to the shoebox. "What do you have there?"

She slowly lifted the cover. My letters sat neatly inside.

I lifted my brows. "Doing some light reading?"

She smiled. "Just getting to know you again."

My eyes drifted shut on an exhale, loving that she'd read them. That she finally knew everything I wanted her to know—everything I needed her to know. Bottom line, she knew me. She was the *only* person who did. "I could think of a lot of ways to get to know me again," I teased.

Though had she said yes, I would've stripped her down right there and then.

She jabbed me with her elbow, abruptly stopping that fantasy.

I nodded to the letters. "So, what do you think?"

"I think you've got potential."

We laughed, and it felt so good to laugh with her again. "Potential?"

"Can you still mash a baseball?"

"Definitely. I've been practicing down at the sports facility," I assured her. "And my swing's better than ever."

"Mr. Humble returns with a vengeance." Her eyes widened excitedly. "Wait a sec. Lorelei knows the baseball coach. I can have her talk to him. Maybe get you a tryout."

I placed my hand on her knee, silencing her sudden enthusiasm. "Vik already took care of it."

She pulled in a deep breath, releasing it slowly. "So, you really are staying." It wasn't a question. It took something like that for it to finally register that I wasn't going anywhere.

I draped my arm around her shoulder, pulling her into my side. In that moment, with my past behind me and my future staring me in the face with gorgeous blue eyes, I knew all was right in the world again. I had my girl. And I had my future. It was mine for the taking. "My girl's here. No way in hell I'm losing her twice."

Hadley turned into me and threw her leg over my hips, straddling my lap so she could look me in the eyes. "If you ever hurt me again—"

I wrapped my hand around the back of her head and pulled her to me, silencing her with my lips. I didn't wait for the go-ahead. My tongue pushed inside, having something to prove. There was no way in hell I'd ever hurt her again, but I needed *her* to know that. She also needed to know I'd never leave her or be dishonest with her again. I'd do everything in my power to hold onto her and kiss her every morning—make that every damn day—for the rest of my life.

EPILOGUE
Two Years Later

Hadley

I sat with Conner's hand tightly clasped in mine. An excited buzz filled the television studio where we sat. A few lucky baseball fans in their favorite team jerseys filled the seats behind us.

Conner had already conducted interviews with all the major sports networks, everyone interested in the story of his past and how he turned his life around. Guys completely ate up the story of the thief who could crack any safe, while women…well women wanted a piece of my man. Who could blame them? He was hot, exuded that same confidence I'd seen the first time I laid eyes on him, and he could mash a baseball like no one's business. And did I mention how his ass looked in those baseball pants?

Today, however, he wore a gray suit with a periwinkle blue tie that brought out the blackness of his eyes. I'd picked it out, teasing him that he didn't have enough female fans and that the blue would push them over the edge. He knew how jealous I got about all the female attention he received—not like it was anything new, but he had no trouble convincing me over and over again in our bedroom that I was it for him.

His agent walked over and whispered something into his ear that I couldn't quite hear with all the noise surrounding us. Conner nodded before his agent disappeared again.

He squeezed my hand. "He thinks New York is gonna make a last-minute trade with Florida."

"What does that mean?"

"It means we may be moving to Florida."

I smiled. "They've got lots of grad schools with art programs I could transfer to."

His brows lifted. "Yeah?"

I nodded. "And Cass, Vik, and Lorelei will all be nearby."

He smiled. "True."

I considered the harsh winters up north. All the snow. The bulky clothes I'd have to buy. The boots. "And…I'd take warm weather over cold any day."

He laughed. "Funny. Because I'd take you anywhere I can get you."

I glanced around the crowded space. "Do we have time?"

He threw back his head and laughed. "Twice this morning wasn't enough? I've definitely created a monster."

I smiled, trying to hold onto this special moment. Trying to capture the feelings of it all. The happiness. The excitement. The accomplishment. It was Conner's time. He'd worked so hard to get there. Sure, he'd made mistakes along the way, but he'd changed because of them. And now, life was granting him his wish.

"What are you thinking?"

I shrugged. "Just how happy I am for you."

He leaned in, his fresh scent wrapping itself around me like a warm blanket. "Oh yeah? Why's that?"

I leaned in, pressing my lips to his. "You're finally getting your dream."

His eyes narrowed, the skin between his brows pinching together. "You think this is my dream?"

I glanced around the room. The excitement was palpable. "Obviously."

He shook his head. "You silly girl. *You.* You're my dream."

A ripple rolled through my belly taking up permanent residency. Even after all the time that had passed, Conner had the power to affect me. To turn me into a pile of goo with a few small words. "I don't believe you."

His eyes flicked around the room. "If all of this didn't happen, if it all just went away, I promise you, I'd be okay. But if you went away, if you never came back into my life, I'd be nowhere near okay."

The sincerity in his eyes and his heartfelt words stole the air right out of my lungs, glazing my eyes with tears. "Conner, I—"

"Conner," a deep voice called.

Our eyes shot to his agent who approached eagerly with his hands clasped together. "You're going number one."

Conner said nothing, just cupped my cheeks and pulled me to him, kissing me gently. When he pulled away he looked to his agent. "Thank God. My girl hates the cold."

Applause ensued as the commissioner of baseball entered the studio and stepped to the microphone behind the podium. "For the first pick in this year's baseball draft, Florida selects…Conner Cartwright."

The fans in the studio erupted in cheers as Conner stood up, pulling me to my feet and wrapping his arms around me. "Was there something you were gonna say before my agent interrupted?"

"Get up there," I urged with a giant grin on my face.

"Nope. Not until you tell me."

"You're crazy."

He smiled down at me, his nose brushing mine. "Yup. Now spill it."

I tried pulling loose, but his strong arms wouldn't release me. "Fine, I love you. Now get up there."

"How much?"

My eyes widened. "You know how much."

"Say it."

"You're my everything, Conner."

He smiled his cocky grin then dropped his lips to mine and kissed me for everyone watching to see. "I love you, too. I'm never letting you go again."

I could feel the impatient eyes in the room on us. "Would you just get up there?"

He laughed and made his way up to the commissioner who shook his hand and handed him a Florida ball cap.

Conner pulled the cap down over his dark hair, staring at me the entire time like no one else occupied the room, forget everyone watching at home. He placed his hand over his heart, tapping it twice. I got it. I completely understood. Baseball was his now. But I was his forever. And Conner Cartwright was without a doubt mine.

THE END

OTHER TITLES BY J. NATHAN

For You
Standalone College Sports Series
For Finlay (Book #1)
For Forester (Book #2
For Crosby (Book #3)
For Emery (Book #4)

Savage Beasts
Rock Star Standalone Series
Kozart
Treyton

Standalones
Seren
Something About You
I Just Need You
You're the Reason
Until Alex
Since Drew
Before Hadley

ACKNOWLEDGEMENTS

Thank you readers for taking the time to read Hadley and Caynan's (and Conner's) story! I hope you enjoyed it as much as I enjoyed writing it.

To my husband for his support and willingness to share me with my imaginary friends. To my awesome little boy for understanding my busy schedule. Just know I always have time for you. To my family and friends for your enthusiasm over this dream of mine. It means the world to me that you care so much. To my fellow romance junkies, Heather, Kim, and Kerrie for reading it before anyone!

To my wonderful editor, author Stephanie Elliot, for not only being a fantastic editor, but also a cheerleader and friend. Can't wait for your next book, *Sad Perfect*, to hit shelves!

To my amazing beta readers for all your thoughtful and constructive feedback. I truly appreciate the time you took out of your busy lives to help me. Author Sierra Hill, bloggers and friends Dali at TJ Loves to Read, and Kat, Neilliza, and Michelle at Four Chicks Flipping Pages. You girls are awesome!

Last, but certainly not least, to cover creator extraordinaire Letitia at RBA Designs for another beautiful cover. You are so fabulous to work with and so patient when I have annoying little changes I need you to make. Thank you for bringing Caynan to life!

ABOUT THE AUTHOR

J. Nathan resides on the east coast with her husband and son. She is an avid reader of all things romance. Happy endings are a must. Alpha males with chips on their shoulders are an added bonus. When she's not curled up with a good book, she can be found spending time with family and friends and working on her next novel.

www.ingramcontent.com/pod-product-compliance
Lightning Source LLC
Chambersburg PA
CBHW030146310726
48970CB00005B/1615